Sunlight over Crystal Sands

HOLLY MARTIN

CHAPTER ONE

Lyra paused at the top of the hill, catching her breath. She loved cycling, but she was very much the kind of cyclist who would throw her lunch in the basket on the front and go out for a leisurely ride, rather than part of the hardcore, high-vis, Lycra-wearing brigade who would spend the whole day cycling for miles through mountainous terrain. Consequently, the hill she'd just cycled up was a lot more tasking than she was used to. But the view at the top was utterly spectacular.

The sea was a gloriously deep sapphire blue today, glittering like thousands of stars had fallen from the skies. She smiled as below her the whole of Jewel Island was spread out in front of her. Soon to be her new home. Up ahead, not too far from where she was now, her little cottage, named Sunlight, was waiting for her to move into in a few days' time. She could see the Sapphire Bay Hotel standing proudly on the headland, a large white house with big glass windows on all sides to make the most of the amazing views. Lyra was starting work there the following week.

Most of the beaches were on the far side of the island but she could see little glimpses of golden sands sparkling in the sunlight. The picture-postcard village looked joyful with its multicoloured houses and cottages, the bunting fluttering in the gentle summer breeze, the fairy lights twinkling as the sun was just starting its descent into the sky, leaving the clouds the palest pink.

A bell rang behind her and she turned to see one of the Lycra brigade cycling past in lurid neon pink on a high-tech black bike that looked like it might be capable of competing in the Olympics. Lyra looked down at the turquoise strapless dress she was wearing and the gold strappy sandals. Her bike was a metallic pale blue with a white wicker basket on the front that she affectionately called Daisy. She definitely wasn't part of that group.

The cyclist waved a friendly hand as she soared past, not taking any time to appreciate the amazing view.

Lyra's stomach rumbled hungrily and she decided she better get a move on if she was going to get back to her hotel in time for dinner. She'd already booked a table in the restaurant. She took another glance at the Sapphire Bay Hotel. She'd tried to get a room there while she waited for her cottage to be ready but they had been full. Her sister Michelle, who had moved to Jewel Island a few months before, didn't have room for her either, as she was completely redecorating and renovating her home, so Lyra had settled for a small hotel further down the coast on the mainland.

Lyra manoeuvred Daisy back onto the road and pushed off, laughing as she started to pick up speed as she sailed down the hill, the wind lifting her long hair off her neck so it trailed behind her. She raised her feet from the pedals, leaving her legs out to the side, and let out a scream of pure joy.

There was something so utterly wonderful about a rare moment of complete freedom. It was exhilarating. As someone who had conditioned herself to be sensible and play it safe, she very rarely let her hair down like this. If she did, it almost always went wrong, and people got hurt. But nothing could go wrong freewheeling down a hill.

As she neared the bottom of the hill, she spotted a man on the side of the road, with a large white and black dog. The man had dark hair and warm, amber-coloured eyes, with a gorgeous warm Mediterranean skin tone. Their eyes locked as she soared towards him and she was struck with a strong sense that she'd seen him somewhere before. She watched in surprise as his mouth fell open in shock. She flew past him, confused by his look – unless he recognised her too? Suddenly she noticed in horror that her strapless dress had slid down and her breasts had been completely on display, flashing the poor guy as she'd cycled past. She tried to drag her dress back up, pedalling away as fast as she could, but the dress was caught in the cogs on the back wheel, pulling it further down her belly. As she carried on pedalling, the bike slowed with the resistance of the dress. She gave the dress one more tug to try to free it and toppled off the bike onto the soft grass on the side of the road.

She swore softly as she struggled to extract herself from the bike, her cheeks burning with embarrassment. She prayed the man hadn't spotted her fall and had carried on his way. She absolutely didn't need him to come and help

3

her when her breasts were still hanging out. The dress was stuck fast in the bike and no amount of wiggling around was freeing it.

Suddenly the large English setter that had been with the man came bounding up to her, shoving his face in hers, his floppy jowls wet as he sniffed her, his tail wagging excitedly. Despite her predicament, she couldn't help but laugh as she stroked his large head.

'Dexter, come away, you big lump,' came a deep male voice from behind the dog, although Dexter did no such thing.

The next thing, the dog was heaved away and the man she'd seen on the corner was standing there. He saw her state of undress and looked away.

'You all right? Do you need some help?'

Lyra desperately tried to hide her breasts, tugging fruitlessly on her dress. 'Yeah, I think only my pride has been hurt. I definitely don't need any help.'

She couldn't think of anything worse.

To her complete surprise, the man tugged off his t-shirt, revealing impressively toned abs and strong arms. It left Lyra almost speechless, which even she had to acknowledge was a rarity. She wondered if he was trying to make her feel better by being topless too, although his gorgeous body did nothing to make her feel better about the part of her body currently on display.

'Here, put this on and then see if you can wiggle out of your dress and I can try to remove it from the bike. It looks like it's caught up pretty bad,' the man said, still looking away from her.

His voice was familiar too; it had a beautiful lilt to it,

suggesting he was from somewhere else in the world, somewhere exotic no doubt. But she knew she'd heard it somewhere before.

'Thank you.' Lyra took the t-shirt, hoping somehow the ground could swallow her up. With a great deal of effort she managed to pull the t-shirt over herself, covering her modesty, but the dress was caught up so badly, wrapped tightly around her hips, there was no way she could get out of it. She tugged and flailed around while the man looked everywhere but at her. Finally she gave up.

'I might need some help.'

She saw his lips twitch into a smirk. He was definitely enjoying her discomfort.

He glanced at her and, seeing she was covered, he knelt down as Dexter continued to sniff around her, obviously wondering if he could help too.

'To be clear,' the man said. 'You want me to take your dress off?'

Amusement danced in his eyes and it struck her then that if it hadn't been the case that right now she wanted to run away from him and die of embarrassment at the very first opportunity, he would have been the kind of man she'd like to get to know better. As it was, she'd be quite happy if she never saw him ever again.

'Yes, I'd like you to take my dress off, but no peeking.'

He held up his hand in a Boy Scout salute. 'I wouldn't dream of it. Although I have to say, I normally take a woman out for dinner before it gets this far.'

She couldn't help smiling.

'I'm Nix Sanchez, by the way. I feel like we should at

least be on first-name terms before I start taking your clothes off.'

Nix. She let the name roll around her tongue for a moment. Surely she would remember a name as unique as that.

'Lyra Thomas.'

He offered out his hand and she shook it. His hand felt warm to the touch.

He turned his attention to her dress, cleared his throat awkwardly, and then started to tug it over her hips, but it was wrapped around her so tightly, there was no give at all. In fact the material was starting to dig into her flesh.

Nix frowned, all humour fading from his eyes. 'I'm hurting you.'

Lyra winced. 'A little, but it's OK, just get it off.'

'I'm going to have to cut it.'

To her surprise, he pulled a penknife from his pocket. He flicked it open and her eyes widened. Christ, that looked sharp.

'I don't think…' Lyra started but Nix was already hacking away at the material, her favourite dress reduced to shreds in a matter of seconds. As she wriggled herself free of the dress and the bike, she realised her unicorn knickers were now on display too. She pulled the t-shirt down over them but it barely covered her bum. Well, this day was just getting better and better.

Nix worked quickly to release the dress from the cogs on the back wheel and then handed her bike back to her. She held the t-shirt down over her knickers with one hand and took the bike with the other.

He quickly grabbed the remains of the dress and

handed them to her, though it was quite clear they weren't going to be good for anything.

'Ah, sorry. I would give you my shorts but I'm not wearing anything underneath. I might get arrested if I start walking around the streets completely naked. Look, I'm camping in that field over there. Why don't you come back with me and I can lend you some more clothes?'

Lyra looked at the tatters of her dress and tied them around her waist like some kind of makeshift loincloth. She couldn't exactly ride back to her hotel like this. She nodded reluctantly; why not prolong her embarrassment a little longer?

They started walking down the road and an awkward silence fell over them. He'd seen her breasts for Christ's sake. What could she possibly say to make this situation better? And she was walking along the road wearing nothing more than a t-shirt, her bloody unicorn knickers and the remnants of her dress like a giant nappy.

She noticed that Nix had a tattoo round his arm, which looked like a series of numbers. She realised they were co-ordinates. She wanted to ask him about them but tattoos were very personal sometimes and she didn't feel they had arrived at that stage yet, despite him having seen her in various stages of undress. She felt like she needed to clear the air somehow before she started asking him what could be very personal questions.

'I'm sorry I flashed you.'

'Oh, I didn't notice.'

'Really?'

'No, I completely caught an eyeful.'

She laughed. 'You should have looked away.'

'Beautiful, half-naked woman sails past me on her bike screaming and whooping like a maniac. Believe me, there's no way I could look away from that, even if I wanted to.'

She tried to imagine what she must have looked like. It was certainly something Nix wouldn't forget in a hurry, but not necessarily for all the right reasons.

Nix unlocked a gate and held it open for her as she wheeled Daisy into the field.

Up against one corner, under a large oak, sat a small shiny blue camper van. 'Is that your van? I love it, she's beautiful.'

'She?' Nix said as they walked towards the van.

'Of course she's a woman. What's her name?'

'Why would I give my van a name?'

'She needs a name,' Lyra said, outraged.

'Does your bike have a name?'

'Yes, it's Daisy.'

He smirked. 'I should have known. Maybe you should name my van for me.'

'Well let's see… something fabulous, glamorous, like one of those old singers from back in the day. How about Judy, after Judy Garland?'

'Judy,' Nix nodded. 'Sure, why not? Hi Judy, we're back and I brought a friend with me.' He lowered his voice and whispered theatrically, 'And please don't judge the way she's dressed, we can't all look as fabulous as you.'

Lyra grinned.

Nix opened the van door and gestured for Lyra to go inside. He followed her in and she was suddenly aware of how small the space was inside when he was standing right behind her. There was a bed up one end, a small kitchen area, a few cupboards, and that was it.

Nix squeezed past her and opened one of the overhead cabinets. He rooted around for a few moments and then pulled out a pair of shorts. He handed them to her. 'They're drawstring so you should be able to pull it tight enough to fit.'

'Thank you,' Lyra said.

'I'll leave you to get changed. I'm sure you don't want me to see your unicorn knickers again.'

She stared after him in shock as he climbed out the van, chuckling to himself.

Lyra quickly pulled the shorts on, tightening the waist, and then stepped outside, feeling slightly less vulnerable now she was fully clothed.

Nix was standing at a small gas barbeque, adding a few sausages as Dexter sniffed hopefully around him.

'Thank you for this and for stopping to help me back there,' Lyra said.

'No problem.'

She paused. 'I should probably go. Are you here for a few days? I can get your clothes back to you.'

'No, I leave tomorrow, I have a meeting in Bristol tomorrow afternoon. But don't worry about it.'

'Oh, I could come back later tonight, drop them off.'

'Honestly, don't worry. But if you don't have to rush off, you can join me for some sausages. I make my own onion chutney and, I'm not going to lie, it's pretty bloody amazing. And with the sausages you're talking five-star cuisine.'

Lyra laughed at Nix's lack of modesty. She was about to politely decline; she had a plan for the evening and she always liked to stick to her plans. But her stomach rumbled loudly again. The sausages did look good, the big fat kind, and they were already starting to sizzle, turning a lovely shade of crispy brown. And she was still trying to place where she'd met him before. Maybe if she hung around a bit longer, it would come to her. Her plan to eat alone in the hotel restaurant didn't seem quite so tempting now. And she was technically on holiday, so she could afford to be a bit more fluid with her plans.

'Sausages and amazing onion chutney sounds good, if you have enough. I wouldn't want to deprive poor Dexter of his sausages.'

'Oh, don't worry, there's plenty for all of us. I couldn't let Dexter miss out. I'd be more likely to go hungry before he does – he's thoroughly spoiled, aren't you Dex?'

Dexter wagged his tail as if he agreed.

'Take a seat, they won't be long.'

Lyra sat down in one of the garden chairs and studied him for a moment as he tended to the sausages.

'Nix, have we met somewhere before?'

He looked at her. 'I thought that too but I haven't a clue where from. Do you work for the trust?'

'The trust?' Lyra said.

He gestured to the t-shirt she was wearing. It was a green one that had some kind of small logo across the left side of her chest. She pulled it out to see what it said. 'The Countryside Trust'.

'Oh no, I don't. I take it you do?'

'I volunteer for them,' Nix said. 'If it's not that, then I have no idea. Maybe we met in another life.'

She smiled. Maybe it was far-fetched but she liked the

idea that they were connected somehow through the passing of time. An eternity of friendship... or maybe more. Back when she was a child, she believed in whimsical stuff like that; fairytales, wishes, soul mates and destiny. And then at sixteen she suddenly had to grow up. Life with responsibility was far more boring.

Nix disappeared back inside the van for a second. He came back out carrying a bottle of red wine and pulling a t-shirt on over his head, which Lyra found herself disappointed by.

'Would you like a glass?' he asked.

She wasn't a big drinker but she did enjoy red wine now and again. There was plenty of time before the last ferry left the island. And as the sun was setting she would try to get a taxi back to her hotel once she reached the mainland rather than negotiate tiny country lanes in the dark on her bike, so she might as well enjoy a glass or two.

She nodded and he poured out two large glasses and passed one to her. Lyra took a sip. It was soothing and very fruity and felt instantly warm at the back of her throat.

'Mmm, this is lovely.'

'Ah thank you. I make my own using strawberries, plums and blackberries.'

'Oh wow. That's so cool. I wouldn't know where to start with that.'

'It's just a little hobby. And believe me, the first few batches I made were not fit for human consumption. But I like experimenting with stuff like that, food, wine; it's fun.'

'And is that what you do as a job, are you a chef?'

'Oh no, I never really fancied cooking for other people – well, other than friends and family. But no, I didn't want to do that as a job. I enjoy it too much to want that to be my nine to five.'

'So what is it you do?'

Nix turned the sausages over. 'You mean other than bum around in Judy?'

'There's nothing wrong with bumming around. My old grandad had one of those brightly painted wooden gypsy caravans and a beautiful horse called Thunder. He would travel from town to town, spend a few days in each place. He'd carve little ornaments out of wood and paint pictures of local attractions and then sell them on. Some days he'd make enough to have dinner in the pub, some days he'd make enough to buy a can of beans and a loaf of bread, but he was happy. No responsibilities, no job, no bills to pay beyond food for the horse and a gas canister for the stove. Maybe it's romantic and silly but I always fancied living that way.'

Lyra had yearned after that lifestyle even more when she'd been forced into a life of responsibility. Things hadn't turned out how she'd hoped. Not even close.

'It's not silly at all,' Nix said. 'I have Judy and I have a small boat – which you'll be pleased to know does have a name – and I'm never happier than when I throw my things in Judy and hit the road, or lift anchor and set sail, see where the wind takes me. It's peaceful. Me, Dex, the sun sparkling off the waves. There's no greater feeling than that.'

She smiled. They were kindred spirits. In a way. The only difference was that Nix had actively pursued that path, whereas she actively avoided it, always dreaming of that lifestyle but never doing anything to achieve it. Dreams were nice but reality was safer.

'I love the sound of that,' Lyra said. 'As a child I always thought that way of life was wonderful. I wanted adventure. I envisaged I would be the next Indiana Jones, seeking out lost treasure and going on exciting quests, travelling around the world.'

'What happened to that dream?'

She smiled – answering that would mean opening a can of worms. But she could skirt around it easily enough. 'Well, it turns out there aren't too many Indiana Jones jobs in the real world. Searching for lost treasure doesn't pay that well.'

'Oh, I imagine it pays very well. Finding lost emeralds and diamonds is surely very profitable,' Nix said.

'Ah, you have to find them first.'

'I think that's about knowing where to look. Sometimes you can find the most amazing things when you least expect them.'

His eyes were locked with hers and her breath caught in her throat. There was something wonderfully exciting about Nix but that scared her a little. She didn't want exciting. Or rather, there was still a part of her that did but, as that was the kind of person her mum was, she'd spent all of her adult life shunning it.

'What's your boat's name?' Lyra asked, needing to change the subject.

'Serendipity.'

Lyra choked on her wine.

'I know you might think it's silly but I've always

believed in fate, in being exactly where I'm meant to be. It seemed fitting.'

'Oh no, I agree. My grandad always used to say, "What's meant for you won't pass by you." And I've always believed that the things that happen to you, the important things anyway, are destined to happen, in some way. I wasn't laughing at your boat's name. It's just that... Serendipity is my first name, but I've always hated it, so I go by my middle name, Lyra, instead.'

His face lit up into a big smile. 'Well maybe it was serendipitous that we met.'

It was a line she had heard many times, meeting men in pubs. They thought it was funny but it just made her cringe. But for some reason, sitting here with Nix, as the sun was setting over the waves, hearing him say it felt significant somehow.

She smiled. 'Maybe.'

'For what it's worth, I think Serendipity is a beautiful name. Why don't you like it?'

Now that was another conversation she didn't really want to have. Her mum had named her for the carefree life she wanted for herself and that was something Lyra had resented when she'd got older.

'I think the life my mum wanted for me when she named me turned out to be very different to the one I have.'

That was a vague answer and one that visibly piqued Nix's curiosity, judging by his expression.

'When I grew up, Serendipity didn't seem appropriate any more. And it was always a bit of a mouthful anyway. My brothers and sisters always affectionately called me

Lyra so I just went with that. When we do speak, Mum still calls me by my first name, almost as a reminder of who I could be.'

'I don't think there's anything wrong with the person you are, Lyra. I mean, we've just met but you seem lovely.'

'I think if Mum had her way, I'd be sitting with her on a beach in Thailand, probably smoking something dubious, drinking copious cocktails and sleeping with a different man every night.'

Nix's eyebrows shot up. 'Well, your mum sounds like a character.'

Lyra nodded. 'That's one way of putting it.'

Nix dished up the sausages into white fluffy rolls and then put a dollop of what must be the much-lauded onion chutney on the side. He passed her the plate.

'So if we are going to leave the rat race and follow the open road together, how would we pay for our food?' he said as he sat down opposite her, and she was relieved he had changed the subject. 'I'm not good at carving or painting so I'm not sure how I would make enough to eat otherwise. And Dexter eats a lot of food. If he was to rely on my artistic side, we'd both go hungry.'

Lyra laughed. 'Me too. Sadly I didn't get that gene passed down from my grandad.'

Everyone said she was like her nan who had liked everything just so, which made her cringe a little. Her nan's favourite saying had been *A place for everything and everything in its place.* Her grandparents' house was always spotlessly clean and ordered. It was little wonder that, when her nan died, her grandad had sold the house and escaped in his little caravan, to finally have the freedom to do whatever he wanted. When Lyra was younger she'd felt she'd been destined to follow in her grandad's footsteps, to have a life of chance and adventure, but that had been silly, whimsical and unrealistic. When she was older and her mum had… retired from parenthood, her nan's genes had well and truly kicked in. She'd had to take life more seriously. Although she missed the freedom, she felt life always ran a lot smoother when there was a schedule or a plan.

Lyra realised Nix was still pondering over how they would make their money.

'I think you could probably sell your chutney and your wine,' she said, gesturing with her glass before taking a drink.

'I could, but there's not much room for my wine-making equipment in the back of Judy.'

'Well, if we're going to hit the open road together, we might need a roof rack and a trailer. I come with a lot of stuff.'

'You don't strike me as the shoes-and-handbags kind of girl,' Nix said, taking a bite of his sausage.

'No, books mainly. I have hundreds of books.'

'Ah. Would you be mortally offended if I bought you a Kindle for our adventure?'

She clutched her heart as if she'd been stabbed and he laughed. 'OK, we can get a roof rack for Judy and all your books. So if I'm cooking and selling chutney and wine, what are you bringing to the table?'

She took a bite of her sausage as she thought. What did she really have to offer? The ability to organise things down to the finest detail. It probably wasn't the spirit of adventure that Nix was looking for.

She grabbed the remains of her dress and draped them over her head like a shawl. 'I could tell people's fortunes.'

She immediately regretted doing that. She had a silly sense of humour and some people thought she was strange. She hadn't known Nix long enough to expose him to it.

But he was nodding, seemingly taking this seriously. 'Now I like the idea of that. If you can see into the future, we could buy the winning lottery ticket. We'd never need to worry about working again.'

'So do I get the job?'

'Lyra, I get the feeling you'd be a great addition to our team.'

She took another bite of her sausage as she watched him, his eyes locked on hers as he ate. Something was happening here and she got the feeling it was something wonderful. And that scared her a little. She certainly wasn't looking to get involved in any kind of relationship. She smiled and shook her head. Her sister, Michelle, always said she got carried away, always seeing what she wanted to see. This was a sausage sandwich with a nice man, she didn't need to make it into something bigger.

She looked away from Nix's amber-coloured eyes, needing to focus on something, anything else. The field sloped away to a small lake at the bottom, which reflected the dusky sky like a mirror. Wild poppies of every colour danced from the trees and bushes at the side of the field. It looked idyllic. As the sun left plum and tangerine trails across the sky, it couldn't have been more perfect.

'This is a lovely place to camp.' Lyra looked around, realising that Nix was the only one camping here and there didn't appear to be any kind of facilities at all. She gasped theatrically. 'Are you camping illegally on private land?'

Nix laughed. 'It *is* private land but… well, I own it so I'm pretty sure I'm allowed.'

'This is yours?'

'Yes, five acres in that direction,' he gestured with his hand.

'Wow.' Lyra looked down at the meadows and fields that followed the course of the river as it meandered down towards the sea. It was tranquil and peaceful. If she owned this, she'd spend every night up here, sitting in this chair looking out on the view.

'Don't make the mistake of thinking I'm rich. I spent every penny I had on buying this land and every penny I didn't. I sold my house, sold almost everything I owned. I now live in Judy or Serendipity, for the time being. Definitely more bum than billionaire.'

Lyra frowned. 'I wasn't thinking about your wealth. I was thinking how lucky you are to own all this. This is a very beautiful part of the world. Strangely, when I meet someone, their wealth has nothing to do with whether I want to get to know them better. Generally I choose my friends because they are kind or fun to be with, not because of how much money they have in their pocket.'

'Sorry,' Nix said. 'I'm used to meeting women in pubs whose eyes practically light up with pound signs when they hear I own land. I bought it to help the important work that the Countryside Trust are doing. It was never about financial gain.'

'See, that makes you infinitely more interesting than if you were just a boring billionaire.'

He grinned. 'I am sorry Lyra; I shouldn't judge you on other people's reactions.'

'It's fine. I'm just glad you're not here illegally. I thought I might have to call the police then for a minute.'

His mouth twitched into a smile. 'Are you a bit of a stickler for the rules? I have to say, when you entered my life in such a dramatic fashion earlier, I kind of figured you for a bit of a rebel.'

She spooned a bit of the chutney onto her second roll and took a bite to buy herself some time. She wasn't sure what to say, because that didn't actually sound like her at all. 'Mmm, this *is* amazing.'

'I've been perfecting that recipe over many, many years.'

'Well, I think you're pretty damn close to it being perfect,' Lyra said.

'Pretty damn close,' Nix echoed in disbelief. 'I don't get ten out of ten?'

'I'd give you nine and a half. If I give you ten, you've got nowhere else to go, nothing to strive towards.'

He grinned and took another bite of his own sausage. 'I'll take that challenge.' He chewed slowly, clearly deliberating over it. 'Maybe it could do with a bit more ginger.'

'Maybe.' She licked a drop of chutney off her finger, considering it. 'So what kind of work are you doing here with the trust?'

'Well, that would be top secret and I'm not sure I can trust you,' Nix teased.

'Now that does sound intriguing. So... you're working with a protected species. Bats?'

'No, but we may see some tonight.'

19

She tried to think of other endangered animals. 'Is it some kind of rare bug?'

'No, I'm not really into bugs. I mean, they play an important part in the ecosystem, but I've always been interested in bigger animals.'

Lyra finished off her roll as she thought. 'I know, hedgehogs… no, red squirrels.'

'Red squirrels in Cornwall would be very rare indeed.' Nix licked his fingers and she felt her eyes drawn to his tongue as he licked his lips.

She glanced down to the lake. Maybe that had something to do with why Nix was here. 'A newt or toad?'

'No, but you're right to focus on the water.'

She gasped. 'Is it Nessie?'

Nix laughed. 'Well, as you're an honorary member of the trust tonight,' he gestured to the t-shirt she was wearing, 'why don't I show you? They should be making an appearance right about now.'

'Oh, so they're a nocturnal animal.'

'The best time to see them is at dusk. I've been watching them here for the last three nights. Let me just put Dexter in the van. Can't have him chasing them away.'

Nix grabbed another sausage from the barbeque and encouraged Dexter back inside.

He looked back at her, his eyes casting down her legs in what felt like an intimate way. 'It's quite boggy down this side of the lake, I fear your poor sandals may get ruined. I have a spare pair of wellies. They'll probably be a bit big for you but better that than your feet getting all muddy.'

'Well, normally I wouldn't care but, as I borrowed these sandals from my sister, and when I say borrowed I mean that in the loosest sense of the word, I probably should take your wellies. She won't be impressed if I return them to her covered in mud.'

He handed her the wellies and she slipped out of her sandals and pulled the boots on.

Nix grabbed a rucksack and closed the van door. He offered out his hand, and she stood and took it, as if it was the most natural thing in the world.

They started walking down the hill towards the lake. 'In all seriousness, Lyra, you can't tell anyone what I'm about to show you. We're trying to educate people about how wonderful this species is, how useful they can be, not only to us but to other wildlife and the environment, but there are still many who think they are nuisances and others who might try to hunt them, so at the moment we're trying to keep the location of some colonies a bit quiet.'

'You can trust me,' Lyra said, suddenly realising the importance of all of this.

He regarded her for a moment. 'Yes, I think I can.'

They neared the lake and Nix gestured for her to be quiet as they made their way through the bushes and trees, which blocked out a lot of the remaining light. He suddenly stopped and gently pulled her so she was in front of him, his hands on her shoulders. She closed her eyes as she felt the warmth of his body against hers. There was something hugely intimate about this even though Nix was oblivious to it.

'Look,' he whispered and pointed through the branches.

She peered into the increasing darkness, her eyes becoming accustomed to the gloom, and then she gasped as she saw it.

CHAPTER TWO

'Oh my god. Is that… is that a beaver?' Lyra squeaked in excitement.

'Yes.'

She twisted to look at Nix, realising they were face to face. She paused for a second, his eyes locked on hers, before she quickly turned back to look at the beaver as it sat in the water, chewing on some wood.

'This is incredible. I'd heard there were plans to reintroduce them to the UK but I didn't realise they'd actually done it.'

'There are actually quite a few colonies in different parts of the UK, but it's still early days. We'll be monitoring them over the next few years to see what their impact is on the environment and local wildlife. But so far all the signs point to having them here being hugely advantageous. This is George, he's the dad of this colony.'

'He's huge,' Lyra whispered.

'Yeah, they grow really big. He's kind of special, at least to me. He is one of the beavers born in Britain in one of the other controlled studies. When he was only a few months old he was attacked by a fox and lost his foot. We had this horrible dilemma of whether to interfere or not. The whole point of reintroducing them to the wild is to largely leave them to their own devices, but we couldn't just stand by and do nothing. We had worked so hard to get our beavers to breed and his mum and dad only had one kit and I hated the thought of them losing him. If left alone, the leg probably would have got infected, so rightly or wrongly I took him and nursed him back to health.'

Lyra turned to look at him with a smile. 'I think you definitely did the right thing.'

Nix shrugged. 'I think there are many who disagree with you but I did it anyway. George had surgery and we looked after him for several weeks and then released him back into the wild. We weren't sure if he would survive with one foot missing, or whether our interference when he was so young would hinder his ability to adapt to the wild, but he's five years old now and you'd never know he had such a rough start to life. His mum and dad were over-joyed to have him back, and he just carried on as if he hadn't been away. He's adapted to only having three feet very easily. He spends most of his time in the water anyway so it's not like he has to move around much on land. When he was old enough to mate, we introduced him to Tilda, another British-born beaver, and they hit it off.'

'And they made a family of their own?' Lyra said.

When he remained silent for a moment, she turned to look at him.

'She didn't care that he only had three legs, she still loved him.'

She studied him for a moment, there was more to what he was saying here.

He cleared his throat. 'The beaver population is thriving because of all the beaver projects around England, but at the moment they're not allowed to be released into the wild. All the projects are on private land and their movements are restricted within that land. With all the beavers breeding, we don't want to get to the point where we are culling the beavers because of overpopulation. I wanted to help in some small way. The beavers are such an important species: they help to prevent floods, they improve the water quality wherever they make dams and the wildlife increases exponentially in all areas where beavers live. So that's why I sold my house and bought the land.'

Lyra stared at him. He was so passionate about this that he had changed his entire life to support the project and help the beavers.

'Nix, you're an incredible man.'

He immediately looked embarrassed and she regretted saying that. That wasn't the kind of thing you said to someone you'd just met, not unless you were wanting to jump into bed with him. She tried to backpedal.

'I don't mean… I'm not flirting with you. This is not, "You're incredible, I want to have your babies," it's just, "You're incredible, no strings attached."'

He stared at her. Yes, she'd definitely made that worse.

Nix cleared his throat. 'So we moved them here so they could start their own colony. I always worry that because of his disability George might be more vulnerable to predators and I can't protect him from that, but at least here, on Jewel Island, the risk might be less.'

She turned back to face the beaver, grateful that the increasing darkness was hiding how red her cheeks were. 'How so?'

'Well, places like the Scilly Isles don't have large predators like foxes, stoats or weasels. There's no way for those species to get there. Jewel Island is similar. You'll see the odd one here because of the causeway joining the island to the mainland, the animals come across that, but the causeway is only accessible at low tide so the risk is a lot lower. Plus George is a big boy now, there are fewer animals that will pick a fight with him.'

'So he has his own family now?'

'There's six here. Tilda, she's the mum, and then four young of varying ages. We rarely see all six of them together but we might see three or four. Oh look, there's Pearl. She's their eldest. She's already showing signs of being ready to leave. She's set up her own lodge further round the lake but she still comes back and feeds with her parents sometimes. A bit like a child going off to university and coming back home in the holidays. Oh, and that's Ruby over there.'

'How can you recognise them?'

'I don't know, I just do. The twins are harder to tell apart.'

'This is all so incredible,' Lyra whispered as she watched them in awe.

Ruby came and started having a chew of the end of George's piece of wood and, like all good, long-suffering dads, George simply let her.

'So the babies are called kits?' Lyra asked, suddenly

wanting to know everything there was to know about this little family.

'Yes, and the older children are called yearlings.'

'And are they actually eating the wood?'

'Yes, they're herbivores. They eat roots, bark, leaves. Contrary to popular belief, they don't eat fish.' Nix was silent for a moment. 'They are monogamous too.'

She smiled, somehow feeling the significance in those words.

'As someone who has been burned quite spectacularly by the opposite sex, I can appreciate that,' Lyra said. 'If one dies, will a beaver find a new mate?'

Nix didn't answer at first. 'Some do, some don't. George's mum died, fairly young for a beaver too. George's dad never found another mate.'

She turned to look at Nix. 'That's so sad.'

'It is. We introduced him to several females but he didn't hit it off with any of them. I guess that's the same for humans too; sometimes they never find another partner either.'

Lyra paused before she spoke. 'My mum and dad split when I was around sixteen. Mum slept with everything that moved over the next few years but Dad has never had another relationship since. Mum had multiple affairs while she was married and I think it broke my dad's heart. I don't think he ever got over that. And I'm not sure what's worse, trying to fill the gap with anyone or everyone just so you're not alone, or staying alone for the rest of your life because no one will ever match up to the one you lost.'

'I wouldn't settle,' Nix said. 'If it was me and I'd lost the love of my life, I wouldn't fill it with random women just so I wasn't alone. A lot of my friends sleep around and that life suits them just fine – there's no commitment or responsibilities – but I've never been like that. I want someone spectacular, someone really special, and if I can't have that I'd rather be alone.'

Lyra stared at him and she got the feeling his response went much deeper than his casual tone suggested.

He shrugged, trying to play it down. 'Maybe that's how your dad feels. Maybe he just never met the right person to move on with after your mum.'

'I think my mum set the bar very low when it came to wife material.'

'Ah, but you can't help who you fall in love with. Or maybe your mum's behaviour put your dad off from ever wanting another relationship again, maybe he decided he was happier on his own. Nothing wrong with that.'

'No, there isn't,' Lyra said, turning her attention back to the beavers as they swam and moved around in the lake and stream. Nix had unwittingly described her to a tee. She had long since given up on having a relationship again, though not because there was some great life partner that she was lamenting losing. She was just happier going through life alone. It was a lot easier that way.

She glanced at Nix and mentally shook her head. If ever there was a man who could tempt her out of her self-imposed celibacy, it would be someone like him, and for that reason she should run a hundred miles in the opposite direction. But there was something about him that had her feet glued to the ground.

They watched the beavers for hours and, when it got too dark to see, Nix fished out some night-vision binoculars which they shared between them while he regaled her with everything there was to know about beavers and the funny little quirks that George and his family had.

Eventually, they made their way back to the van.

'I've had the most amazing time tonight, thank you for sharing the beavers with me,' Lyra said.

'It was my pleasure,' Nix said. 'I presume you're staying on the island? I can walk you back if so.'

'I'm not, I'm staying in a hotel a little way down the coast on the mainland.'

Nix stopped and looked at his watch. 'Lyra, the last ferry left the island over half hour ago.'

'What? No, they run until eleven.'

'On weekends, not during the week.'

'Oh crap. What time is low tide?'

He pulled his phone out of his pocket and swiped his fingers across the screen. 'It's high tide in about half hour. Low tide is at four thirty tomorrow morning.'

Lyra looked around. She would have to stay on Michelle's sofa for a night. Her sister wouldn't mind too much and Lyra's nephew would be delighted.

'You could stay here,' Nix said behind her.

She turned to face him. 'What?'

'You could stay in my van with me.' He shrugged as if it wasn't a big deal. 'I promise to be on my absolute best behaviour but the bed is big enough for the two of us if you want to stay.'

CHAPTER THREE

Nix watched Lyra's indecision for a moment. He wasn't exactly sure this was a good idea either. He had no idea why he offered his bed to her, but for some reason he didn't want her to leave. He'd enjoyed talking to her tonight and he wanted to get to know her better.

He shook his head. He always used to be so confident when it came to women but the sad truth was that he hadn't had anyone in his bed for over three years. He'd dated, taken women to dinner or drinks, but, at the end of the night, he hadn't wanted to take it any further. And now he was inviting Lyra to share his bed with him. Even if it was strictly to sleep, it still felt weird somehow. But at the same time it felt so right. If she said no, would he be relieved or disappointed?

Lyra was gazing out over the sea and it seemed an age before she finally made up her mind; she probably didn't think it was a good idea either.

She turned back to look at him, fixing him with a warning glare. 'No funny business.'

'You have my word,' Nix said, hope blooming in his heart.

She nodded. 'OK. But I sleep on the left side.'

His mouth twitched into a smirk. He really liked this woman.

'That's fine, although I'll let you break it to Dexter. He normally prefers the left side of the bed.'

She smiled.

'Well, I'm not quite ready to hit the sack just yet, fancy a nightcap?' he said.

'Sure.'

He opened the van, letting Dexter out. The dog greeted them both as if they'd been gone for days, not just a few hours. Nix lit a candle in one of the storm lanterns and placed it in the middle of the table, although the light from the van was probably more than sufficient.

'We can finish off the wine if you want, or I have whisky. Or I can just make us two coffees if you'd prefer.'

'Do you have tea?' Lyra asked.

'I don't, I'm afraid. I don't drink it.'

'Coffee is fine,' Lyra said. 'Two sugars please.'

Nix nodded and stepped back inside the van. Coffee was probably better than drinking alcohol. He needed to keep a clear head and not do anything he'd regret.

He quickly made the coffees and took them outside. Lyra was sitting on the step leading up into the van, stroking Dexter as she looked out over the moonlit waves. He sat down next to her, her warmth filling him from the inside. She took her coffee, wrapping her hands around the mug.

'It's so beautiful here,' Lyra said.

'It is. Jewel Island is a very special place for me.'

Lyra watched him for a moment and then placed a finger gently on his arm, right over his co-ordinate tattoo.

He tried to ignore the feeling inside him ignited by her touch.

He nodded. 'Yes, these are the co-ordinates for Jewel Island.'

She studied him, obviously wanting to ask why it was such a special place, but it wasn't something he really wanted to get into tonight.

'Do you live here?' she asked.

'No, not right now. Well, I don't live anywhere right now. But I've spent a lot of time here.'

'So have you heard the story of the lost treasure?'

He watched her, her eyes sparkling with excitement. She was so endearing.

'I have heard the rumours though I think it's more legend and myth than anything substantial,' Nix said.

'It's said that's where the name Jewel Island comes from and that there's a chest of precious jewels buried somewhere here.'

'Maybe we should look for it,' Nix said.

She smiled. 'I'd like that.'

They sat there staring at each other for a moment and he had a sudden realisation that he would sail the stormiest seas on the wildest goose chase if he got to spend more time with her.

Her eyes glanced down to his lips for the briefest of seconds and his heart leapt. God, he wasn't sure if he was ready for this yet. He kept telling himself he was ready to date but he didn't think he was.

'Do *you* have any tattoos?' Nix quickly asked, hoping to divert her.

Lyra grinned. 'Yes, I have a tattoo. I won it in a competition.'

He laughed. 'What?'

'I always fancied having one but couldn't afford to get one when I was younger. And then a new tattoo shop opened in my local town. It was reported in one of those little articles in the local press and they were giving away a fifty-pound voucher for the new shop. It was one of those silly competitions that no one enters – you know, the ones that say something like, "Rattlesnakes, the tattoo shop was named after the tattoo artist's favourite animal", and then at the end of the article it asks what the artist's favourite animal is. Well I entered and I won. So I got my tattoo. My brothers and sisters were convinced that I'd lost my fun side completely and I wanted to show them that I still had that side of me in there.'

'I love that. What did you get?'

She smiled. 'What do you think I got?'

'Well, I'm quickly learning to expect the unexpected when it comes to you,' Nix said. 'So dolphins, unicorns and flowers are probably out.'

'You'd be right.'

'A shark?'

'No, but actually that was a contender. Here, I'll show you.'

She stood up and hoisted the t-shirt up so he could see her shoulder blade. He stood up too, lifting the material to get a better view, his fingers accidentally grazing her skin. He smiled when he saw it. It was a T-Rex.

'You like dinosaurs?'

She turned round to face him, amusement sparking in her eyes. 'I love them.'

He glanced down at her lips, which were very close to his, and he felt an overwhelming desire to kiss her. He took a small step back away from her.

'I was always fascinated by them when I was growing up and I thought I'd become a palaeontologist when I was older, although that never happened. Do you like him?'

'I love him. He's very you. Do you ever regret getting it?'

'Not for one second. I only regret that I had it done where I can't see it.'

'You could get another one, somewhere more visible. A brontosaurus perhaps or a triceratops.'

'Or maybe a beaver,' Lyra said.

Nix's eyes cast down to her lips again. Yes, he definitely wanted to kiss her.

He swallowed and sat back down on the step. 'I think George would be very flattered by that.'

She laughed and took a seat next to him.

What was happening here? He wasn't sure if he liked it. Maybe he should ask her to go. Except he wasn't an asshole and he wasn't going to leave her homeless for the night. But there was an alternative. Why hadn't he told her about the tent? He sighed; he knew damned well why he hadn't told her he had a tent, and now he'd made his bed and had to lie in it, quite literally.

'So tell me, Lyra, do you normally ride your bike topless or was that just for my benefit today?'

She laughed and he loved the sound of it. 'I'm actually

normally a bit more... reserved than that. I'm definitely more of a planner than a pantster.'

'A pantster?'

'Someone who flies by the seat of their pants.'

'Ah, the Lyra I met tonight didn't seem very reserved, and I don't mean the nudity part. You've talked about how much you'd like to cut loose and go on an adventure, follow the open road, you were even brave enough to try my homemade wine and chutney – and let's not forget how excited you were about meeting a group of beavers.'

Nix thought about this for a moment. Previous women he'd talked to about his work with beavers had either feigned interest, politely asking a few questions before changing the subject, or they'd blatantly had no interest at all, or they'd been disgusted by the filthy vermin he'd been working with. He'd never realised before how important it was that he found a woman who was on his wavelength when it came to beavers. He wouldn't say an interest in beavers was a requirement in his relationships, but it was utterly refreshing to have someone who shared his passion. He smiled to himself as he took a sip of his coffee. His brother, Lucas, would be rolling his eyes that Nix was geeking out over finding a fellow beaver lover. But he had loved witnessing Lyra's enthusiasm, squealing in excitement over seeing them, asking loads of questions. She'd looked like she would have been happy to stay there all night watching them and he loved that.

'Tonight has been one of the best nights I've had in a very long time,' Lyra said. 'The beavers were a huge part of that but so were you. I think I've held myself back for so long from fear of the past repeating itself but tonight, chatting and laughing with you, I've felt more like my old self again.'

'Well, if this is the old Lyra, you should let her out more often. She's wonderful,' Nix said.

She stared at him for a moment and he sensed something shift between them. He felt the need to keep talking because he feared, if he stopped, something would happen, something he wasn't ready for.

'Why do you hold yourself back?' he asked.

She let out a deep breath. 'Well, that's probably a long story. My brother, Max, says I have trust issues. I was let down quite spectacularly by my parents and Max thinks I have trouble trusting people because I fear getting hurt. I don't know if that's true. I worry more about letting other people down than being let down myself.'

'I can't imagine you ever letting anyone down.'

'Oh, you'd be surprised,' Lyra said.

He watched her as she took a sip of her coffee. He got the feeling there were many many layers to Lyra Thomas and he suddenly wanted to peel them all away and reveal what was buried inside.

'You can trust me,' Nix said.

She looked at him with wide eyes. He didn't know why he was saying that. He had the feeling if he were to get involved with Lyra it would be something serious and he wasn't ready for that. Hell, he wasn't sure if he even *wanted* that. But there was something about her that he couldn't walk away from.

'I can?'

'I'm not going to hurt you.'

He couldn't promise that. He was woefully out of practice when it came to women and he'd only ever been in one serious relationship in his life. But there was something vulnerable about Lyra – he wanted to take care of her, protect her. That in itself would ensure he wouldn't hurt her, surely?

Her eyes cast down to his lips and his heart leapt in his chest.

'Nix, I think you have the potential to hurt me a lot more than you think. And I feel like if I kiss you now, I'm going to regret it in the morning, but if I don't I think I'll regret it for the rest of my life.'

He found himself smiling. 'Life is too short to live with regret.'

'That is true. We never know what's around the next corner and I don't want to look back at this moment and think why didn't I grab it.'

He took her coffee out of her hand and put both mugs down on the floor. 'Life should be grabbed by the horns sometimes.'

'I agree.'

She smiled as she leaned forward and kissed him.

Looking back on this moment, he liked to think that perhaps he'd paused, that there'd been some consideration that he shouldn't do this. But in reality there was no such hesitation as he kissed her back with as much need as she was kissing him.

His heart thundered with a sudden desire, the taste of her was incredible.

Lyra pulled back suddenly. 'Sorry. I, er…'

He cupped her face and kissed her again, feeling her melt against him. Her fingers caressed the back of his neck and a noise escaped his mouth that sounded like a growl. Christ, he'd be scaring her away. But instead of pulling back, she giggled against his lips. God, he really bloody liked this woman. She ran her hands down his arms and he slid his hands down to her waist, hauling her closer so she was almost lying on top of him as the kiss continued. He wanted her closer, he wanted to feel her skin against his.

Nix pulled back slightly to look at her, his breath heavy against her lips. He stroked her hair from her face. 'I think it's time we went to bed.'

She bit her lip and then nodded.

She was nervous and that was probably a good thing. Her vulnerability and his need to take care of her would ensure he would slow this thing down and not get carried away. It would just be a kiss between them. Nothing more.

She stood up and stepped up into the van, slipping off the wellies.

He stood up and stared at the sky and the moon casting silvery ribbons over the sea for a moment, trying to cool his thoughts. He blew the candle out, then whistled for Dexter. Once his dog was safely inside, he stepped up inside the van and closed the door behind him.

Lyra was slipping out of her shorts and climbing into bed, scooting over to the far side. He kicked his boots off and swallowed. It was just going to be a kiss.

He pulled off his t-shirt and climbed into bed next to her, taking her in his arms and kissing her again. She slid her hands down his back, her touch against his skin igniting a fire inside of him. He ran his hand up her bare thigh and she moaned against his lips. He needed more. He toyed with the hem of her t-shirt for a second and then slowly pulled it over her head. And she let him, lifting her arms above her head to make it easier. He swore softly at the sight of her almost naked in his bed. His need for her erupted through him so strong and so hard, it wiped all sense and reason from his mind. He kissed her again, thanking his lucky stars that his brother Lucas had borrowed the van a few weeks before and there were condoms in the little cupboard above the headboard.

Another soft moan from her brought clarity back to his mind for a moment. No, it wasn't going to be more than a kiss between them… he didn't want to do anything she would regret.

Nix pulled back to look at her.

'Lyra, I have a confession. I have a tent, a pop-up one, and a spare sleeping bag. We don't need to share this bed tonight.'

She stared at him and then smiled. 'I have a confession too. My sister lives on the island. I could have slept on her sofa.'

He couldn't help smiling as he kissed her again.

Her hands slipped down his spine and then into the back of his shorts, squeezing his bum. He made a noise that sounded like an animal about to devour his prey and rolled on top of her.

'We should stop,' Nix said, against her lips, kissing her, stroking her.

'Yes, we probably should,' Lyra said, in between kisses, running her hands over his shoulder blades. 'Why are we stopping?'

He had no idea. 'We should get to know each other first.'

As he continued to kiss her, it sounded feeble to his own ears.

'Yes, good idea,' she muttered, kissing him again. 'What would you like to know?'

He wanted to know everything there was to know about Lyra Thomas but now suddenly didn't seem the right time.

He needed to stop kissing her, put some distance between them, talk to her instead of mauling her, but he couldn't let her go. He searched for a question, something normal and boring, something to cool the passion racing through his veins.

'How many brothers and sisters do you have?' Nix said, kissing her throat.

She giggled against his lips. 'Five.'

The vibrations of that laugh went straight through his body, making his gut clench with desire.

'Michelle, Max, Kitty, Frankie and Ethan,' Lyra said, tracing the indent of his spine with the lightest of touches.

'How old are you?' Nix asked, desperately clinging onto the last fragments of control. But the way she was kissing him, touching him, the feel of her body against his, he was going out of his mind with need for her.

'Thirty, how old are you?'

'Thirty-one.'

'If this is how you talk dirty, you might need a bit of practice,' Lyra said, kissing his shoulder. 'Any other questions?'

'Give me a moment and I'm sure I could think of something.'

He kissed her again, running a hand up her ribs, stroking his thumb over her breast.

She gasped against his lips. 'I promise, I will answer every single question you have for me. But after.'

He kissed her again and the feel of her skin against his was divine. As she wrapped her legs around him, all restraint went straight out the window.

He half rolled off her, sliding down her knickers, as she pushed his shorts off his hips. He wriggled out of them so they were both naked.

Lyra let out a soft moan. His hands were everywhere, touching, stroking, caressing. Nix made her feel alive. He pulled his mouth from hers and started kissing across her shoulders, her chest, her stomach, his hot mouth driving her wild. He kissed across her breast and when he ran his tongue across her nipple she arched off the bed, thrusting her fingers through his hair. Nix slid his hand up her inner thigh and every nerve, every fibre, sparked with need inside her as he touched her. That feeling crashed through her so quickly and so hard she cried out and he leaned up and caught her moans on his lips.

'Nix,' she whispered, trembling in his arms.

He pulled back to look at her, his eyes clouding with concern. 'Are you OK?'

She nodded. 'I'm more than OK.'

He smiled slightly. 'We don't have to carry on if you want to stop.'

'Are you kidding me? You can't tease me with the starters and then not deliver on the main course.'

He grinned. 'Well, I wouldn't get your hopes up too high for the main course, it's been a while.'

She wondered what he meant by a while. A few weeks or months maybe? Someone like Nix probably had a long queue of women waiting for him.

'Me too,' Lyra said, quietly, knowing the last time she'd been with a man would probably be a hell of a lot longer than the last time Nix had slept with someone. 'I don't usually do this kind of thing. In fact, I've never done this kind of thing.'

She normally guarded her heart so fiercely and she always associated sex with intimacy in a relationship. Something she'd typically only ever do in a serious relationship. But her connection with Nix felt unlike anything she'd experienced before. He was completely different to any man she'd been with before. This felt like it was something rare and wonderful.

'We'll take it slow,' he said, softly before kissing her again.

She smiled against his lips, loving how he wanted to take care of her. He carried on kissing her for the longest time, apparently in no rush, whereas her body was humming with need. Finally he reached over her head and grabbed a condom from a cupboard. His eyes scanned hers and she nodded, stroking his face.

He ripped it open with his teeth and a few moments later he was leaning back over her, gathering her hands in his as he pinned them above her head. She wrapped her legs around his hips and he slid carefully inside her in one exquisite movement.

She gasped at the feel of him and his eyes locked with hers as he moved slowly against her. She felt something shift between them, an undefinable, amazing sensation, something she had never experienced before. She knew she was silly to get caught up in the moment like this, she should just enjoy it for what it was, one wonderful night, but she couldn't escape the feeling that this was the start of something incredible. And the way that Nix was staring at her, it was almost as if he felt it too.

He released her hands and gathered her close as she wrapped her arms around him, holding him tight.

'Lyra.'

Her name was no more than a whisper on his lips as he bent his head and kissed her.

This man was going to ruin her. Need for him grew in the pit of her stomach, igniting like little fireworks exploding through her body. She stroked down his back, caressing the dent of his spine, stroking the muscles in his shoulders, and he groaned against her lips. He started moving faster and she clung to him as that feeling spiralled inside her, taking her higher and higher until she was falling over the edge and bringing him with her.

CHAPTER FOUR

Lyra woke with the stars sparkling above them, the moon casting a silvery glow over the waves beneath them. She was wrapped tightly in Nix's arms, her head on his warm chest.

She kissed his bare skin, relishing the scent of him, and she felt his lips touch the top of her head in response.

She looked up at him and he smiled at her, stroking her face.

'Hello,' she said.

'Hey.'

'It's a beautiful night.'

His eyes stayed locked on her face. 'It really is. I've never seen anything as beautiful before.'

She smiled. 'For future reference, that's the kind of thing you should say before sex, not, how many brothers and sisters do you have.'

He laughed. 'I was trying to be respectful. It didn't feel right pinning you to the bed and making love to you without at least trying to get to know you first.'

'And I appreciate that. Normally it takes me a lot longer to be comfortable enough to go to bed with someone.'

'Trust issues?' Nix said.

'Something like that.'

'Ah, come on, you promised to answer my questions.'

'OK, you get one now. I'll answer some more for you tomorrow. So you better make it a good one.'

'Right, let's see. There's so much I want to know.'

She liked that he wanted to get to know her. If this was a one-night stand, he wouldn't care. But she wasn't sure she was ready to open up to him, to share all her darkest secrets. She bit her lip nervously. He'd got enough out of her already about the kind of person she was and about her mum for him to want to follow that up. Did she really want to hand over all her baggage?

'So I get mixed signals from you,' Nix said. 'You said you're not a pantster, you like a plan, you rejected your first name because a life of chance and spontaneity was not you any more. But that doesn't ring true with the woman who got a tattoo just to prove to her siblings that she was fun and daring. You spoke about packing up your belongings and going on an adventure, wanting to be the next Indiana Jones, but it feels like you're too scared to follow those dreams. I get the feeling something happened to make you keep those walls around you, but the wild and free Lyra is still in there, wanting to get out.'

Lyra focussed her attention on Nix's chest, running an absent finger over his heart. That was a very insightful summary of her life.

'So what's the question?' she said.

'Why do you hold yourself back, what happened to make you so afraid of letting go?'

Lyra watched a plane flying far up above them, going off somewhere exotic no doubt. For a while, she didn't speak. She didn't want Nix to think badly of her.

He tilted her chin up to face him.

'You can trust me, remember.'

And for some reason, she did.

She sighed. 'My mum was always a little bit slapdash and carefree. We used to go out for the day with no real idea where we were going. We'd toss a coin or roll a dice to decide what we would do. Mum always said it was much more fun that way. I grew up thinking she was amazing. I loved that spontaneity and life of chance, of going out for the day with no plan, of just seeing where we ended up.

'Dad was always a lot stricter: we had to do our home-work straight from school, we had curfews and we had to stick to them. Until he left, I never realised how Dad was almost single-handedly running the household. Mum fell to pieces, hit the bottle, and I... was too busy going out with my mates with no curfew to even notice. She was angry all the time so I avoided going home, we all did. My brothers and sisters had their own friends they hung out with. I was sixteen and clearly completely self-absorbed. I never noticed that my brothers and sisters went to school for weeks without any lunch or money to buy food and they often went in dirty clothes. I never noticed the bills or the final demand bills piling up. I never noticed that the house wasn't clean, I was barely at home with my sudden new-found freedom. Mum didn't care that I wasn't there so I made the most of it. I never realised my brothers and sisters, especially Max, had started to struggle at school or that he was being bullied. Mum had brought us up to be carefree, to not have any responsibilities, and I was well and truly embracing that lifestyle.'

Lyra pulled the duvet up round her shoulders, suddenly feeling cold despite the warmth of the night.

'It was Max's thirteenth birthday that changed everything. I'd bought him a present but no one else had. With Mum drowning her sorrows in the bottle and Dad completely off the scene, no one had reminded the others or taken them shopping to buy something for him from them. I didn't even see him that morning as I'd been out late the night before with friends and overslept. By the time I'd got up he'd already left for school. No one had cooked him a special birthday breakfast, or even acknowledged his existence at all. No presents, no cards.' She swallowed the lump of emotion in her throat. 'He never made it to school. He... threw himself off a bridge.'

'Shit, Lyra.' Nix immediately cupped the back of her head, rolling towards her so they were lying on their sides facing each other.

'He's OK,' Lyra said, brushing away the tears, because even now it hurt her to think her brother had sunk so low that he'd thought death was the only way out. And that she had played some part in that. 'He broke his leg and two ribs, smashed up his face pretty good. He was in a wheelchair and then crutches for weeks, but he was OK. Physically at least. He's fine now, happily married, lives in Australia. But it was a huge wake-up call for me. I should have been there for him, for all of them. I was the oldest, I should have—'

46

'You were sixteen Lyra; you were still a child yourself. You can't take the blame for that. Your dad walked out on you and your mum more or less abandoned you herself when she left you all to your own devices. Regardless what was going on between your parents, they had a responsibility to you and the other children and they dropped the ball, not you.'

Lyra shook her head; she should have done more. She could never let go of that guilt. Her brother had nearly died because of her.

'Did your mum step up after that?' Nix asked.

Lyra shook her head. 'Obviously Mum was distraught that he'd done it but it wasn't enough to bring her out of herself. If anything, it made her worse. She was always moaning that she was a terrible mum but she never did anything about it. From that moment on I pretty much raised my brothers and sisters single-handedly. Got up early to make them packed lunches and give them breakfast, made sure their clothes were always washed and ironed. Passed my driving test as soon as I could and bought an old banger so I could drive them around their after-school clubs. There were so many of them that I ended up making a timetable that I stuck to the fridge so I knew where I had to be at any given time to collect them or drop them off. I made sure their homework was done and that I was always there to help them with it. I quit college and got a job to help with the bills. Dad sent some money every month – that was his contribution to his children's upbringing, but I did everything else. There were six of us so it took a lot of organisation and planning to make sure none of them missed out. It was exhausting but that was my life for the next eight or nine years, at least until they'd all moved out or went off to university.'

'And your parents never helped out?' Nix was incredulous.

'Dad moved to America pretty soon after he left. He lives over there now. I've only seen him twice since; he has nothing to come back here for. He sent money, quite a lot of it actually – maybe it was guilt money, but we never went hungry. And when I was twenty-one, Mum went backpacking around the world. She lives in Thailand now, where she has fully embraced the carefree life. I rarely speak to either of them. Ethan was only fourteen when she left. I mean, she hadn't exactly been mum of the year since Dad left but at least she'd been there in some capacity. For her to walk out on Ethan when he was still so young, I hated her a little bit for that.

'Eventually, my brothers and sisters all moved out, had their own lives, but I've never really been able to let go of that need to organise and plan. I guess I'm scared that if I let go, I might turn out like my mum who only ever cared about herself. Spontaneity and a life with no responsibilities sounds wonderful but quite often there are repercussions for those actions, and I don't want anyone to ever get hurt from something I've done. I want my brothers and sisters to know they can rely on me, no matter what.'

Nix was staring at her as if he didn't know what to do with all this baggage she'd suddenly dumped at his feet. He probably hadn't been expecting this.

She wanted to let him off the hook.

'Let's change the subject. Tell me something about you.'

'Let's not. I think you're amazing, Lyra Thomas.'

She shook her head. 'I'm not, I just did what I had to do.'

'You raised five children on your own when you were still a child yourself. That's pretty bloody incredible in my eyes.'

She smiled sadly. It wasn't true but it was nice of him to see it that way.

'You don't see it; you don't see what a wonderful thing you did.'

'What was the alternative? Let my siblings go hungry, let their lives fall apart just because my parents couldn't care less? Thankfully it was only a few weeks before I picked up the slack or I'm damned sure social services would have been called. They might even have been taken into care, and there was no way I was going to allow that.'

'I think a lot of sixteen-year-olds would have taken that road rather than take on that responsibility. But I'm quickly realising how utterly unique and spectacular you are.'

He cupped her face and kissed her and she melted against him. She'd told him something hugely personal, something she'd never told anyone before, and he was here, kissing her like he truly believed she was spectacular. No one had ever called her that before.

Lyra had always wondered if she was perhaps unloveable. Her dad walked out on them, her mum abandoned them. Even her brothers and sisters had left home as soon as they possibly could, leaving her in the family home alone, until her dad had finally sold it. The fleeting relationships with the men she had dated briefly had all ended after a few dates. The three semi-serious relationships she'd had all ended because her boyfriends had cheated on her. She wondered if the issue was her. But the way Nix was kissing her now – like he adored her – it felt like maybe she was loveable after all.

She stroked round the back of his head, touching his hair around his neck.

He slid his hands down her spine and then pulled her tight against him, holding her in a big hug as he kissed her.

The kiss very quickly turned from something sweet and loving to something needful and urgent.

He moved his mouth to her throat.

'Christ Lyra, what are you doing to me?' he whispered, trailing his hot mouth over her collarbone.

He swept his hand down her ribs and over her thighs and then slid it between her legs. Her body instantly awakened at his caress, still sensitive from the last time he'd touched her there. She arched against him, stretching out her body as she lay in front of him, and he used that opportunity to hook her leg over his. His touch was gentle but confident, he knew exactly where she needed him to be. It took mere seconds before she was moaning against his lips.

He pulled away, reaching over her to grab another condom. She could barely catch her breath but a few seconds later he was inside her. She moaned at the sensation and he kissed her as he held her close. He felt so good, *this* felt good. Their bodies entwined, the touch of his bare chest against hers, his heart beating hard against her. His hands were everywhere, relishing in the feel of her, his mouth against hers, it was complete sensory overload.

How was it possible that this man fitted her so perfectly? How did he know exactly where she liked to be touched without being told? She'd never had this kind of connection so early on in a relationship before. In fact, she'd never had this kind of connection at all, despite having been with her previous boyfriends for months.

Nix rolled her so she was on top of him, sitting astride him as he held her hips. He stared up at her in awe like she was some kind of goddess. She rolled her hips and he let out a groan of pure animalistic need. It made her feel powerful.

He sat up and cupped her face, kissing her with a desperate need. He moved his hands back down to her hips, holding her tight as he moved inside her harder and faster.

She felt the change in her body at the same time she felt his breath hitch against her lips, that need for him ripping through her so hard she could barely catch her breath. He moaned against her lips, trembling in her arms.

He pulled back slightly to look at her, his chest heaving as he stroked the hair from her face, and she knew she wanted more than just one night with this wonderful man. In fact she wanted forever.

CHAPTER FIVE

Lyra woke as sunlight poured in through the windows and skylight, dusting Nix with a golden shimmer. He was beautiful. She wanted to reach out and stroke him all over but she'd let him sleep.

She couldn't keep the smile from her face. The night before had been incredible and she knew that Nix felt the same way; she'd seen it in his eyes.

She couldn't wait to see what would happen next for them. Meeting Nix and falling into bed with him had not been part of any long-term plan, but suddenly none of that mattered. She had held herself back for so long and with Nix it felt like she was finally stepping into the light. She wanted to get to know him, every little thing that made him tick.

She climbed out of bed and stretched. Nix stirred, mumbled something in his sleep and rolled over to face away from her.

Dexter looked up sleepily at her movements and then

stood and stretched, wandering over to his empty food bowl.

Lyra looked around the little kitchen area and saw a can of dog food. She had no idea how much a dog of Dexter's size would eat but she opened the can, poured some into a bowl and put it down for him. Dexter snaffled it all up.

She looked out the van window and saw the sunlight sparkling off the lake below. It looked inviting. Feeling like she needed to freshen up, she pulled on Nix's t-shirt and shorts. Nix was still sleeping, so she grabbed a piece of paper and wrote him a quick note.

Gone for a swim, come and join me. Love Lyra.

She signed it with two kisses which was how she ended most notes or texts to people.

She stared at the note. Signing it from Lyra was a bit stupid – who else would be leaving him a note? Was putting *Love* and the kisses too much? But they had certainly been a lot more intimate the night before than two simple kisses on a note would indicate. And *Love Lyra* didn't mean she was in love with him. That was a fairly common way to end a note. Urgh, why was she second-guessing everything?

She propped the note up against a mug so he would see it. She opened the door and breathed in the fresh sea air for a moment. A strong warm breeze swept in around her, lifting her hair around her face. There was still no movement from Nix so she stepped outside, closing the door behind her so Dexter wouldn't get out.

She stood looking over the fields and meadows, the stream glittering as it made its way out to the sea. It was a beautiful day.

She turned towards the lake and glanced at Daisy, who was lying exactly where Lyra had left her the night before. There was mud and grass all caught up in the wheels and on the side of the frame, probably from Lyra's little tumble onto the grassy verge the night before. She decided to take Daisy down to the lake and clean her off too.

The birds were singing, little rabbits hopping around in the undergrowth and iridescent dragonflies darting through the trees and across the surface of the lake as Lyra wheeled her bicycle down towards the water.

Lyra spent a few minutes cleaning the leaves and mud off Daisy's frame and wheels, then stripped off and walked into the lake. The water was freezing and she laughed at the exhilarating buzz of it. She started swimming across the lake. It felt so completely liberating and freeing. Nix had awakened a side of her she'd kept buried for so long and she felt like she was stepping out from the fortress she had built around her to protect herself.

It was completely secluded here; no one could see her from the road or any other part of the island. In fact, she couldn't even see Judy at all.

She rolled on her back and floated on the surface of the water, staring at the sun-drenched turquoise sky as wisps of clouds floated gently by.

It was crazy to feel this way, this complete sensation of happiness. It really was serendipitous to meet Nix... it was almost as if they were supposed to be together.

She lay there for a while as the cool water licked her skin, hoping he would come and join her, but as she started to feel the cold, she swam to the shore and climbed out. She sat on the grassy banks for a few moments as she dried off in the early morning sun, then pulled on her clothes and wheeled Daisy back up the hill. She felt sure Nix would be awake by now, maybe even cooking her breakfast. She was ravenous.

She was waiting for Judy to appear over the brow of the hill as she walked up the slope but frowned as she neared the top because that didn't happen. Lyra dropped Daisy and quickened her pace, her heart plunging into her stomach as she got closer to the road. She looked around frantically in case she'd walked up the wrong part of the hill but the van, Nix, Dexter and any sign that they'd ever been there had completely vanished.

Nix was gone and he'd taken her heart with him.

CHAPTER SIX

'I'm such an idiot,' Lyra said, miserably, as her sister Michelle dished up more of her homemade Danish pastries onto Lyra's plate. These were apple and custard and tasted like heaven. She'd have liked to be able to say that after Nix left she was completely off her food but in reality she was drowning her sorrows in Michelle's delicious baked goodies.

'You're not an idiot,' Michelle said, loyally. 'You're an optimist. You always see the good in people. I just wish you wouldn't give your heart away so easily. A man flashes you a smile and you see marriage and babies, and then you always inevitably get hurt.'

That wasn't exactly true. Lyra had envisaged the happy ever after with her last three serious relationships but that was after months of being together. She hadn't seen a happy ending with the men she'd dated briefly, there hadn't been time for that. Although the hurt and disappointment part was definitely right. She had been let down quite badly by all of them.

Zach, Michelle's little son, ran past, stark naked with a nappy on his head, giggling loudly as Michelle's husband Ben chased after him, but Zach was fast, darting right underneath the table before heading out through the open doors and into the garden. Ben scrambled round the table to try to catch his son.

Michelle's home was a mess. There were pots of paint, planks of wood and rolls of wallpaper stacked up in the corner of the kitchen ready for the mass redecoration and renovation that was underway. The rest of the floor, cupboards and walls were taken up with toys, baby paraphernalia and baby clothes in various stages of cleanliness, ranging from needing washing to freshly washed. There were still many boxes from when they'd moved house a few months before that hadn't yet been unpacked. The house was complete chaos, which kind of made Lyra, who liked things orderly and tidy, twitch a little. But despite all this, she was still envious of Michelle's life. She had a wonderful husband. Ben Olney was clumsy and loud and unbelievably messy, but Michelle and Zach were his entire world. He loved Lyra's sister with everything he had. Michelle had met Ben when they were only sixteen and they'd been completely head over heels in love with each other ever since. The Olneys, as Ben and Michelle called themselves, were a perfect little team. Despite the chaos on the surface, Michelle's life was completely full and happy. Lyra wanted that more than anything. A soul mate to traverse life's adventures with.

Michelle was a year younger than Lyra and the fact her little sister had her life so completely sorted while Lyra was still lost at sea hurt a little. In fact, all five of her younger siblings had their lives sorted. Kitty was married to a wonderful woman and they lived in a big house in the heart of the Devon countryside. Max had got married to his long-term girlfriend a few months before and was living happily in a beach house in Australia. Frankie had a fabulous boyfriend and was very successful in her job as a lawyer in London. Even the youngest, Ethan, had just got engaged to his girlfriend, just after his twenty-third birthday. Lyra had celebrated her thirtieth birthday and she was no closer to finding her happy ever after.

She was happy that after their parents' divorce, and the tumultuous years that had followed, her brothers and sisters had all turned out as normal, well-adjusted, happy people. It was just a shame the same couldn't be said for her.

Out of all of her siblings, she was closest to Michelle, despite their differences. Michelle had been a child who embraced the noise, chaos and mess, while Lyra had turned out completely the opposite. Lyra loved a good list and there was always a plan for everything.

Well, if truth be told, it wasn't that she loved those things, but they had helped her to forge a life a million miles away from the one her mum led. Her mum had dropped the ball spectacularly when their dad had left, and never picked it back up. Lyra never wanted to turn out like her. That need for adventure, for fun and a life filled with travels around the world was always there, like an itch she couldn't scratch, but she couldn't give in to it. Max had nearly died because of Lyra's careless attitude and she'd never forgiven herself for that.

But maybe if she stopped planning ahead for once,

jumping forward to the final page before she'd finished the first chapter, she wouldn't keep getting so disappointed when her story didn't turn out how she envisaged it.

Michelle was right: Lyra fell in love very easily and every time she ended up with her heart broken.

'Nix was different,' Lyra said, wondering why she was still standing loyal to him when he'd left without saying goodbye. But they'd shared this incredible connection, and it was hard to just dismiss that. Or had she totally imagined all that, seeing something that wasn't there just because she'd wanted it to be? Anger pushed past the disappointment and sadness. If it really had been just a one-night stand to him, the very least he could have done was be honest with her and have the guts to explain in the morning, rather than leaving her wondering where she'd gone wrong. Or had he seen the way she'd looked at him, seen the kisses on the note and thought he'd hotfoot it out of there before she dragged him down the aisle?

She felt her cheeks burn red. Had she been that desperate and needy, was that why he'd run?

'He seemed so lovely,' Lyra said. 'He said he doesn't sleep around and hadn't had sex in a while... Maybe he'd been hurt in the past and then woke up this morning and got worried about getting involved in a relationship again.'

Michelle stared at her. 'Or he was a complete turd and he trotted out that vulnerable line to hook you in.'

Lyra sighed and took a bite of another Danish.

'I could talk to him so easily. I even told him about Max, and I never tell anyone about that.'

'Why did you?'

'I don't know. He's so insightful and he picked up on a few

things I'd said and he asked me about it and then it all came tumbling out. God, maybe that's why he ran. He realised I have a ton of baggage and he didn't want to deal with it.'

'I doubt that's the reason. What was his reaction when you told him?'

'Umm, he said I was spectacular.'

'Well, you are.'

'And then he made love to me again.'

'Wow, he really ticked all the boxes for you, didn't he?' Michelle said.

'He did. We had something special. Well, at least I thought we did.'

Her sister sighed. 'Men are the worst.'

Lyra eyed Ben as he chased a giggling Zach around the garden. 'Not all of them.'

'No, I definitely picked one of the best.'

'I honestly thought that about Nix too.'

'I can't believe you slept with him.'

'Wow, slut-shamed by my own sister.'

'No slut-shaming here. If women want to go out and sleep with a different man every night, good for them, it's no one's business but their own. It's just not you. You've only slept with three men and all of those were when you were in a serious relationship. I've just never known you to jump into bed with a man you only met a few hours before. There's nothing wrong with it, but that's not your style.'

'I know, I don't know what came over me. He made me feel things I've never felt before. When he started kissing me, it just felt so right.'

'Please tell me you used protection.'

'Yes, he took care of that. He had a whole stash of condoms, actually.'

Michelle narrowed her eyes. 'That doesn't sound like a man who hasn't had sex in a while. That sounds like someone who has sex every week.'

Lyra reached for one of her sister's brownies. She'd thought about that too. Not at the time, because she'd been too caught up in the moment. But why would a man who said he didn't sleep around have a cupboard filled with condoms? Had Nix really just been feeding her what she wanted to hear to get her into bed?

'Maybe Dad has the right idea: give up on the opposite sex completely. Maybe I'm better off on my own,' Lyra said as she watched Ben throw Zach up in the air, catch him and then blow raspberries on his belly. She swallowed down the lump in her throat.

'Don't give up on men. Just because you've been burned a few times doesn't mean they are all pigs. There are some wonderful men out there. Just... tread carefully. Get to know them before you give away your heart.'

Lyra nodded sadly. She was clearly a terrible judge of character. Maybe she should get her sister to choose her men from now on.

Just then Michelle's tablet sprang to life with a video call from Frankie in the little group chat she had with her siblings. There were calls to the group at least once a week, mostly at weekends. Sometimes there were only two or three of her siblings in the chat, depending what they were doing (or in Max's case, depending on the time zone), but sometimes they were all there. Lyra loved talking to her siblings but right now, feeling sorry for herself, she didn't know if she could face them.

'I'm not here,' she said.

Michelle shook her head. 'Except they know you are. I might have messaged them and told them you'd had your heart broken again.'

Lyra groaned. 'Why would you do that?'

Her sister shrugged. 'We're a team, we always have each other's back.'

Michelle answered the call and waved at Frankie. Lyra held up her hand to say hi just as Ethan joined the call.

'Wow, Lyra, you look like shit,' Ethan teased.

Before she could respond, Kitty and Max suddenly joined the conversation.

'Oh good, we're all here,' Lyra said, dryly.

'What's going on?' Frankie said, getting straight to the point.

'Nothing, just a misunderstanding,' Lyra said, wanting to downplay it. She didn't want them to think she was like their mum, jumping into bed with someone she'd just met, even though that was exactly what she'd done.

Michelle was having none of it though. 'Long story short, Lyra met someone last night, fell in love with him, he lured her into his camper van where she spent the night having amazing sex, and then, when she got up the next morning and went for a swim in the lake, the guy did a runner.'

There were various cries of outrage on Lyra's behalf.

'I think *lured* is a bit of an exaggeration. It's not like he tricked me into bed, I went willingly,' Lyra said. Though she couldn't deny the rest of that summary was true, although it made her sound so naïve.

'I don't think you'll find your soul mate by jumping into bed with someone you've just met,' Frankie said.

Frankie had been best friends with her current boyfriend for two years before they'd finally got together. She was a big advocate of getting to know someone inside and out before even considering them for a relationship.

'That's bollocks,' Max said. 'Me and Zara slept with each other the first night we met, and we've been together six years now.'

'Me and Jen were the same,' Kitty said. 'Sometimes you just have an undeniable connection with someone and you just know they're your forever.'

Lyra smiled. She loved listening to Kitty talk about her wife – she was so completely in love with her.

'No judgement here,' Ethan said. 'We've all had one-night stands.'

'I haven't,' Frankie said.

'Me neither,' Michelle said.

And until the night before, Lyra could have said that she hadn't either. What had it been about Nix that had pulled down all her inhibitions so quickly?

'So anyway,' Kitty said. 'This guy just left you, standing in the middle of the field?'

Lyra nodded and felt the tears smart her eyes again. She took a swig of her tea as a diversion. Nix had said he could trust her and she had and then he'd run away.

'What a scumbag,' Frankie said.

'Exactly,' Michelle said.

'I think this comes down to your trust issues,' Max said.

'I think you're subconsciously choosing crappy men because you don't want a proper relationship for fear of being let down and hurt.'

'I think if Lyra thought he was special enough to go to bed with, then he must have been something extraordinary,' Ethan said.

Lyra smiled with love for her little brother. He had a way of seeing things that her other siblings didn't. He had a real sensitive side.

'What was the sex like?' Kitty asked without a hint of embarrassment.

They all had a very open relationship with each other but Lyra still wasn't comfortable talking to her siblings about stuff like this. Kitty was a counsellor and mostly dealt with couples' therapy. Part of that involved openly talking about sex, which helped explain why she had no scruples about bringing this up in front of her siblings.

Lyra cleared her throat. 'The best I've ever had.'

'I'm not sure I want to hear details about my sister's sex life,' Max said.

'Don't be such a prude,' Kitty said. 'The point is, sex is almost never great the first time a couple get together. I mean, sure it can be satisfying and nice, but it's almost never the most amazing sex of your life. That kind of sex only happens when you truly know the person. For you to feel that kind of connection, I guarantee he felt it too. Something else is going on here.'

'What do you mean?' Lyra said.

'You don't walk away from something like that easily. My guess is that he freaked out over finding something so special. Maybe he hasn't been in a relationship for a while for one reason or another, and then got scared when he fell in love with you after only one night.'

'That's what I said,' Lyra said, almost triumphant that someone else shared that view. 'Well, the freaking-out part, not the falling-in-love bit.'

'I think the guy is just a git,' Michelle said.

'We talked about so much, really personal stuff, and he listened to everything I said. He was so patient and kind.'

'What's his name? Maybe we can stalk him online,' Frankie said.

'Good idea,' Max said.

'I'm not stalking him.'

'If you find him, you can ask him what happened,' Ethan said. 'I bet your ass he's regretting running away right about now.'

'I'm not chasing after him. Don't you think that's a bit creepy?'

'What if he has a wife and three kids?' Frankie said. 'At least if you find out he's a dick, you can put your feelings to bed rather than raising him up on this pedestal.'

'If you give me his name, I know someone who can get his address for me,' Max said.

'And do what, go round and beat him up?' Lyra said in exasperation.

'Tempting. Fortunately for him, I live over ten thousand miles away. I'm just saying, you could go round and—'

'No. I'm not stalking him or turning up at his house. It is what it is, I made a mistake, saw something that wasn't there. It's not his fault I saw marriage and a happy ever after. It was a one-night stand for him. So we'll just draw a line under it and move on.'

Lyra's siblings were silent for a moment.

'OK, OK, we love you, that's all,' Kitty said. 'Like Grandad used to say, "What's meant for you won't pass by you." If this is the real thing, love will find a way.'

'I think I just threw up a little,' Frankie said.

'Shut your face,' Kitty said and Frankie laughed, not remotely offended.

'Look,' Frankie said. 'I think it's good you found out now that he was that kind of man, rather than in three months' times when you'd already picked out the wedding dress.'

'That's true,' Lyra said, glumly. It would be a lot harder to get over Nix if she'd had all his loveliness for several months.

'I still think he'll look back on this morning and regret it for the rest of his life,' Ethan said.

'I still think if you liked him that much, he's worth finding,' Max said. 'And if it turns out he's still an asshole then at least we know where to send the heavies.'

Lyra smiled with love for her family. 'Well, thank you all for your wonderful pearls of wisdom. I'm going to go and drown my sorrows in Michelle's cakes and we all know that will make everything better.'

She held up one of the delicious brownies and her siblings all moaned in protest before she pressed the button to end the call. They would all probably continue talking about her now she was gone, but she didn't care.

She took a bite of the brownie and moaned appreciatively. 'These are amazing, you should definitely think about selling them.'

Michelle arched an eyebrow. 'Don't think I'll let you

change the subject that easily. You can't hide away from love for the rest of your life.'

'I know, but let me change the subject for now, this is all too depressing,' Lyra said. 'How's the house getting on?'

Michelle nodded and then smiled. 'Slowly. I love my husband but decorating is not his best quality. It's not mine either so I can't complain. We're bumbling along. We might be finished by Christmas. When are you moving into yours?'

'Day after tomorrow, first of July. I can't wait to get all my stuff in and make it mine. Everything is sitting in the back of my car at the moment outside the hotel. There's a lot of unpacking.'

'And then you start at your new job on Monday?'

'Tuesday actually. Clover, my new boss, isn't there on Monday and she wanted to be there for my first day so she asked me to start on Tuesday instead.'

'That only gives you the weekend and Monday to get your new house sorted.'

Lyra smiled. The house would definitely be sorted before Tuesday, she would make sure of that.

Then Tuesday would be a fresh start. New job, new home, new beginnings. Definitely no men.

CHAPTER SEVEN

Lyra walked into the Sapphire Bay Hotel on Tuesday morning with a spring in her step and a smile on her face. It was a gorgeous sunshiny day and she couldn't wait to start work as a co-ordinator on the events team – so much so, she'd turned up at work twenty minutes early.

She'd spent the weekend cleaning, unpacking and making her little cottage into a home. Sunlight, her cottage, had the most spectacular view over Crystal Sands, a tiny cove with turquoise waters and white sands. She'd even seen seals playing around in the water the night before.

The cottage wasn't in the main village, something she hadn't noticed when she had taken a virtual tour online. But, sucked in by the incredible view, she'd put a deposit down and paid two months' rent before she realised that it was in a secluded spot on the opposite side of the island. But actually, she quite liked that. It was peaceful, quiet. And the village and hotel were only a fifteen-minute walk away and she enjoyed a nice walk or a cycle so it wasn't really a problem. She felt almost sorry for her little car that was parked outside the cottage, it didn't look like she'd be needing it any time soon.

The cottage was a little too close to Crystal Stream and Nix's beavers for her liking, but she guessed he wouldn't be there that often to check on George and his family and, if he was, he had no reason to come to her cottage. Hopefully, she could largely avoid him.

She pushed thoughts of Nix away. She was looking forward to starting her new job. Event planning was something she'd done in various different jobs for the last few years, organising parties and weddings down to the finest detail was completely up her street. She was also looking forward to working with Clover and her sisters Skye and Aria. She liked the fact that it was a family-run hotel; family was important to Lyra and she appreciated that it was obviously important to the three sisters too.

Lyra waved at Clover Philips, who was leaning on the reception desk. Clover was the current conference and banqueting manager at the hotel and due to go off on maternity leave in five or six months. Lyra hoped that Clover and Aria, the hotel manager, would be impressed enough with her work to promote her to that role, even if it was only while Clover was off.

'Lyra, hi.' Clover came over, showing the tiniest baby bump. She was wearing leggings and a t-shirt, which wasn't what you'd expect to see a conference manager wearing, although Lyra knew that Clover was also the hotel's dance teacher, offering classes to the guests and the islanders. It was a weird job arrangement but Lyra guessed it came with the territory of a family-run hotel.

'Hi Clover, it's good to see you again.'

'You too! I'm excited to be working with you. You're early, I wasn't expecting you until ten. I've just had a dance class, so I was going to have a quick shower.'

'Oh please do. Don't worry about me, I'm just keen to start. I can have a wander round the hotel, get my bearings.'

'Oh come in and have a little chat for a few minutes, then I'll arrange for you to have a tour while I have a shower.' Clover walked into her office and Lyra followed her.

There was a dark-haired man in there, tapping away on his laptop.

'Angel, this is Lyra, my new events co-ordinator. Lyra, this is my husband, Angel; he's also our marketing manager,' Clover said.

Angel stood up and offered out his hand. He had eyes that held permanent amusement and Lyra liked him immediately.

'Good to meet you, Lyra. I'll get out of your way so you two can talk.'

'Oh, don't leave on my account.'

'It's fine, I'm happy to work anywhere and this office is small enough when it's just me and Clover, without adding more people to the mix. I'll be in the lobby.'

Angel picked up his laptop, flashed Lyra a warm smile and left.

'Your office is across the other side of the reception,' Clover said as she sat down behind the desk. 'I'll take you there in a few minutes. As we are employing more staff, we ripped out one of the downstairs bedrooms and converted it into an office. It's lovely in there, you even have sea views. I was tempted to take that office myself and let you

70

have this one, but Angel is right, there's not really enough room for two of you in here.'

Lyra sat down. 'Two of us?'

'Oh yes, there's two conference and banqueting co-ordinators, so we have two desks in the new office. It's quite big though, plenty of room to spread out. You're both starting today so I'll give you both the tour in a minute. The conference and banqueting side of the hotel is still relatively new. We've only been holding events here for the last nine or ten months. We have several weddings booked for this year and a few other events too, but I haven't really given over as much time as it needs to develop that side of things. So we'd like you both to oversee the organisation and smooth running of the events that have already been booked, but also to try to secure more events for us in the future. We can talk more about that later. Angel has some ideas for marketing and you two can work with him to try to put us on the map.'

Lyra nodded. There were wedding fayres they could attend, where there would be photographers and florists for the new couples to choose from, as well as locations to have their weddings. If they could get a stand at one of them that could help, especially if they could show photos or videos of weddings that had already been held at the hotel. She dug around in her bag and found her notebook and pen, jotting down a few notes about looking into wedding fayres. Advertising would be key; she'd have a chat with Angel about different things they could do.

Just then there was a knock on the door and there was a lady who Lyra recognised as one of the receptionists that had been there on the day of her interview. She couldn't remember her name though.

'Hello Tilly,' Clover said.

Tilly, that was it.

'Hey, your new co-ordinator is here.'

'Wonderful, show him in,' Clover said, standing up.

Lyra stood up too to greet her new colleague, hoping he or she would be lovely and they could work well together. But all those hopes were immediately dashed as she saw that the man being shown into the office was Nix.

Nix swore under his breath at the sight of Lyra standing in the office. The first woman he'd slept with in over three years, the woman he'd been unable to forget since that incredible night.

And suddenly he realised where he'd met her before. She'd been dressed in a suit, her beautiful red, wavy hair pulled neatly back in a bun, just like the first time they'd met, the day of his interview six weeks before. They'd sat together as they'd waited for their interview. He'd said a few words to her but she'd been too nervous and distracted to engage with him properly and he hadn't exactly been on top form himself. He hadn't recognised her when they'd met the week before because she had been dressed completely differently, her red hair loose as she sailed past him on the bike, a pretty turquoise dress instead of this very dull suit. Lyra probably hadn't recognised him for the same reason, plus he'd also been wearing his glasses in the interview.

And now she was here, staring at him in horror. Life was spectacularly unfair sometimes. He'd been looking forward to this job and now he'd have to see her every day.

'Nix, lovely to see you again,' Clover said, holding out a hand.

He turned his attention to his boss and shook her hand, hoping he could somehow block out Lyra, although that wasn't likely.

'Lyra Thomas, this is Nix Sanchez, your new partner in conference and banqueting.'

Lyra didn't make a move; she didn't even break a smile. It was quite clear that she was about as thrilled to see him as he was to see her. She'd said before that she'd been hiding from her past; it had well and truly caught up with her now.

He was going to have to be professional about this. But should he admit that he knew her? He could hardly say that the last time he'd seen her, she'd been in his bed, her red hair splayed across his pillow, as he'd made love to her.

Christ, he rubbed his eyes to get rid of that image.

Nix cleared his throat and forced a smile on his face. 'Nice to meet you.'

Lyra's eyes widened in surprise.

'Hello,' she muttered, before looking away and sitting back down again.

'Well, I might as well give you the tour myself and then I'll show you your office,' Clover said.

Of course he'd be sharing an office with her. Fate wasn't just going to rain on his parade, there was going to be thunder and lightning too.

'Sounds great,' Nix said.

Lyra, it seemed, had lost the power of speech altogether as she grabbed her bag and shoved her notebook and pen back inside.

Clover didn't seem to notice anything was amiss as she moved out of the office, and Nix and Lyra reluctantly followed her.

He chanced another look at her as they walked side by side across the reception, trying to listen to Clover as she talked about using the reception area for welcome drinks for various events.

Lyra appeared to be distraught at seeing him again. She honestly looked like she was going to cry and he just didn't know what to do with that. She was probably embarrassed while he felt... confused.

They would have to clear the air at some point, especially if they were going to be working together. But right now, he didn't want to talk to her at all. He had no idea what he could say to her.

Clover showed them the restaurant and some of the smaller function rooms, the boardroom, the swimming pool which Clover said they'd used for a few functions – serving drinks and nibbles at the side, not in the actual pool itself – and then she took them out into the gardens which were blooming with every flower imaginable. The views of the beaches were spectacular and it certainly had a lot of potential for different events to be held here.

'OK, let me show you your office,' Clover said.

She took them back into the hotel, chatting away about upcoming functions and events, but Nix barely heard any of it. All he could focus on was Lyra, her scent, the warmth from her body as she accidentally brushed up against him, causing his arm to erupt in goosebumps. His brain was filled with images of the last time they were together. Working with her was going to be torture.

Clover walked along the corridor, opened the first door and stepped inside.

'This is your office,' she said, as if showing off a fabulous prize – which in many ways she was. Two large desks sat on either side of a room with the most stunning views over Sapphire Bay. So why did he feel like he'd actually been given the booby prize?

'Well, these files are the events that are happening in the next few months, so you can have a look through them,' Clover said. 'Each file has a bullet-point checklist of things that need to be done for each event. You can see what things need to be taken care of and what's already been sorted. Some you'll have to outsource, like fireworks for example. Some things, like most of the catering, will be done in house, but if the clients have a specific menu or dietary need, that will need to be tied up with the kitchen, or Skye and Jesse down at Cones at the Cove for any dessert requirements. This wallchart shows all the events this year and this one shows the upcoming events for next year. All the files for next year are in the cupboard in here, in these hanging files, in date order. Most of them are fairly empty right now, they'll fill up as we confirm different arrangements, but you can have a look through them too. Anyway, I don't want to overwhelm you on your first day so have a look through the files for the immediate events and I'll be back soon and we can have a chat about anything you're not sure of.'

Clover paused, looking between them to see if they had

anything to say. Lyra was silent so Nix just muttered his thanks.

Clover frowned slightly. 'Well, I'll be back in a bit.'

She left the room.

Lyra moved over to the window and stared out at the view and an awkward silence fell between them. He had no idea what to say to her.

Eventually she spoke. 'I imagine you were hoping you'd never see me again.'

Nix sighed. He wished he could say he'd hoped for that, but his sad and desperate side had thought about her constantly since he'd last seen her. Although he certainly wasn't going to admit that.

'This wasn't exactly how I envisaged my first day in my new job,' he said, eventually.

'No, quite,' she said, still not looking at him. 'Well, it doesn't have to be awkward. We can divvy up the files between us and then just work on our own projects. That will reduce the time we have to spend with each other, which I'm sure you'll appreciate.'

She walked over to the files and started spreading them out on the desk. 'Here, why don't I take all the weddings and you can take all the other events – the parties, the conferences. There are twelve weddings this year and ten other events so it's about even. I'm sure romance isn't your sort of thing anyway.'

Lyra piled up half of the files and walked over to him, dumping them in his arms, then went back to the desk and sat down, pulling one of the remaining files towards her. After a few moments she pulled her phone and headphones out of her bag, plugged them in and put the headphones in her ears. A few moments later the faint sound of music filled the air, making it very clear that she wanted nothing to do with him, which was no real surprise after what had happened the last time they'd been together.

He went over to his desk and sat down. It was going to be a long day.

❦

'He's here,' Lyra hissed into the phone as she walked across the lobby towards the restaurant. She'd nipped out under the pretext of getting coffee but, in reality, she just needed some space away from Nix. She looked around to see if anyone could hear her. There was an elderly lady dressed in a satin green cloak with seashells all over it, sitting on one of the sofas tapping away on a laptop, a large white fluffy dog lying at her feet. The lady was engrossed in whatever was on the computer and hadn't seemed to have heard Lyra talking. There was no one else around; they were probably all outside enjoying the glorious sunshine.

'Who's there?' Michelle hissed back.

'Nix!'

'At the hotel?' her sister said.

'Yes, and would you believe my bad luck, he's my new partner in conference and banqueting. And I don't know what to do.'

'Oh my god, that's a bit awkward.'

'Just a bit. I want to ask him why he left but I'm not sure if I really want to know.'

'I would ask,' Michelle said.

'Really? Don't you think that would make me look

pathetic and needy? It was just one amazing night, there was never any talk of seeing each other or starting a relationship. He didn't give me any promises. I suppose technically he hasn't done anything wrong.'

The elderly lady looked up from her laptop, watching her as she walked across the reception. Lyra hurried into the restaurant. It was empty at this time in the morning so she went to the coffee machine and started making two coffees. She'd offered to get one for Nix as she was trying to be polite and professional, when inside she was hurt and angry.

'He left you standing in the middle of a field without having the decency to say goodbye. Do I need to remind you that you had to climb over a gate with your bike to get out? That was hardly a nice thing to do.'

Lyra had thought about that. It just didn't make sense. Even if Nix had woken up in the morning and wanted nothing more to do with her, why would he hightail it out of there and leave her locked on his property?

She thought back to her last boyfriend, Greg, who'd told her sex with her had been really bad. She'd hadn't had a ton of experience in that department, only two men before him, but she'd always thought the comment about bad sex was just Greg being really spiteful. Had sex between her and Nix been so bad that Nix had run away as fast as Judy would carry him, rather than face her again over breakfast?

'I'm not asking him why he left,' Lyra said, decisively. Her self-esteem didn't need to hear that kind of answer. 'I'm sure the fact that I was looking at him with that stupid loved-up expression was part of the reason why he ran. He doesn't need me being clingy and desperate now, not when I have to work with him every day.'

'I don't think it's clingy and desperate to ask what went on. It's not like you're going to welcome him back with open arms even if he apologises and comes up with some feeble excuse. But at least it will clear the air between you, especially if you have to work together.'

'I'm not asking him. I'm going to remain cool and aloof, as if him leaving doesn't bother me at all.'

'And how long do you intend to be aloof for?'

Lyra sighed, knowing it would probably take some time for her to stop looking at Nix and feeling hurt and embarrassed. 'As long as it takes.'

'Come round for dinner tonight and we can come up with a plan of attack, even if that's leaving a kipper in his desk drawer as revenge.'

Lyra laughed. 'OK, I'll see you later.'

She finished making the coffee and turned, coming face to face with the elderly lady in the green cloak. She wondered how much of the conversation she'd heard.

'Sylvia O'Hare,' the lady stuck her hand out. 'I just fancied one of those nice cappuccinos.'

Lyra shook it. 'Lyra Thomas.'

Sylvia moved to the machine. 'You and that nice lad are the new events co-ordinators, aren't you?'

'Yes, that's right. His name is Nix. It's our first day today.'

Sylvia watched her carefully. 'But you and Nix have met before. I saw the way you two were looking at each other on your tour this morning.'

'I, er... briefly.'

'Sounds like it was a bit more than brief.' Sylvia waggled her eyebrows mischievously.

'Were you listening to my conversation?'

'Honey, you're not very discreet. Besides, I'm an author of romance stories, I get all my inspiration from watching and listening to people. I've also been married six times in my very long life, so I do have some understanding of matters of the heart. Want to talk to me about it?'

'I mean no disrespect but I don't tend to talk about my private affairs with strangers.'

'Let me guess.' Sylvia tapped her chin, thoughtfully. 'You had a one-night stand, you thought it was something more, he clearly didn't, and he left the following morning before you'd even woken up.'

Lyra didn't like the way their amazing night together had been summarised to sound so… meaningless. But that was it in a nutshell: they'd had a one-night stand, simple as that.

'Sort of. But it's in the past, it doesn't matter.'

'Except you seem to be bothered by it more than you're letting on. And, judging by the way he was looking at you earlier, I'd say he's regretting it.'

'He's probably embarrassed that he has to face me, but don't confuse that for regret,' Lyra said.

'You mark my words, he'll be begging you for a second chance soon enough.'

'He can beg all he wants, he won't be getting one,' Lyra said.

'Ah, but if it's upset you that much, you obviously thought he was special,' Sylvia persisted.

'And I *obviously* thought wrong. I'm sorry, I'm a big fan

of happy-ever-after romances, but I really don't think this is it. Now, I must be getting back.'

'I'll be here for the next two weeks, so if you want to talk, I'm sure you'll be able to find me,' Sylvia said, clearly not to be put off.

Lyra gave her a polite smile and then, keeping that smile fixed in place, she walked back to the office.

~

'So you'll never guess who I'm partnered with in my new job,' Nix said, twisting a paperclip around a pencil as he listened to his brother turn down the TV.

'Who?' Lucas said. 'Wait, is it Jennifer Lawrence?'

'In your dreams.'

'A man can hope. I'd definitely be bringing my visit to you forward if it was. So who has got my little brother all worked up? Oh hang on. Is it that woman you fell in love with?'

'I did not fall in love with Lyra.' Nix was quick to put that rumour to bed. 'But yes, it is her.'

'I beg to differ. She's pretty much been the topic of conversation ever since that night,' Lucas said.

'That's... not entirely true,' Nix said, shaking his head. Had he really been talking about her that much? Probably. He was such an idiot.

'So what's the game plan, beg her for a second chance?' Lucas said.

'No, that's not on the list of how to deal with suddenly seeing her again.'

'What is on the list?'

81

Nix sighed. 'I have no idea.'

'In all seriousness,' Lucas said, losing all his usual sarcasm. 'You said she was someone special, she's the first person I've heard you talk about since Emily. Isn't that worth fighting for?'

'It takes two people to fight for a relationship and, after what happened the last time we were together, and seeing how she reacted to me this morning, I can't see her fighting for me somehow.'

'Is this just an excuse because you're scared of risking your heart again?'

Nix twisted the paperclip between his fingers and it suddenly snapped. 'I guess there's a tiny element of that.'

There was probably more truth to that than he'd care to admit.

He heard footsteps coming down the corridor and somehow knew it was her. 'I have to go.'

'Is that an excuse too?'

Nix laughed. 'No, it's Jennifer Lawrence.'

At a wail of protest from his brother, Nix quickly hung up and pasted on a smile as Lyra walked back into the room. It seemed she had a fake smile fixed on her face too.

She gave him the coffee and without a word went back to sit down at her desk, plugging in her headphones again.

He sighed. This was going well.

CHAPTER EIGHT

Lyra was busy working her way through the list of things to do on an upcoming wedding when Clover popped back in.

'How's it all going, are you two getting on OK?' Clover said.

Lyra was fairly sure her boss was asking about the work rather than if the two of them had hit it off. If she wasn't, Lyra had no idea how to answer that question. She was sure Clover didn't want to know she and Nix had barely spoken a word to each other since they'd met earlier that morning and that you could cut the atmosphere in the office with a knife.

Lyra fixed on her polite smile again. 'We're fine.'

She glanced over at Nix and saw him suppress a smile, obviously knowing that *fine* covered a multitude of sins. She suddenly wanted to let out a giggle herself, because this was ridiculous. Of all the people she could have been landed with on her first day of work, why did it have to be him? Nix had said that he was a firm believer in fate and destiny, that he always trusted he was where he was meant to be. She wondered what he thought of fate now for bringing them back together.

'You've made this very easy for us,' Nix said. 'Your lists of what to do are very detailed. It's hard to go wrong really.'

Lyra suppressed the urge to roll her eyes at Nix sucking up to Clover. Why was she finding everything he did so irritating?

But she knew why. Because he genuinely seemed like a nice guy. She'd heard him on the phone earlier to an elderly lady who'd had concerns about her upcoming eightieth birthday party and he'd just been so lovely and patient with her, despite having to repeat himself several times. Lyra had expected him to roll his eyes when he came off the phone or laugh at the lady but he hadn't. And not forgetting he'd sold his house, and almost everything he'd owned, to help some beavers and support a project he was passionate about. She wanted him to be an arse so she could hate him more easily but he was lovely and that pissed her off no end.

And annoyingly, Nix was right about the work that Clover had left for them, he wasn't just being nice. It must have taken weeks to make sure all of this was ready for them to pick up so easily.

'All of this is incredibly straightforward to follow,' Lyra said.

'Oh, I wanted to make it easy for you. I'm pregnant with my first child and me and my husband have decided we're going to do a bit of travelling before the baby arrives. We leave at the end of next month so I wanted to make sure everything was in order for you before we left. And then when I come back I'll probably be going on maternity leave. That's why we got two of you – so you could support each other. You both come with so much experience, I know you'll fit in perfectly. Do you have any questions, anything you're not sure of?'

Nix looked through the files on his desk and shook his head.

'Only one for now.' Lyra rifled through a file on her desk until she found what she was looking for. 'This wedding, Jack and Heather – they want to hold the reception in Cones at the Cove. Is that viable?'

'That wedding has come in very last-minute, and they want to get married as quick as possible,' Clover said. 'You get those sometimes; they get engaged and want to walk down the aisle the next day. They actually met in Cones at the Cove, when she was here for the day and he was here on holiday. They were sitting at tables next to each other and just hit it off, one of those instant, love-at-first-sight-type moments.' Clover smiled and shook her head as if she didn't believe in that kind of thing.

Lyra couldn't help glancing over to Nix and his eyes locked with hers. She quickly looked away.

'The call about using Cones at the Cove for the reception came in yesterday and I haven't actually checked with Skye yet,' Clover said. 'To answer your question, I'm not sure and I've said that to Jack and Heather. I think a lot of the tables and booths are fixed so we might not be able to accommodate a party, and I don't know if we'd have room for any kind of dance floor. Alternatively, we could set up some ice cream machines in the main restaurant here, but I think the newly engaged couple have their hearts set on holding their reception there. Why don't you give my sister, Skye, a call – or better still, pop down and have a chat with her? Then you can see the place for yourself.'

Lyra nodded. 'Good idea.'

'Well, I have a dance class shortly, so I'll leave you to it. But please come and find me if you have any questions, or phone through to my office or drop me an email. I'm happy to talk through anything if you're not sure. The contacts list is in your top drawer, that has all the extension numbers and emails for the different parts of the hotel.'

Lyra smiled and Nix nodded his thanks as Clover left.

She glanced over at Nix and realised he was watching her.

'Your clients sound interesting,' he said.

'They sound foolish,' Lyra said.

'You don't believe in love at first sight?'

'No, I think it's nonsense. You can't really fall in love with someone after only a few hours. You have to get to know the person first – the good, the bad, the ugly – before you can fall in love. Lust at first sight is much more likely but real love takes a lot longer.'

'I agree that you have to get to know a person before you can really fall in love with them. But sometimes you meet someone and you have an instant connection and you just know that that person is going to change your life.'

Lyra swallowed, unable to take her eyes off him. 'And you've had this with a woman?'

Nix nodded. 'Two actually.'

'And what happened?'

'The first woman we had seven glorious years together.'

'But you're not seeing her now.'

'No, she... I haven't seen her for three years.'

'So it didn't work out,' Lyra said.

'It worked out absolutely fine for those seven years,' Nix said, somewhat defensively.

She decided to move on. 'And what happened with the second woman?'

He stared at her for the longest time. 'I don't know, maybe it's a work in progress.'

Did he mean her? Had he felt that amazing connection too? Then why the hell had he run? None of this made any sense. And if he was talking about her then his assumption that he still stood a chance with her after what he did was very misguided.

'If you're talking about me, then it's more like finished business,' she snapped, grabbing the file on Jack and Heather's wedding and standing up. 'I'm going to see Skye.'

And with that she walked out of the office.

Cones at the Cove was a bright blue wooden building with large glass windows to make the most of the beautiful view over Emerald Cove. There were oversized chessboards and Jenga outside, which would probably prove popular with the children. The café was currently closed but thankfully the door was open and, as Lyra walked inside, she could hear music drifting out from the kitchen. There were large booths and smaller tables dotted around the room and the driftwood-style tables, seaside paraphernalia hanging from the ceilings and beautiful paintings on the walls gave the whole place a distinctive coastal vibe. One entire wall was taken up with lots of ice cream machines that no doubt held lots of different flavours. This place definitely looked fun and she could see why Jack and Heather had been charmed by it.

Lyra moved over to the kitchen door and stopped as she peered through the little window. There was a woman – presumably Clover's twin, Skye, as she looked so much like Clover – and a very large man dancing together. The woman was quite visibly pregnant and the man had his hands on her belly as they moved around the room, with eyes only for each other.

Lyra swallowed down the lump in her throat because they were so obviously completely in love with each other. She'd never had anything like that. She'd had men she was in love with and who she'd thought had loved her, but she'd never had a man look at her like that.

She pushed the thought from her head that said Nix had looked at her like that when they'd laid in bed together.

She didn't know whether to interrupt them but Jack and Heather's wedding was coming up quite quickly and there was a lot to sort out before then. Having given herself all the weddings to take care of, Lyra didn't even feel she could ask Nix for any help.

She knocked on the door of the kitchen and watched the couple quickly break apart.

The woman came to the door and opened it.

'Hello, I'm so sorry to interrupt. I'm Lyra, part of the new events team.'

A large smile spread across the woman's face and she stuck out a hand. 'I'm Skye and this is my husband, Jesse. Great to finally meet you. Clover has been going on about you and Nix for weeks, about how impressed she was with you. She's been dying for you both to start.'

'Well that's nice to hear. I've been looking forward to starting here too.'

Lyra gave a little sigh because she *had* been looking forward to this job so much and now it felt tainted. She couldn't let Nix ruin it for her.

She moved forward to shake Jesse's proffered hand. 'This place looks great. It's not just a café, it has real character.'

'Thank you,' Skye said. 'I know I'm biased but I love it. Anyway, what can we help you with?'

'Well, we have a wedding, one of those last-minute jobs, and it's a couple who met here in your café,' Lyra said.

'Heather and Jack? Yes, we know them. They've been here so often since that first night, they're regulars now. They even got engaged here.'

'Yes, it seems they love the place too. So much so they actually want to get married here.'

'Here?' Jesse said. 'Is that legal?'

'Well, not actually tie the knot here, I think they'll do that up at the hotel, but hold the reception here. I came to see if you think it's a viable option.'

'Oh, how exciting,' Skye said, turning to see what Jesse thought.

'We'd have to close the café to the public,' he said. 'But it's only for one day.'

'How many guests are we talking about?' Skye said.

Lyra consulted the file. 'It's quite a small wedding, currently forty-eight guests.'

'We have seating for sixty so it's doable,' Skye said, thoughtfully. 'But what are their plans, are they wanting a proper three-course meal here?'

'Yes, that's the idea.'

'Oh wow,' Jesse said. 'I've never done a wedding menu before. I help out in the hotel kitchens twice a week so I have experience of cooking food other than desserts, but this might be a bit beyond my skills.'

'No it isn't. You could do this, and me and Melody will be here to help you,' Skye insisted.

'What kind of food are we talking about?' Jesse said.

'I can send you over some sample menus from previous weddings and events we've held in the hotel to see what we normally do,' Lyra said. 'And that's the kind of thing we'll be sending to Jack and Heather for them to choose from, though they might have more specific ideas.'

Jesse nodded. 'But what about a dance floor? We don't really have anywhere big enough to accommodate that in here and the tables are all fixed in place.'

'The hotel has its own marquee that we've used for different events before,' Skye said, visibly getting excited. 'We could put it up outside. We can push the bifold doors back and have a large doorway between here and the marquee. They can dance in there and have desserts on tap in here.'

'This sounds promising,' Lyra said. 'The request to use this place only came through yesterday so why don't I invite them down here to have a chat and we can discuss what they would like for their day? Then you can decide whether we can accommodate them or come up with an alternative. We might even be able to pin them down to a menu choice too.'

'Good idea. It'd be great to chat through with them how they envisage it,' Skye said. 'Oooh, this is exciting. Bea will be delighted.'

'Bea?'

'Our daughter,' Jesse said.

'She loves watching the weddings at the hotel, I think she has a bit of a romantic heart,' Skye said.

'Ah, every little girl loves a good old-fashioned fairytale wedding,' Lyra said.

'And Jack and Heather are definitely the fairytale couple,' Skye said. 'It was one of those love-at-first-sight moments, it's very romantic.'

Lyra cleared her throat and hoped she didn't look too disapproving; she would have to keep her pessimism to herself.

'Right, well I'll get back to the office and give them a call,' she said. 'I'll keep you posted.'

She waved goodbye and walked back through the gardens. It was a glorious summer day and an array of colourful flowers were in full bloom as she made her way towards the hotel.

She looked down at the file and sighed. This love-at-first-sight wedding was going to be a touchy subject for the next few weeks. It wasn't that Lyra didn't believe in it, because she did; she was a big romantic at heart. She loved reading all those lovely romance books with the guaranteed happy ending, she was a sucker for wonderfully cheesy romantic movies, and she'd seen enough of her friends and family tie the knot and get their big happy ending to know it did exist. But for her it just never happened. She'd fallen in love too many times to count and had her heart broken too many times too. She'd vowed she wouldn't be so foolish and give away her heart again, and then along came Nix and her carefully constructed walls had been yanked down.

She *had* felt that connection with Nix, it had been unlike anything she'd ever felt before, but yet again she'd ended up hurt.

So she would arrange this wedding and she'd pour her heart and soul into it because someone ought to get their happy ending, even if for her that door was now firmly closed.

Nix was typing up a table plan for an upcoming fiftieth when there was a knock on the office door, which was a bit odd. If it was Clover or any other member of staff they would have just come in. As Lyra still had her headphones in and hadn't heard the knock, he stood up to answer it.

There was an elderly lady on the other side, wearing a stunning emerald cloak with shell patterns sewed on it.

'Sylvia O'Hare,' the lady said, sticking out her hand.

Nix couldn't help but smile at the bold introduction. However, the name rang a bell.

'Nix Sanchez.' He shook her hand, finding her grip surprisingly strong.

'Ah, the other half of the events team. I met your partner earlier, she seems lovely.'

Nix nodded, politely. 'She is.'

Of course, *lovely* didn't come close to describing Lyra. There was something about her that made him smile so damned much. Well, at least that's how he'd felt when he first met her. Today's Lyra was very different to the one he'd made love to the week before.

'We had a nice chat before, very... enlightening,' Sylvia said, fixing Nix with a look that suggested Lyra had told Sylvia every single detail about their wonderful night together, which he highly doubted. Although it was clear she certainly knew something, or at least thought she did. 'But in all the excitement of our little chat, I forgot to talk to her about my party.'

'You're having a party?' That was why the name seemed familiar: he'd seen it on one of the files.

'Yes, it's a book launch, the publication of my hundred and fiftieth book.'

'Wow, that's quite some achievement – that definitely needs a big celebration. I wrote a book once, a children's book about beavers. I tried to get it published but with no luck. To get a hundred and fifty books out there in the world is a really big deal.'

'Ah, children's publishing is notoriously hard to get into. Fortunately for me, I write about sex and love and there's always a huge appetite for that.'

He felt the smile spread across his face. 'Maybe that's where I'm going wrong.'

'If you ever fancied trying your hand at writing romance, I could definitely give you a few pointers. But I'm sure you could find your own inspiration. Maybe your lovely colleague could help you with that.'

Nix smirked. Sylvia definitely knew something. He decided to move the subject away from sex. He was pretty sure Lyra was listening to at least some of this conversation.

'So you wanted to discuss your party. Come in for a second and I'll just grab your file.'

Sylvia followed him into the office and Lyra smiled and waved. 'How nice to see you again.'

Nix suppressed a snort of laughter. Judging by Lyra's tone of voice, the last conversation with Sylvia hadn't been an entirely pleasurable one. Maybe Sylvia had talked to her about sex too.

He flicked through the files on his desk and found Sylvia's. 'Why don't we go outside into the reception to discuss this, leave Lyra in peace?'

'Oh, I thought I'd discuss it with both of you.'

'Lyra is in charge of weddings, I'm in charge of all the other events,' Nix explained. 'So it will be me who will be handling your party.'

'Well that's a very efficient way of handling the events.' Sylvia tapped her lips thoughtfully. 'Although I know that Clover hired the two of you so you could work together, not separately. Wouldn't it be better to work as a team, discuss the events with each other, help each other to carry the load?'

Lyra smiled sweetly. 'We decided that this way worked better. Then the clients will always have the same point of contact.'

'And this new arrangement is nothing to do with not wanting to work together after your... last meeting?' Sylvia said.

Nix watched Lyra blush furiously. He hated that this conversation was making her feel awkward.

'We discussed it and, based on our previous experience in this role, we both thought it was for the best,' he said. 'But you don't need to worry, I'm more than capable of helping you plan the most amazing launch party for your book. Shall we?' He gestured for her to leave the office, which Sylvia did.

Lyra flashed him a grateful smile as he went out.

Sylvia slipped her arm into his as they walked into the reception area. 'Nix, I'm very much looking forward to getting to know you properly.'

Nix kept the smile fixed on his face. Why did he get the feeling that getting to know him was going to involve asking lots of personal questions about his relationship with Lyra? Or the lack of one.

CHAPTER NINE

There was a knock at the office door later and the door was tentatively pushed open before Lyra could even get up.

She recognised Aria, the hotel manager, instantly; she'd met her at the interview. Lyra knew that Aria was the oldest sister, though she didn't look anything like the twins.

'Hello,' Aria said. 'Sorry to interrupt. It was so quiet; I wasn't sure if anyone was in here. Thought you'd both gone out to lunch.'

'No, just... working away,' Lyra said, standing up as Nix did the same. Obviously he recognised Aria too.

'I'm Aria, the hotel manager.' Aria stuck her hand out to Lyra who had reached her first.

Lyra shook her hand. 'I remember you from the interview, it's good to meet you again.'

She noticed there was a man outside the office holding the hand of a little girl.

Aria shook Nix's hand. 'And this is Noah, the co-owner of the hotel and my husband.'

Noah stepped forward and shook their hands too. 'Great to meet you both, I've heard only good things about you. Clover has been singing your praises ever since the interview.'

'Thank you,' Nix said. 'That's nice to hear. And who is this lovely young lady – one of the hotel receptionists perhaps?'

The little girl burst out laughing. 'No, I'm too young to be a receptionist and I'm going to be an astronaut anyway. I won't have time to look after the hotel when I'm in space.'

'No, good point,' Nix said, seriously. 'Being an astronaut will take up a lot of your time.'

'This is our daughter, Orla,' Noah said.

'Pleased to meet you, Orla,' Nix said, holding out a hand. 'I'm Nix.'

Lyra smiled as Orla shook it so firmly she almost bounced Nix's arm out of his shoulder.

'Nix is a funny name.'

'It's short for Phoenix,' Nix said.

Lyra didn't know that. In fact there was a lot she didn't know about Nix, which begged the reason why she'd felt the need to jump into bed with him.

Orla's eyes lit up. 'There's a Phoenix in my class at school.'

'There's quite a few of us around. I bet there aren't too many Orlas though.'

Orla smiled proudly. 'I'm the only one.'

'Then I'm even more delighted to meet you,' Nix said.

Orla turned her attention to Lyra and offered out her hand in the way the Queen might offer hers out to be kissed.

Lyra suppressed a smile as she shook it. 'I'm Lyra. Do you have any of those in your class?'

Orla wrinkled her tiny nose as she thought. 'There's a Laura.'

'That's a pretty name.'

'I don't like her,' Orla said.

'Orla!' Aria said. 'We don't say things like that.'

'She's mean, she splashed water over me this morning.'

'I'm sure she didn't mean to,' Noah said.

'I splashed her back and then she cried and told the teacher.'

'Orla, that isn't very kind,' Aria said. 'When you next see her, I want you to be nice, ask her if she wants to play with you.'

Orla sighed theatrically. 'OK.'

Aria turned her attention back to Lyra and Nix, obviously a bit embarrassed by Orla's proclamation. 'We, er... wanted to invite you both to lunch, introduce you properly to the whole team.'

'That sounds great,' Nix said. 'I was just thinking how hungry I was.'

Lyra wanted nothing less than to have to socialise with Nix, but she knew she couldn't turn down the invite from her bosses.

'That'll be lovely,' she said.

'We can eat in the restaurant,' Aria said, gesturing for them to go out of the office ahead of her. 'It'll be fairly quiet this time of day. Orla will be joining us. She's not normally part of the management team meetings, but her school closed early today. Apparently there was a burst pipe.'

'Will Bea be at lunch too?' Orla said, excitedly.

'No, her school did not have a burst pipe.'

'I wish it did,' Orla said, grumpily.

Lyra hid a smile as she looked down and, as she glanced across at Nix, she saw he was struggling to suppress a smile too.

They walked into the restaurant and Lyra noticed Clover, Angel, Skye and Jesse were waiting for them.

Aria made the introductions and there were lots of handshakes all round. Nix hadn't met Skye, Jesse or even Angel before.

There were a few stragglers in the restaurant finishing off their lunch but it was mostly empty. Lyra couldn't help being impressed by the amazing view over the sea.

Aria and Noah sat down with Orla, leaving the only space in the booth for Nix and Lyra to sit together. Definitely not awkward, Lyra thought as her leg brushed up against his.

Orla was given an activity book to work on and was soon busily colouring and sticking stickers everywhere.

They spent a few minutes discussing the menu options before placing their order with one of the waitresses.

Aria turned to them. 'So, we know quite a bit about your professional lives and the jobs you had before coming here, but we don't know much about your personal lives. Are you married, do you have children?'

Lyra shook her head and then found herself holding her breath waiting for Nix to answer. Please don't let him be married, she couldn't handle that.

'No, not married, and… no children,' Nix said.

He seemed almost sad about that. Something the others around the table seemed to pick up on as well.

'Oh I'm sorry, I didn't mean to pry,' Aria quickly back-tracked. 'We're obviously a family-run hotel here and I'm always happy to meet other people's partners and families.'

'No it's fine, don't worry,' Nix said with a smile, though it didn't quite meet his eyes.

There was an awkward silence for a few moments and Lyra quickly leaned forward to fill it. She wasn't sure why, but she suddenly wanted to protect Nix from feeling uncomfortable.

'Is it just the three of you in your family?' Lyra asked the sisters. 'Or are there any other brothers and sisters?'

'Just the three of us,' Clover said.

'Eight of us,' Orla corrected. 'When Bea is here. And there will be two more babies soon.'

'That's right,' Aria said. 'You'll have lots of cousins soon.'

Lyra smiled as Orla continued with her colouring, clearly happy she had set the record straight.

'I come from a big family,' Lyra said. 'I have five brothers and sisters. I'm the eldest.'

'Oh, I imagine that was wonderful growing up with such a big family,' Skye said, giving Jesse a hopeful look.

He grinned, resting a hand on her bump. 'Let's just concentrate on this one first.'

Skye smiled before turning her attention back to Lyra, who realised she'd now have to come up with an answer about how great it was to have so many brothers and sisters.

'It was certainly a lot of fun when I was younger. When we all hit the teenage years, things were... different. But now it's certainly nice to have a team in your corner. When you have a problem there's always someone there to listen to you.'

'Or interfere?' Nix said, with a smile. 'I only have one brother but he has an opinion on everything in my life.'

Lyra nodded. 'Yes, there is definitely an element of that. The last man I was involved with, they certainly had a lot to say about him.'

His eyes widened in surprise. 'That doesn't sound good.'

Lyra shrugged, trying to downplay it. This wasn't something she wanted to discuss in front of the others. She turned her attention back to the three sisters. 'You know what siblings are like, they want what's best for you.'

They all nodded.

'And what brought you to Jewel Island specifically?' Aria said. 'We're quite far off the beaten path down here.'

Lyra wondered what Nix would say. He had the co-ordinates of Jewel Island tattooed on his arm, so it must have had some significance for him, although whether or not he would share it was another matter.

'Jewel Island has always been a special place to me for various reasons,' Nix said. 'I actually came on holiday here when I was a child.'

Lyra gasped. 'I did too.'

Nix fixed her with a look. 'That's interesting.'

Lyra focussed her attention on her napkin. 'I doubt we were here at the same time.'

'How funny that you both came here,' Clover said. 'Did you stay here in the hotel?'

Nix shook his head. 'Mostly we'd stay in a holiday cottage on the far side of the island.'

'We used to camp here,' Lyra said. 'Not many places could accommodate a family as big as ours. I have such fond memories of those times.'

She frowned because, just a few years, later everything changed.

'Me too,' Nix said, softly.

She glanced at him to see he was watching her and she quickly looked away again.

'Lots of good things have happened to me here,' Nix said. 'I've always wanted to live here. I was... quite ill a few years ago and it kind of hit home for me that I really needed to make my dreams come true. I don't want to look back on my life and wish that I'd done this or that. So I knew I needed to stop wishing for it and instead make it happen.'

Just then the food arrived and everyone tucked in. Lyra frowned, wondering what he meant when he said he'd been ill. She hoped it wasn't something horrible like cancer. She wouldn't wish that on anyone. Her own sister, Kitty, had recovered from lymphoma years before; it had been a very stressful and upsetting time but it had completely changed the way Kitty looked at her life and what she wanted from it. Having a brush with death had a tendency to do that. But whatever Nix had gone through, it would have had to be something serious for him to decide he needed to make his dreams come true.

'I actually own a bit of land up by Crystal Stream,' Nix said. 'And although I don't intend to use it for property or anything like that, it's nice to be close to it.'

'Oh, the land borders the back of the hotel grounds,' Aria said. 'I always wondered what the new owner intended to do with it once it sold a few years ago. Do you plan to keep animals on it?'

Nix cleared his throat and Lyra smiled into her food as she thought about George and his family, sitting up there in the stream, probably chewing a branch right now.

'Yes, I... um... definitely want to do that at some point. Sometimes it's just nice to have your own bit of space.'

'I get that,' Angel said. 'I always wanted to have my own plot of land. Have some horses, maybe some goats, pigs and sheep. We have the horses – although technically they're not ours, we sort of look after them – and a cow, plus there's also a donkey, but no luck on the pigs, goats and sheep yet. Or the land. I always fancied myself as a bit of a farmer.'

Nix nodded. 'I like the sound of that.'

Clover smiled at her husband. 'Well at least I know what to get you for your next birthday.'

Angel grinned.

'I'd like to be a farmer too,' Orla said as she coloured in a picture of a cow. 'I'd have llamas on my farm and hedge-hogs too.'

'That sounds like a fun farm,' Nix said.

'And what about you, Lyra?' Noah asked. 'What brings you to Jewel Island?'

'Well, similar to Nix in a way. We used to come here so often as a child and me and my sister, Michelle, she's the one closest to me in age, always used to plan how we would live here when we grew up, which cottages we would live in and how we planned to marry Leonardo DiCaprio or Will Smith. And when we were teenagers and things were... difficult at home, we talked about this place like it was some pot of gold at the end of the rainbow. I didn't honestly believe we'd end up here. But Michelle moved here a few months ago and we've always been close. She has a little boy who I adore and I don't want to miss out on him growing up. I missed her like crazy too. When this job came up, I knew I had to apply. And here I am, living the dream.'

Apart from the fact that the man next to her had sort of taken the shine off all of that.

'Well I'm so glad we managed to make your dreams come true,' Clover said.

Lyra glanced at Nix and mentally shook her head. The week before, her dreams for the future involved him, which was ridiculous. Now she just had to focus on the original plan: move to Jewel Island, start a new life. Getting involved with a man was not part of that.

Lyra had spoken to Jack and Heather and, as they lived locally, they'd been able to pop down that afternoon. They were every inch the loved-up couple she had imagined them to be. They held hands as Lyra escorted them through the gardens, Heather excitedly talking about their wedding, Jack looking at her adoringly. It made Lyra's heart hurt to watch them together.

'So you two met at Cones at the Cove?' Lyra asked, feeling like she was torturing herself asking for details.

'Yes, and we just hit off right away,' Heather said.

Jack smiled at his fiancée. 'I knew, as soon as we met, I

knew then we were going to get married. We had this...
connection, this spark that I'd never felt before.'

Heather blushed. 'It was incredible. It wasn't like we'd
just met, it was like we'd found each other again, our other
half. We spent the whole day talking to each other, in the
café, on walks down on the beach, and then he came back
to mine and... well, the chemistry was off the charts.'

'I moved in with her a week later,' Jack said. 'Our family
and friends all thought we were crazy. Mine especially, as
the morning I'd met Heather, my divorce had finally come
through. I wasn't ready for another relationship, I certainly
wasn't looking for one, and then there was Heather and I
knew she was going to change my life.'

'It was fate. I had an unexpected day off and I'd seen
adverts for Cones at the Cove so thought I'd treat myself to
a dessert. Jack was only staying at the hotel because the one
he was supposed to be staying at had double-booked. Six
months ago, if you'd asked me if I believed in the stars
aligning or some divine power watching over us, I'd have
laughed you out the door, but I know we were supposed to
meet that day. We were exactly where we were meant to be.'

The echoes of what Nix had said to her rang in Lyra's
ears. The morning after the night she'd spent with him, as
she lay in his arms, she'd have said that she was exactly
where she was meant to be too. That somehow she and Nix
had found each other, despite all the odds. Look at how
badly that had turned out. God, she was such an idiot. Why
did she let herself fall in love so quickly? Why did she
never learn?

'That's very romantic,' Lyra forced herself to say.

They were now approaching Cones at the Cove, which was closed again for the short lull between lunch and dinner. Skye was busy cleaning the tables when they walked in but her face lit up at seeing Jack and Heather. She came over and hugged them both.

'Hello again. I'm so excited you guys are getting married and that we might be able to help here in some small way.'

'We were kind of hoping it would be in a big way,' Heather said, looking at Jack. 'We talked about it on the drive over here and this place is so special to us. It's where we met, where we got engaged, and although it'd be nice if we could hold our reception here, we'd actually really like to get married here too.'

'I would love that,' Skye said. 'But I don't think legally you can.'

'There are ways round it,' Lyra said. 'The hotel is licensed to hold weddings in two of our rooms, and the Diamond Lounge is the one most commonly used. We legally can't hold a wedding in a room unless we have a licence for that particular room. However, most registrars will be happy to perform a ceremony anywhere you want – on the beach, here in the café – as long as you do the legal bit in one of the licensed rooms either before or after the big ceremony. It really is just a formality; a few questions, a few legal statements, you'd be in and out before they started serving the ice cream. But at least you can then have the real ceremony how you want it.'

'What do you think?' Jack asked Heather.

'I like the sound of it. Even if we got married in a church, we'd have to go off and sign the certificate and do the formal bit. This is no different. And the registrars would be willing to do a full ceremony in here after?'

'Me and Jesse did that for our wedding,' Skye said. 'We did the legal bit first at the hotel and then got married down in Emerald Cove at sunset. It was beautiful.'

Lyra nodded. 'This is more normal than you think, many people get married this way.'

Heather squealed a little in excitement. 'We could get married over there by the windows, overlooking Emerald Cove.'

Lyra started writing things down on her notepad. 'We can borrow some chairs from the hotel and can push those doors back if it's a nice day – make the space a bit bigger.'

'Maybe we can hang up some fairy lights,' Heather said. 'Have some flowers around the place. Keep it simple.'

'Skye suggested we have a marquee outside for the dancing. The hotel owns one so it wouldn't be a problem,' Lyra said.

'Oh yes, I like that idea. What do you think, Jack?'

'I like the idea too. But whatever makes you happy. As long as I get to call you my wife, we can do this any way you want.'

They talked for a bit longer about how they'd like to set up for the ceremony and how best to utilise the space, and then, while Jack and Heather were in such an accommodating mood, Lyra thought she might try to tie them down to a few other decisions too.

'So I wonder if you've had a chance to look at the menu choices that Clover sent over?' she said.

'Yes, but to be honest none of them were quite what we were looking for,' Jack said.

Lyra's heart sank. She'd dealt with customers before who wanted something completely different to eat and, while that was normally fine, she knew indecisive ones would take weeks of taste-testing to come to a decision. In Jack and Heather's case, they just didn't have that time.

Heather giggled. 'We just want fish and chips. It was the meal we had after leaving here the first time we met – we wandered into town and bought fish and chips and sat on the beach and ate them. And then for dessert, we'd really like it if people could build their own desserts, just like the normal customers do here. They can choose which flavour ice cream they want, add their own toppings. We just want a really simple affair.'

Lyra smiled in relief. 'I'm sure we can do that.'

'I hate to throw a spanner in the works but we're primarily a dessert café, we don't have fat fryers here,' Skye said.

'That's not a problem,' Lyra said. 'I'm pretty sure we can hire them. Let me look into prices and possible solutions. Are you wanting some kind of buffet for the night time?'

'Yes, but just sandwiches, chicken drumsticks, nothing too fancy,' Heather said.

'OK, I can send over some options for you to choose from,' Lyra said, writing it all down. It was something of a relief that the couple knew exactly what they wanted from their special day, and they had quite simple tastes, but sometimes the simple things were the hardest to organise.

Lyra rang the bell of her sister's house and smiled when she saw the name card under the bell. 'Mr and Mrs Olney'. Michelle had been so excited about taking Ben's surname when they got married. She wanted everyone to know they were part of the same team. Lyra wondered what it would be like to be part of a team.

Ben answered the door, Zach flung over his shoulder, giggling wildly.

'Hey Lyra.' He kissed her on the cheek. 'Welcome back to the madhouse. Come in, my world-famous chicken pie is almost ready.'

Lyra stepped inside and relieved Ben of his wiggling load.

'I can never turn down one of your pies. Hello you,' she said to Zach.

'Ra!' Zach said, grabbing hold of her lips. She smiled at his name for her. The word Lyra was too hard for Zach to get his little tongue around when he was still trying to perfect other words in the English language. In the end, he'd settled for Ra.

'Leave Aunty Ra's lips alone, she needs them.' Ben ushered them both through to the kitchen and he returned to attempting to cook the dinner. Every pot, plate, pan and bowl had been used in the making of the famous pie, and Michelle was sitting at the table looking very calm about all the mess. Although she was sipping on a glass of wine, which might have had something to do with it.

'Can I help you with anything, Ben?'

'No, just keep that little one occupied for a few minutes,' Ben said.

Lyra kissed her sister on the cheek. 'How was your day?'

'Good. Well, busy.'

'Tell her about your plans,' Ben said, excitedly.

'Oh, you have plans?' Lyra said, sitting down with Zach on her lap. She grabbed a squeaky bear and gave it to her nephew to play with. He immediately shoved it in his mouth.

'I've been thinking about what you said the other night about selling my brownies and cakes,' Michelle said. 'I get so many of my friends requesting I make them batches for this and that, and ever since I've moved down here, I've had to post the cakes to them, which hasn't always ended too well for the cakes. After a few trial and errors, I've found some packaging that can protect them through the post and now I'm thinking of making more of a business out of it. Selling my baked treats online. Ben has been helping me design a website and I've spent a lot of the day making small batches of different-flavoured cakes and biscuits and taking some nice photos of them to upload on the website and see what kind of interest I get from it.'

'That sounds like a wonderful idea. Your cakes are amazing, you definitely should be making money out of it. Are you thinking about posting on places like Etsy or Not on the High Street too?'

'Oh yes, I hadn't thought of that. That's a good idea.'

'And if you need me to trial any new flavours, I'm more than happy to step up to the plate,' Lyra said.

Michelle laughed. 'You're so brave.'

'Pie is ready,' Ben said, coming over to the table with two plates of steaming hot chicken pie, served with mashed potatoes and gravy. He placed the dishes down. 'Could you strap trouble into his high chair?'

Lyra plonked Zach on her hip as she wrestled the high chair out from the corner of the room and Michelle started clearing away some of the debris from the table. To Lyra's surprise, Zach went into his chair very easily, his hands greedily reaching out for the small plate of pie Ben was bringing over.

Lyra sat down and tucked into her food. 'Ben, this is delicious, as always.'

'Thank you. How was your day?' Ben asked.

Lyra puffed her cheeks out and let out a big sigh. 'Pretty crappy if I'm honest, which is a shame as I was really looking forward to this job.'

'Is Nix that bad to work with?' Michelle said, taking a big bite of her pie.

'I just don't know how to be with him. He seems really nice but then I remember what happened and I just can't seem to let that go. And I don't know what bothers me more, that it was just a one-night stand for him when it felt like so much more, or that he left without having the decency to say goodbye.'

'I still think you should talk to him, ask him what happened,' Michelle said. 'What do you think, Ben?'

Her husband chewed on his pie thoughtfully. 'Lyra, I love you, I think you're brilliant and this guy clearly had no idea what he was walking away from. But I think for your own sanity, you need to put that night behind you and move on. There's no point in dwelling on why he ran away and I don't think you'd like to hear the answer anyway. Finding out the truth won't make you feel any better. So I

111

think you go back to work tomorrow and treat him like any other colleague. You dazzle him with your lovely Lyra kindness and well… maybe he'll come to regret walking away from you in the first place.'

'Yes!' Michelle said. 'Show him what he's missing out on.'

Lyra sighed. She had no interest in playing games with Nix but Ben did have a point, she had to let it go and move on. They were colleagues, working together in the same room. They had to have a good working relationship. Starting from tomorrow she was going to start a new leaf with Nix Sanchez.

Nix put Dexter's food down and then went out on deck as the sun left pink candyfloss clouds across the sky and turned the sea a beautiful crimson. Little sailboats dotted the horizon as people went out on sunset boat trips. Most of the boats in the harbour were empty. Unlike him, no one else was living on their boat, which seemed a real shame as this was one of the most beautiful parts of the world in his opinion.

He took a sip of his beer. As first days went, that certainly hadn't gone to plan. The atmosphere between him and Lyra had been awful, so much so that he hadn't even wanted to be in the same room as her. He had to make it right between them but he had no idea how.

When they'd first met they'd got on so well, and conversation had been really comfortable between them. He wanted that ease back, even if a proper relationship between them was completely off the table. He wanted to be able to laugh with her, or at the very least discuss the different events together.

He had to talk to Lyra about what happened, because the sense of angst he was getting from her was way more extreme than it should have been under the circumstances. They'd had a great night together, they didn't need this bad feeling between them. If she didn't want to pursue a relationship then that was fine, but surely they could be grown-ups about it.

His phone rang in his pocket and he fished it out as Dexter wandered out on deck too, licking his lips and wagging his tail, ready for his post-dinner fuss.

Nix sat down and Dexter nestled between his legs demanding to have his back stroked. Nix obliged, massaging the dog's neck with one hand and answering the phone with the other.

'How did your first day go?' Lucas said. He was slightly out of breath, as if he'd been running.

Nix sighed. 'In terms of the job, fine. The upcoming events have been organised to the finest detail, so it's very easy to see what is left to do. I think the job will be fun. In terms of working alongside Lyra, not great.'

'That's not good. Do you think she feels embarrassed?'

'I don't know, I think it's way more than that.'

'Maybe the sex was crap,' Lucas said, knowing the exact thing to make his brother feel better.

Nix rolled his eyes and shook his head. 'That's entirely possible – it's been a while – but still it seems like a bit of an overreaction if that's the case.'

'Maybe it was really really bad.'

'She seems angry.'

There was a pause from Lucas. 'Well, that's weird.'

'I know. We had this lovely night and she certainly didn't seem angry when we were making love. In fact, she seemed pretty into it.' Nix sighed. 'She told me some stuff about her mum that night. She was let down by her parents very badly and it makes her hold onto the reins really tight. I wonder if she's angry at herself for letting go. Maybe she feels like she shouldn't have done it.'

'Maybe. You need to talk to her.'

'Yeah I do,' Nix said, although he was really not looking forward to that conversation. 'I had an idea actually. I was thinking about doing something for her that might make her... relax a little.'

'Get her drunk,' Lucas teased.

'That's more your style than mine,' Nix said. 'No, something fun.'

'What did you have in mind?'

He did have a plan but he had no idea whether Lyra would be up for it, especially as she was barely talking to him right now. That spirit of adventure she'd had the night they'd met had gone, but hopefully it was just hidden away rather than gone for good.

'I'll let you know once I've given it some thought. How are things with you?'

'Good, just finishing my run before I go out on my date.'

'Anna?'

'No, Helene.'

'What happened to Anna?' Nix asked.

'She asked me to meet her parents.'

'Is that really a bad thing?'

'Serious relationships are your thing, not mine. You made love to the first woman you've slept with since Emily, I have sex with the women I date, and there is a really big difference.'

Nix rolled his eyes. Lucas was never going to settle down. Maybe that was a better way to be, then he'd never get hurt.

'Right, I better go, I need to take Dexter for his walk. Enjoy your date.'

'Always do.'

Nix hung up. Life would be a hell of a lot simpler if he adopted Lucas's attitude and then he wouldn't be dwelling on this thing with Lyra. He'd just have slept with her and moved on. Instead he was worrying over how he'd upset her and how he could make this right.

CHAPTER TEN

Lyra walked into the office the next day with a smile forced on her face. 'Good morning Nix.'

She could hear how stiff and formal it sounded but it was the best she could do. Every time she looked at him she recalled how he'd touched her, the affection in his eyes as he'd made love to her, the way his kiss had made fireworks erupt inside her. She remembered that connection which had felt deeper than anything she'd ever experienced before, even after only a few hours together. She sat down with a sigh. To find out the next morning that he hadn't felt any of that and it hadn't meant anything to him hurt like hell. And although Ben's advice had made sense and she knew she had to move on and put it behind her, it wasn't as easy as that.

She glanced across to see he was watching her warily like she was a deranged wild animal. He cleared his throat. 'Morning Lyra,' he said, softly.

Her name on his lips was like a kick to the heart. The last time he'd spoken her name was when they'd been in bed together, her arms and legs wrapped around him as he stared at her as if she was the missing piece he'd been searching for. And it had all been a lie.

Maybe they should have discussed the parameters before they'd jumped into bed together, laid out some ground rules so she knew what to expect. She was a big fan of rules but for some reason all of that had gone straight out the window when she met Nix. But maybe he'd thought they were on the same page. If she was the kind of woman who jumped into bed with a man she'd just met, then she was probably not the kind of woman who was looking for a serious relationship where love and trust were built up over time.

OK, she just had to treat him like a normal colleague, and not someone who had broken her heart. She could do that.

'How's George?' Lyra asked, as if asking after his first-born.

Nix stared at her, visibly confused by her attempt at polite conversation. 'He's fine. I think, I haven't seen him for a few days... But yes, he seems to be fine.'

She nodded and turned her attention to the files on her desk, although she could sense he was still staring at her.

'Lyra, that night...'

Her eyes snapped up, locking with his. Were they really going to talk about it? So much for trying to go back to normal and pretending it never happened. She waited and eventually Nix spoke.

'Did I... hurt you?'

She frowned in confusion. She hadn't been expecting that.

'When you made… during sex?' she quickly corrected herself. She couldn't call it making love because it clearly hadn't been that. It had been sex, nothing more.

'Yes, did I do something you didn't like?' Nix asked.

Lyra's frown deepened. How could he think that? It had been incredible. Her heart had broken the next day when she'd found him gone but she couldn't take anything away from the night itself. And although she hated him a little bit for leaving after the wonderful night they'd spent together, she could never let him think that he'd hurt her in any way, or that she'd been anything but completely willing.

'No, completely the opposite. There was quite a lot I did like.'

He gave her a sad smile. 'Me too.'

This conversation was getting more and more confusing.

'So you woke up the next morning and regretted it?' Nix asked.

Did she regret what happened between them? If she knew then what she knew now about how it would come to a crashing end, would things have been different? Would she have said goodnight after visiting the beavers and made her way to Michelle's house? That was like asking whether she'd turn down the best chocolate cake in the world knowing she could only ever taste it once. Definitely not. Not even knowing the cake was unhealthy and bad for her would put her off. She'd devour every mouthful and then lick the plate afterwards. So, no, she couldn't regret the night she'd spent with Nix, no matter what had happened the next day. She knew if she had the chance to make that decision again, it would be exactly the same, only this time she would agree to spend the night with her heart firmly locked away so she could enjoy the night for what it was: an incredible moment never to be repeated.

'I don't regret what we shared,' Lyra said.

He stared at her. 'So why—'

The office door opened and Clover walked in, carrying cups of what looked like two frothy cappuccinos. 'How's it all going?' she asked. She placed one of the cups on Lyra's desk and then took the other over to Nix's desk.

Lyra cleared her throat as she tried to get her mind back in professional mode. The conversation with Nix had completely thrown her and now she had to pretend that everything was fine and she hadn't just been thinking about the best sex in her life while at work.

'We're getting on well,' she said, plastering on a smile. 'We've decided to split the files for efficiency. I'm currently looking after weddings and Nix is doing all the other events. That way the clients can always have the same point of contact going forward.'

'Oh, good idea,' Clover said. 'And in that case, Nix, Elsie McLaughlin just called – she's the hundredth birthday party in the middle of August. She's asked if someone can go to her house to talk through menu options and a few other details for the party. She's not as mobile as she used to be, although her mind is still as sharp as a pin.'

'Not a problem,' Nix said, easily.

'Her address should be in the file, but it's just behind the school, bright pink cottage, you can't miss it.'

'I'll go as soon as I've finished my coffee,' he said, taking a sip of his drink. 'I need to drop some details round to Seamus for his party, so I can do that on the way back.'

'That's great, thanks. And I've actually got another event I wanted to talk to you two about. Last year we reopened the hotel after extensive refurbishments under the new name and the Sapphire Bay Hotel will be one year old at the end of August. We hadn't thought about doing anything, but we had a management meeting yesterday and thought we could hold a party or some kind of event. A two-day event actually. Lyra, you can take day one, and Nix, you can take day two.'

'OK,' Lyra said, somewhat relieved that they would still be working relatively separately for their day of the party.

'Sounds good,' Nix said.

'We'll be inviting our regular guests to come and stay for the weekend. Most of the party will be done in house,' Clover went on. 'Especially all the catering, but there will be a reasonable budget for entertainment or decorations or other things you might want for the party. It won't be crazy high, but I suspect Noah will be quite generous.'

They both nodded.

'Now here's the fun bit. As you know, I'm going to be taking a step back from the conference and banqueting side of things and initially we thought we would just have two events co-ordinators. But Aria and Noah feel that we actually need an events manager who would be in charge and make final decisions about things, but who would also play a key part in the hotel managerial team, reporting back to the rest of our team about events and anything we need to be aware of. The two of you are very experienced and we couldn't choose between the two of you. Personally, I can see both of you shining in that role, so we thought we'd have a little competition. You have a few days to prepare your ideas for your day of the party. On Monday, you can present your ideas to us and the best presentation and ideas will get the job.'

Lyra frowned slightly. Were her new bosses really going to promote one of them based on the outcome of a competition? That didn't sound particularly professional or efficient.

'It'd mean a small pay rise,' Clover went on. 'The two jobs won't be that different in the day-to-day workload, as you'll both still be co-ordinating your own events and working together to come up with ways to encourage people to book their events with us. It'll just be co-ordinating with management that will be the added element. The winner will also get a five-hundred-pound one-off bonus.'

A pay rise would be very welcome, and five hundred pounds would almost pay Lyra's rent for an entire month; Jewel Island was not a cheap place to live. But she still didn't feel good about this. She glanced across at Nix. They were barely speaking and now they were going to be in competition against each other. This didn't exactly bode well for a harmonious professional relationship. She'd opened her mouth to say she wasn't sure if it was a good idea when she spotted Nix nodding.

'Sounds like a great idea,' he said.

Lyra swallowed her objections. She was hugely competitive. Whenever she got together with her siblings and they played board games, she would do everything in her power to win. If Nix wanted to take her on, she was definitely up for it. And at least that would give her something else to focus on rather than healing her battered and bruised heart.

She smiled sweetly at Nix. 'Bring it on.'

~

There was a knock on the door shortly after Nix had left to go and see Elsie McLaughlin. Lyra got up to answer it and found Sylvia on the other side, today wearing a glittery gold cloak embroidered with flowers. She looked spectacular. She was accompanied by the big white fluffy dog again.

'I have to ask, if you wear this kind of thing on a normal day, what will you wear to your party?' Lyra said, stepping back to let her into the office.

'Oh, something fabulous, I assure you.'

'I have no doubt. And who is this?' Lyra stroked the fluffy dog's head.

'Snowflake. He's very good at sniffing out a good romance story,' Sylvia said.

Lyra smiled. 'I'm afraid Nix has popped out to see another client, but I can take a message for him.'

'I came to see you actually,' Sylvia said.

Lyra grabbed Nix's chair, wheeling it around his desk for Sylvia to sit down on, before returning to her own desk. 'I'm guessing this isn't related to your party?'

'Well, strictly speaking it's linked,' Sylvia said, settling herself in the chair. 'You see, how can Nix plan me an amazing party if the boy is sitting in here being miserable for the next few months? I feel the party will be tainted somehow.'

'Ah, I see. I'm to blame for that, I suppose?' Lyra said.

'Well, that boy has it bad for you, I can tell. And I think you feel the same way, so just let him apologise and take him back. Then at least he'll stop moping about the place.'

'I don't think he's moping,' Lyra said, although Nix certainly wasn't the happy, chatty man she'd met the previous week. 'And even if he is, this is of his doing. It's not my job to make him happier.'

'But men are fools who have no idea which path to take through life. It's our job as women to guide them.'

Lyra smiled at this simple view from an octogenarian. 'I'm not sure someone who has been married six times is really the kind of expert I need in matters of the heart.'

'I think that's exactly the kind of person you need to advise you,' Sylvia said, unperturbed. 'I have a wealth of experience. Tell me, was the sex good?'

Lyra shook her head with a smile. Realising that Sylvia was here purely for a salacious bit of gossip, she wondered whether, if she gave her something, she might go away and leave her to do her work.

'It was the most incredible night of my life,' Lyra said.

Sylvia clapped her hands together in triumph. 'I knew it, I could see the connection between you. I was watching you at lunch yesterday and it just sparkled in the air. Why are you not fighting harder for this, if it was so incredible?'

Lyra sighed; her tactic evidently hadn't worked. 'Have you spoken to Nix about all this, about what happened?'

'No, he's been very discreet about it all, not like you.'

Lyra burst out laughing. 'Oh my god, you're terrible. I was hoping if I gave you a little nugget you'd go away.'

'Perhaps the nugget should have been smaller,' Sylvia

said. 'I'm not going anywhere after that. In my experience, you don't walk away from that kind of sex unless he did something unforgivable.'

'Well, after six marriages, you obviously found some things unforgivable,' Lyra said.

'Two of them cheated on me, one stole my money, one tried to kill me, one turned out to be gay. All pretty unforgivable. Well actually, I forgave my lovely gay husband for breaking my heart. Even went to his wedding when he found himself a nice fella, but the others I couldn't forgive. I'm presuming Nix didn't cheat, steal or try to kill you?'

'Well, no,' Lyra said.

'What did he do that you can't get past?'

'He ran away,' she said simply. 'The next morning he left without even saying goodbye.'

'OK, but have you asked him why?'

'No of course not, how sad would that make me look?'

'Can I ask him?'

'No you cannot. And if you breathe one word of this conversation to him or anyone, I'll take that gold cloak and put it through the shredder.'

Sylvia gasped. 'You wouldn't.'

'I would,' Lyra said, grabbing a piece of scrap paper and putting it through the shredder next to her desk, relishing the noise it made as it destroyed the paper.

'OK, OK,' Sylvia said. 'This goes no further than these four walls. But what are you going to do?'

'Nothing. Try be civil to him and hope that we can put it behind us and work together.'

'That doesn't sound like a good plan. What if Nix is your soul mate? What if he's your happy ever after?'

'I'll guess we'll never know,' Lyra said.

'No, this is heartbreaking. You two are supposed to be together.'

'Look, I'm not the one in the wrong here. He left me. He has to be the one to offer the olive branch, not me.'

'And if he did?' Sylvia leaned forward eagerly. 'If he apologised, would you take him back?'

Lyra thought about it. 'Honestly, probably not. I've been hurt too many times in the past to want to go through that again.'

Sylvia opened her mouth to protest but Lyra stopped her.

'*But* if he had a good enough reason for leaving then I might consider it.'

Sylvia nodded. 'Yes, it has to be a good reason. You can't let these men walk all over you.'

'No, definitely not.'

'OK, let me see if I can do some digging. Subtly,' Sylvia quickly reassured. 'I won't mention this conversation but let me see if I can find out his side of the story.'

'It better be subtle, Sylvia O'Hare. Your precious cloak is at stake.'

CHAPTER ELEVEN

Nix got back to the office after several hours with the charming Elsie McLaughlin and some time with Seamus, the town mayor, to find a sandwich wrapped in clingfilm on his desk. He cocked his head in confusion and glanced over at Lyra who was hard at work, but thankfully not with her headphones in this time.

'Is this from you?'

She looked up. 'The restaurant is now closed until dinner. I thought you'd be hungry as your meetings seemed to overrun.'

She turned back to her work as if it wasn't a big deal, when it was a really thoughtful gesture.

Unless it was poisoned. The air was still distinctly frosty between them and he had no idea why. 'Thank you.'

Lyra shrugged.

He didn't want to tell her that Elsie had plied him with enough biscuits that he didn't feel remotely hungry. And then, while visiting Seamus and his wife Kathy to discuss their anniversary party, he'd been given several slices of cake as well.

Nix sat down and bit into the sandwich, making appreciative noises for good measure. It did taste good so he took a few more mouthfuls and then discreetly moved it to the side.

'What's with the teabags?' Lyra asked, gesturing to the small plastic bag he'd brought in with him.

He stared at the bag. Seamus had been helpful in *so* many ways when Nix had told him about his plan, and, when Kathy had handed Nix the bag of teabags with a wink as he'd left their house, he'd laughed at their meddling. Although he couldn't tell Lyra any of this.

He cleared his throat. 'Oh, me and Seamus were talking about special teas. I'm not a tea person so Kathy suggested I try some.'

Lyra looked like she didn't quite believe him and Nix decided to quickly change the subject.

'I've been thinking about this competition,' he said. 'I think we should liaise with each other about what we're doing.'

Lyra frowned. For someone who'd seemed so easy-going and happy the first night they'd met, she sure did frown a lot at work. He wondered if that was all his doing.

'It's hardly going to be a fair competition if we're telling each other our ideas,' she said.

'Well, no, but it doesn't need to be a fight to the bitter death. It's a friendly competition. May the best man or woman win.'

She eyed him sceptically.

'My point is, if you present that there's going to be a

chocolate fountain on day one they won't want to see a chocolate fountain on day two. It makes sense that we have fireworks on day two, so by me telling you that I plan to do that, then you won't go ahead and plan them for day one.'

'I've already added fireworks to my plan.'

He sighed. 'Fireworks are always the grand finale, everyone knows that. It makes sense to have them at the end of day two.'

'Fireworks are used at the opening of events,' Lyra said. 'Even the Olympics have fireworks at their opening ceremony.'

'It doesn't make sense to have fireworks on both days – it's too costly for the hotel for one.'

'No you're right, which is why it makes sense to leave it on day one.'

Nix bit his lip to clamp down on his frustration. So that's how she wanted to play it. 'Well, I guess we'll let them decide which day they want the fireworks.'

'I guess we will,' she smiled at him.

He sighed. 'So you don't want to liaise on what we're having on our respective days?'

'I think it's probably best if we keep our ideas separate. I'd hate you to think I was stealing your ideas or vice versa.'

He felt his eyebrows shoot up. 'I would never steal your ideas.'

She sighed, the fight seemingly going out of her. She rubbed her eyes. 'I know, you're way too nice for that.'

It sounded like she wished he wasn't.

'Fireworks on day two probably makes more sense,' Lyra said.

He hesitated, not quite sure what to do with this sudden U-turn. 'Thank you.'

Lyra nodded and then gave him a small smile, the first genuine one he'd seen since that wonderful night. 'It won't matter anyway; I intend to win this competition with or without the fireworks.'

He met her challenge with a smile. 'Oh, we'll see about that.'

Lyra shone the torch on the road ahead as she walked back to her cottage. The moon was gleaming brightly above her, the stars twinkling against a velvet sky. She loved going for a walk at night. It was something her mum always used to do, bundle Lyra and all her siblings into their coats and go out for a walk before bed. And though Lyra had worked very hard to make sure she didn't end up like her mum, and though they barely spoke at all now, it was a habit that had seemed to stay with her. This time of night there was no one around, it was peaceful and quiet and it gave her time to think. And maybe it was naïve, but here on Jewel Island she felt safe.

Except... up ahead there was a man in a hoodie climbing over a gate. The gate leading from Nix's field and the beavers. Her heart leapt in her chest as the man pulled his hood down further over his head and walked away up the hill. She felt sick at the thought that he might have done something to the beavers. Nix had told her that some people didn't like the ideas of beavers in the wild, and that in some parts of Scotland the beavers had been culled. What if this man had snuck in and hurt them?

'Hey, what do you think you're doing?' Lyra said, chasing after him. 'Oi!'

The man kept on walking, and she caught up with him and grabbed his arm. He leapt at her touch and turned around and she came face to face with Nix.

'Lyra, shit, you scared the crap out of me,' he said, pulling his headphones out of his ears and turning the music off on his phone.

She stepped back in surprise. 'Oh, I saw you climbing over the gate and I thought... I thought you were someone else. You looked dodgy.'

His eyes widened slightly. 'Did you see what I was doing?'

She frowned. 'Why, what were you doing? Is there another poor unsuspecting woman in there?'

She glanced over the fence to see if there was another woman abandoned in the middle of the field after having the best sex of her life. The moonlit meadow was completely empty.

'Unsuspecting?' he said, clearly alarmed. 'How were you unsuspecting?'

'Oh come on, we both know you made it seem more than it was.'

He stared at her in confusion. 'And how did I do that?'

'You... pretended to care, you listened.' Embarrassingly, she felt tears smart her eyes. 'You held me as I told you things I've never told anyone before.'

Nix was looking at her as if she'd grown an extra head and she felt like an idiot.

'It doesn't matter, water under the bridge,' Lyra said, hurrying past him to get to her cottage.

'Wait—'

'Please, forget I said anything.'

There was silence behind her for a moment as she walked away and then he was running to catch up with her.

'What are you doing out here alone at night?' Nix said, as he fell in at her side.

'I'm going home.'

'You live round here?' he asked in confusion.

'I moved to the island a few days after we...' she trailed off. 'My house is just up here.'

'The little cottage? What a great place to live.'

'It has a wonderful view,' Lyra said.

'Shall I walk you back?' Nix said.

'Thank you, but that's not necessary.'

'Well, I'm going this way anyway. I'd prefer to know you were safe.'

They continued on in silence for a while and it was just painfully awkward.

They approached her cottage and she headed straight up to her door. She opened it and switched the light on inside, letting it pour out into her tiny front garden.

'Well, I'll see you tomorrow,' Nix said.

'Thanks for walking me back,' Lyra said.

He paused. 'Lyra, I didn't *pretend* to care.'

She stared at him. This was ridiculous. Ben said she had to put it behind her but she couldn't, she had to know. She moved back out to stand in front of Nix. He was watching her warily.

'Look, I think we should talk about this, because we're never going to move on unless we do. And I've told myself a hundred times that I'm probably better off not knowing, but I just can't let it go. So let's just be brutally honest and then we can move on once and for all. Because I thought we were getting on really well that night and you seemed so bloody lovely. And we talked about stuff that I've never told anyone and you seemed interested, like you genuinely cared. If I'm honest, I haven't been with a man for so long and you just pulled down all my walls and now I feel like you were playing me just to get me into bed. Was that it? Was that always the endgame – just sex? And then what? You saw how I looked at you and panicked that I saw something that you didn't? Or did you see all my baggage and think you didn't want to deal with that? Because I'm a big girl, I would have understood. But you didn't even say goodbye.'

Nix was looking thoroughly confused.

'Or was it the sex? Was it really bad, is that why?'

She definitely didn't want to hear the answer to that.

Nix's mouth fell open in shock. Then he cleared his throat. 'Lyra, the sex was incredible. I wish it wasn't because it would be easier, but it was. We had this connection that I've never felt before.'

She frowned in confusion. 'Then why? What happened?'

'What do you mean, what happened?'

'You left!' Lyra said in exasperation.

His eyebrows shot up in surprise. 'That sure in hell isn't how I remember it.'

Lyra sighed. 'Go on then, how do you remember it?'

'I woke up after the most amazing night of my life and you were gone,' Nix said.

She felt her eyes widen, her heart crashing into her stomach as doubt and uncertainty started creeping in. 'No, I left a note,' she said, her voice no more than a whisper.

He folded his arms. 'I can assure you there was no note.'

She swallowed. 'I went for a swim in the lake. I suggested you might want to come down and join me.'

His eyes widened and when he spoke his voice was broken. 'Lyra, no!'

'And when I came back you were gone and I wondered if you'd looked at the part of the note that said, "Love Lyra" and thought that I'd fallen in love with you and so you ran away before I could march you down the aisle.'

'No, I would never just go. I mean, sure, if I'd woken up and you suggested we got married I probably would have been a bit shocked, but I wouldn't have just left.'

Had she completely got this all wrong?

Nix shook his head. 'But hang on a minute, Daisy was gone as well.'

'She was dirty after my little fall so I took her down to the lake to clean her off too. I can't believe you didn't see the note, I left it by the door.'

'Well I'm guessing that when you opened the door it blew away,' Nix said.

Her heart sank. That was entirely plausible.

'I was gutted when I found you gone,' he said, softly. 'After what we shared…'

'I was too. When I came back up from the lake to see you, Dexter and Judy had gone, I felt sick because I felt that connection as well. I know people have one-night stands all the time but it didn't feel that way for us. I thought I'd done something wrong, that you didn't want anything more to do with me. And, honestly, that made me feel pretty crap.'

'I'm so sorry Lyra, I hate that I made you feel that way.'

'I'm sorry too,' she said, quietly.

They stared at each other for the longest time. She actually wanted to cry. All of this disappointment and pain had been completely unnecessary. She had hurt him too and she hated that. And she had been almost rude to him since starting work at the hotel the day before and he hadn't done anything wrong. But where the hell did they go from here?

Nix moved his hand to touch her shoulder and she instinctively stepped back out of his reach. 'Maybe it was for the best,' she said, defensively.

He let his hand fall to his side.

She felt her shutters going back up. It didn't seem to matter that there had been a genuine misunderstanding, that Nix hadn't deliberately tried to hurt her. Her self-preservation was kicking in and she didn't want to get hurt again.

She took another step back. 'I've never done that before; I've never jumped into bed with a man I'd only met a few hours before. I've only ever had sex in a serious relationship and, well, they never turned out well either. I always end up getting hurt. For some reason, I let my guard down with you and I ended up hurt yet again.'

'Lyra, it was a misunderstanding.'

'I know, but I should never have... After my last boyfriend I swore to myself that I would never get involved with a man unless I had taken the time to get to know him first, and all those precautions just went straight out the window when I met you. If we'd known each other properly you never would have thought that I'd run away when you woke up. Not just because we had something special, but because you would have known that's not the kind of person I am. And I wouldn't have spent the last week feeling heartbroken yet again.'

'Lyra, I'm sorry.'

'No, you have nothing to apologise for – it wasn't either of our faults. But I think we recognise it for what it was, one spectacular night, and we draw a line under it and move on. I'm rubbish at relationships. I'm terrible at picking men. I think I attract the bad apples and I think honestly I'm probably better off alone.'

Nix let out a heavy breath and then eventually nodded. 'OK. I get it. I was hurt and disappointed when I woke up to find you gone, but after I'd driven off and had some time to think, and despite the fact I've thought about you every single day since that wonderful night, I started to think it was for the best as well.'

She swallowed a lump of emotion in her throat. He'd thought of her every day.

He looked away over the moonlit sea. 'I... I haven't been in a relationship for a long time either and I don't know if I'm ready to start one,' he said.

She stared at him. 'That night, you said you hadn't had sex in a while, I thought it was just a line. You had this big stash of condoms and...'

He smiled. 'My brother's. He borrows the van from time to time and I think he uses it as some kind of sex-

135

mobile, driving round different places, a different woman every night. That's not my style at all. No, when I said I hadn't slept with anyone for ages, it was the truth.' He brushed his hand through his hair and didn't speak for the longest time, as if struggling with what to say. 'My wife died over three years ago. I've had a few dates but nothing serious. I haven't slept with another woman since.'

Her heart ached for him. 'Oh God, Nix. I'm so sorry.'

'Thank you. It's… tricky, you know, starting again.'

'I can only imagine how hard it is,' Lyra said.

He looked down, fiddling with the zip on his hoodie. 'Part of me feels like I'm ready to have another relationship again, but then there's a part of me that feels like… I don't know if I want to fall in love again.'

She didn't know what to say. She couldn't even begin to imagine what he'd been through, what he was still going through.

'I understand that. To fall in love leaves you open to getting hurt.'

He nodded. 'That's exactly it. I feel like, I just need something fun, something casual to get me back in the saddle again. I'm not sure I'm in the right place for a serious relationship and, after the night we shared, if I got involved with you it would be something serious. It couldn't be anything else. We'd have something big and life-changing and I'm definitely not ready for that.'

Lyra stared at him with wide eyes, her breath catching in her throat. She didn't know whether to be scared or excited by the prospect of something big and life-changing. This conversation had taken a very unexpected turn.

'So yes, I agree,' Nix went on. 'We had an amazing night,

we had this crappy misunderstanding which hurt us both, we've apologised and neither of us is ready to start something serious so we draw a line under it, but that doesn't mean we can't be friends.'

She hesitated before speaking because being just friends suddenly didn't seem like enough.

But she knew this was for the best – she wasn't ready for a relationship. And they had to work with each other. After the angst of the last two days, if they pursued a relationship and it came to an end, it was quite obvious things would be awkward between them at work.

She nodded. 'I think I'd very much like to be friends with you, Nix Sanchez. This tension between us is exhausting and it turns out you are rather lovely after all.'

He smiled and stuck out his hand. 'Friends then.'

She took his hand, and shook it, ignoring the spark that flashed between them as they touched. 'Friends.'

CHAPTER TWELVE

Lyra was sitting at her desk early the next morning when Nix walked in carrying a bunch of yellow roses. He came over to her desk and offered them out to her.

She couldn't help smiling. 'What are these for?'

'Well, yellow roses symbolise friendship and I thought we should celebrate our new arrangement,' Nix said.

She took them. Some were just starting to bud; others were in full bloom. 'Thank you, they're beautiful. I brought you something too.'

He grinned. 'You did?'

'Friendship brownies. Although I can't take any credit. My sister makes them, but she makes the best brownies in the world so you're in safe hands.'

'Thank you, I can't wait to try them. I was also wondering if, as friends, you'd let me take you out for lunch today.'

She hesitated. Flowers and lunch seemed a bit more romantic than friendly, but she was keen to put the angst of the last few days well behind them. She was determined it wasn't going to be awkward any more. 'I'd like that.'

'OK then.'

Nix smiled as he walked back towards his desk and she watched him as he opened the tin of brownies, carefully unwrapping them and taking out one with pink sprinkles on the top. He took a bite and moaned with appreciation. 'These are amazing. Thank you.'

'Almost as good as your sausages with homemade chutney.'

He grinned. 'Better, I think. Please pass on my compliments to the chef.'

Lyra focussed her attention on the roses for a moment. She'd had a hard enough time that morning getting Michelle to part with her brownies once she knew who they were for. Lyra had tried to explain how it had all been a complete misunderstanding but her sister hadn't been convinced. If anyone hurt Lyra, there were no second chances. She decided to change the subject.

'What were you doing up at the field last night?'

He paused for a fraction too long. 'I was checking on George.'

'Oh, you made it look like you were up to something when you asked if I'd seen what you were doing.'

He laughed. 'I promise you it was nothing dodgy. Just Countryside Trust stuff.'

She studied him for a moment, but he was so open and honest that she knew she believed him.

'I've been thinking about the competition,' Lyra said. 'I think your idea of liaising with each other about what we intend to do on our respective days is a good one.'

He looked thoughtful for a moment. 'OK. Let's share what we have.'

She nodded. Nix grabbed his chair and pushed it over towards her desk and then went back and took a small file from his desk before coming over to join her.

'OK, hit me with your brilliance,' he said.

'Well, I have quite a few ideas, but I need to narrow them down. I thought it should be a classy event. We're showcasing the hotel and what a great place it is now. I thought we could have some old black and white photos of how the hotel used to be so people can see the transition. For the party I thought we could have some ice sculptures, maybe a champagne fountain. I was thinking we could have a ball, maybe even a masked ball, so the guests can dress up in their finest clothes. We'd have a cocktail bar and people can even design their own cocktails. I thought for the entertainment we could run a casino or a horse-racing event too, one of those with videos of old horse races on the big screen so that people can bet on it. We can give them some fake money so they can spend as much as they want but the person with the most money at the end of the night can win some prizes.'

She looked down her list of ideas. She had a few more she could use, but she couldn't go crazy with her ideas. Clover had said there was a budget, after all. Lyra had spent most of her years in the events business organising parties, weddings and events, but to the clients' specifications, and while she was good at coming up with different suggestions to help the clients get what they wanted, she'd never before been given completely free rein to organise something from scratch. It was a bit scary and she had to make sure she got it right.

Nix was nodding as he studied her list of ideas. 'This all sounds great but...' he trailed off.

'But what?'

He brushed his hand through his hair. 'When I was talking to Sylvia the other day she was telling me all about the different events that are held on the island. There've been lots of new ones since the hotel renovations, like the autumn and Halloween fair, but some traditional ones too, like the festival of lights. And in the spring this year they brought back the tradition of a pudding parade, which they used to hold on the island seventy-odd years ago. The hotel is a big part of the community and the islanders are all heavily involved in the events being held here or down in the village.'

'OK,' Lyra said, slowly. 'What did you have in mind?'

'Whatever we do needs to involve the villagers, and I think the celebrations need to be in keeping with the island and the hotel. This is a seaside resort so I'm wondering whether we should do something simple like a beach party, or a barbeque on the beach or in the gardens overlooking the sea. But I also think we need to do something in the day too, something for families and children. Maybe something fun like one of those inflatable obstacle courses or a fair or an outdoor cinema. We can get some of the shops in the village to man stands selling their goods. There are lots of things we could do to keep it casual.'

Lyra thought about it for a moment. Nix was right: involving the villagers was important.

'I like your suggestions. I love the idea of doing something fun for the families. What about some kind of treasure hunt? I used to do stuff like that when I was a kid.'

'Oooh, I like that idea. There's certainly a place for your kind of classy celebrations. And we have got two days to fill. So I think it's great we're bringing something different to the table.'

She nodded. They both had different styles but they might complement each other.

'I'd also really like it if we could work together on the other events rather than separately, pool our expertise,' Lyra said. 'I think it's a good idea if I stick to weddings and you do other events, but we can help each other.'

'I'd like that too.'

She nodded. 'OK, good.'

Nix watched her for a moment.

'I'm very much looking forward to working with you, Lyra Thomas.'

His eyes were locked on hers and she forced herself to look away. Why did she get the feeling she was going to be really bad at being just friends with Nix Sanchez?

Nix had just popped to the restaurant to get some drinks for him and Lyra when Sylvia and her huge dog collared him.

'Hello, Snowflake,' he said, crouching down to give the dog some love.

'Nix, I need a word with you,' Sylvia said, sternly.

'Is this about the party? Let me just nip back to the office and get your file,' he said, wondering what he could have done to deserve such a sharp reprimand. He'd only spoken to her about the launch party two days before.

'It's not about the party, it's about you and Lyra.'

'Oh,' Nix said, smiling to himself at Sylvia's audacity. 'Shall we take a seat?'

She ushered him into a nearby booth. Thankfully the restaurant was currently closed because this looked like it was going to get interesting. She'd tried to pin him down on his first day in the job as to what had happened between him and Lyra but he hadn't said a word. He'd soon managed to distract her with talk of her party, which she was very excited about. But it looked like he wouldn't be able to deflect her so easily today; she was clearly a woman on a mission.

Sylvia settled herself into the booth opposite him. 'Right young man, do you like Lyra?'

He smiled. 'Very much.'

'Well you have a funny way of showing it.'

'I don't know, she seemed to like the roses I bought for her this morning.'

Her eyes lit up in delight. 'You apologised?'

He wondered how much she knew about his relationship with Lyra and what had happened between them the week before.

'What would I apologise for?'

'For leaving her!' Sylvia said, in exasperation.

She'd certainly wheedled something out of Lyra. Sylvia would be good at torturing people for information, she was completely relentless.

'In actual fact, she left me,' Nix said, deciding he was going to mess with her rather than capitulate.

She frowned in confusion and Snowflake put his head on Nix's lap, probably hoping that if they were sitting at a table there must be some food around. Nix stroked his soft velvety head.

'I don't understand,' Sylvia said. 'She was upset because *you* left her.'

Nix relented. 'It was a big crappy misunderstanding, Sylvia, but we've sorted it all out now.'

Sylvia's face lit up with a big smile.

'Yes, we had a long chat about it last night. We both apologised and drew a line under it all and we've decided to be friends.'

Her face fell. 'Friends?'

'Yes, neither of us are ready for a relationship.'

Nix had lain awake for most of the night thinking about their agreement to stay just as friends. It was true that he didn't feel ready for something serious. After what happened with Emily, he wasn't sure if he could face a proper relationship yet, but it was always going to be hard moving on and starting anew with someone else. He had to take that step some time and there was something about Lyra that he just couldn't walk away from.

'What's there to be ready for?' Sylvia said, apparently not happy with this answer. 'It's not like running a marathon where you have to train for months to be ready for it. You either want to be together or you don't. And judging by the fact that Lyra said the sex was the most incredible she'd ever had, I'm pretty sure she wants a repeat of that sometime soon.'

Nix felt the smile spread across his face. 'She said that?'

'Yes, but if you tell her I told you, me and you are going

to fall out. Trust me, you don't want me as an enemy, I know people,' Sylvia said, ominously, which made him smile even more. She was so small; the threat could hardly be taken seriously.

'I'm sure you do.'

'I mean it. She threatened to put my gold cloak through the shredder if I told you and it's my favourite one.'

'I won't say anything. If it makes you feel better I thought the same about making love to Lyra. Best sex I've ever had. And that comes from someone who was happily married for over seven years. I feel guilty for saying it, but it's true, me and Lyra had an amazing connection I've never felt before.'

'So why are you accepting just being friends with her?'

A question he'd asked himself – and he'd been the one to suggest it. But after the amazing night the week before, he'd needed something more than just being work colleagues with Lyra Thomas, so being friends had seemed like a good compromise. Or a good start.

'Were you ever friends with any of your husbands before you married them?' Nix asked.

Her face softened. 'My current husband and I were friends for three years before we got married. Best thing I ever did. I know he is my forever now.'

Nix nodded. 'I think being friends will be good for us, it will allow Lyra to trust me, for us to become comfortable with each other rather than jumping straight back into bed again. We can focus on really getting to know each other when sex is out of the equation. And I have a plan. She doesn't like who she really is, and she keeps that part locked away. I want to show her that that part of her isn't something to be afraid of. If she learns to love herself, maybe she'll let someone else love her too. And then, maybe in time, we'll both be ready to take that step.'

Sylvia nodded. 'Don't take three years though. This is one wedding I'd like to be invited to.'

Nix laughed. 'I promise, if it gets that far, you'll have front-row seats.'

Nix put his menu down after giving his order to the waitress and watched Lyra as she tried to decide what she wanted. The morning had been a huge improvement on the day before. They'd laughed and chatted and worked together on the upcoming events. She had a keen mind for detail and clearly had a ton of experience in event planning. They got on well, and the more he talked with her, the more he regretted his offer of just friendship. But like he'd said to Sylvia, it was for the best – he just wasn't ready for something serious.

Finally Lyra made her decision and placed her order. The waitress smiled and walked off to the kitchen.

'For someone who makes brilliant snap decisions at work, I expected you to know what you wanted as soon as you walked in here,' Nix said, noticing that her hand was on the table just a few inches from his. He had an overwhelming urge to bridge the gap and entwine her fingers with his own.

'Ah, food is very different. I'm very good at making decisions for other people, not so good at making them for myself. And when it comes to food I don't want to miss out on something wonderful.'

'I get that.' Although he was starting to think he'd done just that by agreeing to draw a line under that perfect night. He had hurt her and she had gone scuttling back inside her shell again. He had to get to the bottom of her fears if he was going to coax her out again. 'So, Lyra, you know a little about my past, and I know a little about yours – about your parents abandoning you and why you prefer control over spontaneity. But why are you guarding your heart so fiercely?'

She let out a heavy breath, tracing the condensation on her water glass. Eventually she spoke. 'I've dated a few men in my life. Most of them ended it before it really started, probably because the men I date seem to only be interested in having a bit of fun and I'm always looking for something more than that. I'd like to say that these men didn't matter, that I wasn't hurt by getting dumped repeatedly, but I was. I always give my heart away very quickly and easily and always get hurt.'

She picked up a bread roll and started picking at it. 'I've had three semi-serious relationships, if you could call them that, which lasted a few months. The first two cheated on me; I literally walked in on Mitch with another woman in *my* bed.'

'What? That's a bit... crap.' That was putting it mildly. Nix had a lot worse he could say for a man like that but he didn't want to ruin their lunch.

'I know,' Lyra went on. 'He was almost living at my house because after he'd split with his previous girlfriend he'd moved back in with his parents, so he preferred to spend his time with me, although it was never official. One day, I came home from work early and there they were. I suppose he couldn't sleep with her in his own bed at his parents' house – his mum adored me, she would have given him hell – so he probably thought my house was the better option. But it made the situation so much worse.'

'I can imagine. That's really shitty. And the third boyfriend?' Surely it couldn't get worse.

'Greg, well everything seemed pretty damned perfect to start with. Although he was away a lot with his job, we made it work when we were together. Things were good. Turned out he wasn't away with work; he was going home to his wife.'

Nix swore under his breath.

'I certainly know how to pick them,' Lyra said. 'I was so upset over Greg, because I was the other woman and I had no idea.' She stared at the table. 'I threatened to tell his wife, I thought she should know, but Greg got really nasty and spiteful about it all. He said some really unpleasant things, like how bad I was in bed and that nobody would ever want me, let alone get married to me. That he'd only slept with me out of pity. It was really awful. He became really angry and threatening. So I never told his wife, I suppose out of fear of what he would do if I did. And I just wanted to get as far away as possible from him. But it really showed me that I didn't know him at all, because I would never have gone out with someone who was so horrible. I must be a terrible judge of character, or just gullible, because I was taken in by him completely. And it just put me off dating altogether and, well, I haven't been with anyone since. I do wonder if I'm just not loveable. I'm not someone who men see as long-term, marriage material. Even my parents didn't want to stick around.'

Nix instinctively reached across the table and took her hand. She looked up at him in surprise. 'Lyra, I'm so sorry you've dated such awful, crappy men. But please don't take those men's issues or your parents' issues on yourself. You are very very loveable.'

She focussed her attention on her bread roll again, picking the crispy bits off the soft bread.

'And I don't blame you for being reticent about starting a relationship again after what happened with Greg and your other relationships,' Nix said.

'It's just easier being on my own,' Lyra said. 'I like my own company. I don't need anyone else.'

'I don't think there's anything wrong with being single,' Nix said. 'Being single is pretty bloody brilliant actually – you can watch what you want on TV, you get the bed to yourself, you can do what you want without being answerable to anyone else. Me and Dexter can take off for a weekend, go wherever we want.'

'I think that's it,' Lyra said. 'Dating has just made me miserable. I think I'm happier on my own. I mean, I do get lonely sometimes, but I have my brothers and sisters, friends. And I can always adopt a family of beavers like you.'

He laughed. 'I get lonely too, sometimes. I miss having someone to laugh and chat with, but I think it'd take someone really special to make me want to give up that single life.'

He didn't mention that after that incredible night he'd

149

spent with Lyra he'd started to think she might be that special person.

He stared at her; their fingers still entwined. He suddenly didn't want to just be friends with her. Having a serious relationship again scared him, but this felt too big and too important to walk away from. He knew it was going to take a lot to get her to take a chance on him. She was going to have to trust him first and he was prepared to wait until she did.

'If you ever did go out with someone again, what would you be looking for in a relationship?'

'Honesty,' Lyra laughed.

'Yes, that's important.'

'Someone kind, who can make me laugh. Someone who is amazing in bed.'

He laughed again. 'Glad to see you've got your priorities straight.'

'I guess, ultimately, I'd want someone who was there for me, no matter what. Someone who's on my team. I was on my own for so long, raising my brothers and sisters, which meant every little decision was down to me, the good, the bad, the awful. It would be good to have someone to rely on, to hold my hand when things got tough.'

He nodded. 'I totally get that.'

'What about you? You said you've found moving on after your wife died really hard. How do you ever really move on from that?'

Nix thought about that for a moment. His emotions surrounding Emily's death were more complicated than simple grief, if there was anything simple about grief. 'In the spirit of honesty, things were not great between me and Emily before she died.'

'Oh, I'm sorry. But you said you had seven wonderful years with her.'

'We did, although we were together for eight.'

She squeezed his hand. She didn't ask him any questions, she just waited to see if he wanted to talk, and he liked that.

'We wanted kids; it was something we always talked about but we could never get pregnant. We told ourselves that it wasn't the right time, that things at work were stressful and we didn't really have the money, so maybe it was for the best, but secretly we were disappointed. Then one day she took a test and the dream we'd always wanted came true. We were over the moon but, erm... she lost it a few weeks later.'

'I'm so sorry.'

'And then I got sick and... things became difficult between us. I kind of figured it was the stress of it all, losing the baby and me being in hospital a lot. When I started to get better and there was light at the end of the tunnel, she told me she wanted a divorce. When we said our vows and promised to be there for each other in sickness and in health, it turned out she wasn't too keen on the sickness part.'

He hadn't told anyone this, because he hadn't ever faced up to the real reason Emily had left. It was something that he'd never wanted to admit. Even now, when Lyra was sitting here, holding his hand, and he wanted to be honest with her, he couldn't say the words. Because it wasn't exactly true that Emily had left him because he'd got sick, it had been the repercussions of that sickness that had made her run. As far as everyone else was concerned, she'd died while they were still happily married and it was easier to go along with that than tell people he hadn't been enough for his wife.

'That must have been so hard,' Lyra said.

'It was. She always said I was her missing piece, two halves of a whole, which I never really understood. I saw it more as us being two individuals who loved each other completely but it was always nice that she said those things. It made me feel safe in her love, like we were forever. So it came as a bit of a shock when she wanted to end it between us. We decided to take a break for a few months. See how we felt when life had got back to normal for me. She went on holiday with a friend to the States and, four days after I'd said goodbye to her, she died in a helicopter crash.'

'Oh my god,' Lyra said.

'Yeah. Of course I grieved for her, we'd been together for years, but there was also the added complication of knowing that our marriage was probably over. Or maybe it wasn't, maybe we'd have had a few months apart and got back together, maybe it was just a tiny blip that we'd have got over… I'll never know. So yes, it's hard moving on with someone else, not only because my wife died, and it's tough to get over that, but also because there's this feeling of… I wasn't enough for her. Will I be enough for someone else?'

Lyra stared at him in shock. 'Nix, I'm so sorry.'

'It's OK. It's been over three years and I wasn't ready to move on before, but then I met someone who changed that.'

She smiled, cautiously. 'You said you weren't ready for another relationship. We agreed to be friends.'

'I do want to be friends but I feel like everything changed when I met you. After Emily died, I sold our house, bought the land here for George and ran away from the rat race. I took jobs, but a lot of it was working from home so I had the freedom of working from anywhere. I took this job so I could be closer to George, but I kept Judy and Serendipity because I still wasn't ready to settle down and having the boat and the van gives me that freedom. I dated but my heart wasn't in it. I was happy being single, I just wasn't ready for anything more. Then I met you and for the first time I wanted more than that life. For the first time since Emily died, I could finally see myself in a relationship again. Yes, it is a big step and it's scary and I know you're not ready for that – hell, I don't know if I'm ready for it – but meeting you makes it feel like I'm on the road to recovery. Before you, I didn't know if I'd ever be ready for something serious again, but now it feels like a possibility. Meeting you gave me hope where before I had none.'

She stared at him with wide eyes and just then the food arrived, which was a much-needed distraction.

It felt good that he was taking that step and he felt relieved that he'd told Lyra the truth about Emily.

Well, almost all of it.

CHAPTER THIRTEEN

Lyra stepped outside the restaurant and Nix followed her. It was a gloriously sunny day and the little village was charming in the sunlight. Bunting was fluttering in a gentle sea breeze above them and the multicoloured houses looked so joyful. Tourists and villagers were walking around the shops and stopping to chat with each other. There was a definite community feel about the place.

But after talking to Nix over lunch her heart was in turmoil. Nix had been through hell and she hated that when he'd been sick and at his lowest, his wife hadn't been there for him. No wonder he'd lost all confidence in love.

It made her happy that she had given him hope about having a relationship again, that she had helped him to see a future he hadn't been able to look forward to before. She wanted to take that step with him and explore something wonderful but it *was* scary. She felt like with Nix she had a lot more to lose.

She mentally shook her head. She was a mess.

'I've got an idea,' Nix said as he fell in at her side. 'Why don't we talk to a few villagers about the party and try to gauge a feel for what kind of things they would like to see? Whether they would like something more formal or casual or a bit of both.'

'That's a good idea – we want them to feel a part of this celebration too.'

'Come on then, we can go and talk to a few of the shop-keepers first. Let's start with the bakery.'

'Wait, you mean now?' Lyra said, checking her watch. 'Don't you think Clover might get a bit annoyed with us taking an extended lunch break on only our third day at work?'

'Why don't I call her and ask her?' Nix said, fishing his phone out of his pocket.

She pulled a face. 'Oh, I don't know if we should.'

'Why not? Unless you think it's better to ask for forgiveness rather than permission?'

Lyra laughed. 'I'm not that kind of person, at least not any more. Go on then, ask her.'

Nix dialled a number on his phone and then moved off a little to take the call.

Lyra looked around the shops. Perhaps it wouldn't hurt to talk to a few shopkeepers now. Clover might quite like the initiative.

Nix came back to her with a grin on his face. 'She loved the idea, she's totally happy for us to spend a little time talking to some of the villagers. She recommended we start with Kendra in The Vanilla Bean – she said if we want dessert after our lunch, that's a great place to visit too.'

'I was just thinking we should start there. I've been past

there many times but not been in yet. The cakes look amazing,' she said.

They walked across the cobbled street but Lyra stopped outside the antique jewellery shop.

'Oh, I love this place, there are so many unusual pieces in here. I just love imagining the stories behind these pieces. Who wore them? Where did they wear them? Who gave the jewellery to them? Look at that ring, it's so pretty and unique,' she said, pointing to a gold ring studded with tiny white crystals which then split into two branches of emerald green leaves. 'I think most of these rings are costume jewellery rather than precious jewels, but I think their worth comes from their sentimentality and their history rather than what they're made of. Look at that pocket watch, can you imagine what kind of gentleman would have worn that?'

'Let's go in and have a look around,' Nix said.

Lyra laughed. 'We're supposed to be canvassing, not shopping. Come on, if I go in there, you'll never get me out.'

They walked down the road and pushed open the door to The Vanilla Bean. Immediately they were met with the wonderful warm smell of baking. There was a lady behind the counter with blonde hair in a loose bun, wearing a bright red apron dusted with flour or icing sugar. Her name badge said she was Kendra. She was chatting to a man who could have easily doubled for Santa with his white beard and rounded belly. He was dressed in a bright flowered shirt.

Kendra turned her attention to them. 'Hello, can I help you?'

'Oh no, it's fine, we can wait,' Lyra said, gesturing for her to finish serving the man.

'It's OK. We're just talking,' Kendra said.

The man turned round from inspecting the cake cabinet and his face lit up at seeing them.

'Nix, hello,' said the man, excitedly. 'And this must be the lovely Lyra.' He stuck out his hand and Lyra shook it in confusion. 'Nix has told me all about you.'

'He has?'

Surely Nix hadn't given a blow-by-blow of their wonderful evening the week before?

'Just that we're partners at the hotel,' Nix said, awkwardly.

Seamus blushed. 'Yes, that's what I meant. Well, we've all heard about the new events team; Clover's been talking about you for weeks.'

'Seamus is the village mayor,' Nix quickly explained. 'And he and his wife are having an anniversary party in October so I came round to his house yesterday to give him some menus.'

'Ah, I see,' Lyra said.

'I'm Kendra, nice to meet you,' the lady behind the counter said.

Lyra smiled at her. 'Good to meet you too. I haven't met too many of the islanders yet, but hopefully that will change soon.'

'And are you both living here on the island?' Seamus said.

'Yes, sort of, I have a boat in the harbour,' Nix said. 'I'm hoping eventually I can afford to buy or rent a place here, but for now the boat is my home.'

'I've always wanted to live on a boat,' Kendra said. 'Although I wonder if the realities of that would be far different from my romanticised view.'

'It's very small, but I love the possibility of adventure, of setting sail and seeing where the waves take me.'

Seamus nodded. 'Me and my wife went on a cruise last year and we loved it. But I think that wouldn't be quite the same as living on a small boat.'

Nix laughed. 'My boat is significantly smaller.'

Seamus turned his attention to Lyra. 'Lovely to finally put a face to the name, Lyra. And you're living in Sunlight, aren't you, overlooking Crystal Sands?'

'Yes I am,' Lyra said, laughing. She knew everyone knew everyone's business in such a small village but for the mayor to be aware exactly where she lived felt a bit weird.

'Oh, that cottage has so much history. I didn't know much about it until recently. But I've just picked up a few local history books and there's so much I didn't know about the house. It used to be called Smuggler's Cottage, which I thought was just a nice seaside-themed name, but it turns out there is an actual tunnel that goes directly from the cottage to Crystal Sands.'

Lyra's heart leapt with excitement. 'Is there?'

He nodded. 'It was how a lot of rum and other contraband goods were smuggled onto the island and later taken onto the mainland and sold.'

'I was in Crystal Sands the other day,' Nix said. 'I was sailing my boat round the island and you can see a cave at the back. Is that the tunnel?'

'It could be, I've never been in it myself. There's no way down to the beach and rock falls from the cliffs over the years have made it hard to get boats in. I'm not sure where the tunnel is in the cottage – it's been used as a holiday let for many, many years and the owners don't live here on the island. It's been sold several times too. And of course there's the legend of the missing treasure.'

'Yes, I'd heard something about that,' Lyra said, excitedly.

'Well, it's linked heavily with your cottage,' Seamus said.

'I never knew that,' Kendra said, in surprise. 'I'd heard the rumours about the lost treasure on the island but I didn't know it revolved around Sunlight.'

'Oh yes,' Seamus nodded emphatically as if trying to convince Kendra. 'There was a ship that ran aground on the rocks nearby and a group of fishermen went out and looted the ship, bringing most of the goods to the house through the tunnel they'd been using for years for smuggling. Apparently the ship had a lot of precious jewels on board. Legend has it they were kept in the house for a few days but, before they could sell them on, someone stole them from the house. Although some say one of the fishermen, the one that lived at the cottage, double-crossed the others and stole the jewels for himself, but the other fishermen were on his tail so apparently he hid the jewels somewhere else.'

'On the island?' Lyra said, feeling herself getting caught up with the story.

'I think so. Or maybe somewhere else. I know several people have been up to the garden with metal detectors and never found anything.'

Lyra stared at him with wide eyes. 'That's a bit exciting.'

Seamus nodded. 'It is a bit. Look, why don't you pop by

my house later and I'll give you some of the books that mention the cottage? Maybe you might be able to solve the mystery as you're now living there.'

'I would love that,' Lyra said, feeling like a kid at Christmas.

Seamus fished a business card out of his pocket. 'That's my address, pop round whenever you want this evening. I'll be in all night. Anyway, sorry, got a bit carried away there. Were you here on hotel business?'

'Well, we're organising a party for the hotel to celebrate the Sapphire Bay Hotel being one,' Nix said. 'It'll be one year since it reopened after all the renovations.'

'Yes, the hotel has changed a lot,' Kendra said. 'The place was so badly run-down that tourists had stopped coming here. Noah, Aria's husband, completely saved the place and the island too. Aria, Clover and Skye have all worked so hard as well to turn the hotel around after their dad died. It would be nice to celebrate everything they've achieved.'

'Well, that's what we wanted to talk to you about,' Lyra said. 'We wanted to gauge what kind of party the villagers wanted. Obviously all the islanders will be invited so we'd like their input. We're not sure whether to do something more formal like a ball or casino night, or something fun and casual like a beach barbeque.'

'Oooh, I think everyone likes an excuse to dress up in their best clothes,' Kendra said.

Lyra flashed Nix a triumphant smile.

'I'm not sure,' Seamus said. 'I kind of think there's more of a laid-back vibe here. I think people will enjoy having some sort of beach party. There are a lot of families here too, and I think we need to cater for everyone.'

Lyra laughed at the smug grin that Nix gave her.

'So maybe we do a bit of both,' Nix said. 'We could do the beach barbeque and fun stuff on day one, and the casino or a more formal party on day two. Then people can pick and choose which one they would prefer.'

'I think that sounds like a great idea,' Seamus said. 'I mean, talk to some more of the shopkeepers and villagers, get more of a feel than just us two, but I think that gives us the best of both worlds.'

'Right then, come on, let's ask around,' Lyra said. 'Thank you for your time.'

'Wait, before we go, can we get a couple of cupcakes?' Nix said. He looked at Lyra. 'My treat, what would you like?'

'Oh.' She approached the counter and peered through the glass at the multicoloured cakes topped with a range of Maltesers, Minstrels, Smarties and other sweet treats. 'The coconut cream please.'

'I'll have the marshmallow dream please,' Nix said.

Kendra bagged up the two cakes.

'I'll get these,' Lyra said.

'No, let me,' Nix said.

'No, you paid for lunch, let me.'

Lyra handed over her card before there was any more argument and then took the cakes, handing Nix his bag.

'Thank you,' he said.

Lyra waved goodbye to Seamus and Kendra.

'Don't forget to come over later for those books,' Seamus said.

'Oh I won't.'

They walked out onto the street and Nix nudged her as he tucked into his cake.

'What?'

'You,' he said. 'Your face lit up like a child in a sweet shop when Seamus mentioned there was a secret tunnel and a legend about missing treasure. I think you really do have an inner Indiana Jones waiting to come out.'

Lyra grinned. 'Come on, secret treasure is the stuff of everyone's dreams, right? Plus I adore a good mystery to solve. Me and my brothers and sisters love doing those escape rooms where you have to work together to solve the puzzles.'

'Well, I think we should definitely work together to solve this one.'

She smiled to herself. She liked the idea of that.

'Any idea of where the tunnel could be in your house?' Nix said.

Lyra shook her head. 'It's a small cottage, I would think I'd have noticed a hidden door or a secret hatch.'

'In the garden maybe?'

'It could be, but again, it's very small. It'd be hard to miss.'

Nix was quiet for a moment. 'Maybe we take a look at the cave at the back of Crystal Sands one day. We could take the boat out and sail round to the cove.'

'You heard Seamus; he said the beach was really hard to access because of the rocks.'

'That's not to say we couldn't swim to it from the boat.'

'That's not a bad idea.'

'I do have them occasionally,' Nix said.

'I think you're full of them.'

'Or full of it.'

Lyra laughed. 'Are you coming with me to collect the books from Seamus tonight?'

He paused for a moment before answering. 'Why don't I come round to yours tonight after you've been to collect those books? Say eight? I have some stuff to do first. We can search the garden and house together for any signs of the tunnel.'

'OK, I'll cook you dinner if you like. Bring Dexter as well.'

'Sounds great. We'll find you your treasure, Lyra Thomas.'

She smiled. She got the feeling finding the treasure was going to be like searching for a needle in a haystack. But they would have a lot of fun looking.

Back in the office, Nix finished counting up all the responses to their research. From their impromptu survey of the locals, it had become very apparent that there was a definite even split between Nix's original plans, which were for something fun that would involve the community, and Lyra's ideas, which involved something a bit classier.

'Well?' Lyra said, as she finished printing off the table plan for Jack and Heather's wedding.

'I think we need to do both,' Nix said.

'So classy on day one and fun on day two.'

Nix was silent for a moment as he looked out over the turquoise sea. 'I'm wondering if we combine it into one day, on the Saturday. Something fun for families during the day, something classier like the horse racing or casino night on the evening.'

He watched her as she thought about it. She was such a stickler for the rules but that wasn't the real Lyra. She had this inner spirit that she'd sometimes let out but for the most part kept locked away for fear of turning out like her mum.

'What are you suggesting?' Lyra said.

'I think we should work together on one great celebration.'

She frowned. 'But what about the competition?'

'I want to work with you, not against you. We can tell them that we're not doing it. We can easily both be part of the management team if that's what they want, split the increase in pay and the bonus between us. We're a team Lyra, they shouldn't be pitting us against each other like this.'

She was visibly torn. 'I would love to work with you on this. I think you have some wonderful ideas and I think we could be of real benefit to each other, pooling our experiences and different styles.'

'Why do I get the sense there's going to be a *but*?'

She smiled. '*But* they were very clear about the brief. They wanted separate days, they wanted us to compete against each other.'

'What kind of way is that to find out who is the best? If they truly want just one events manager then let them decide that based on our work for the next few months, not one silly competition.'

Nix could see she was wavering.

'Don't you think it's a bit of a risk? We don't want to piss them off after only one week,' Lyra said.

'Life is a risk sometimes.'

'But when I take a risk, when I let go, things go wrong, people get hurt, or I end up embarrassing myself. Last week I ended up flashing a really cute guy on my bike when I freewheeled down a hill.'

He laughed. 'But what was the moment like before you flashed him, the freewheeling part?'

She smiled. 'Exhilarating.'

'Sometimes we have to take a risk to create something beautiful and unexpected.'

He watched her smile. They both knew he wasn't just talking about the party.

'And this is a small risk in the grand scheme of things,' Nix said. 'We already know they're impressed by us; they've been singing our praises for weeks.'

She looked down at her notes for the party for a moment and then she nodded. 'OK, I do think we'd be better off together. I mean, working together.'

He grinned.

'Although I was looking forward to whipping your ass in this competition,' Lyra said.

A smile spread across his face. 'Why do I get the sense that you're very competitive?'

'Oh I am, something else you need to know about me.'

He stared at her. 'I think I'm going to enjoy getting to know everything about you.'

She smiled and turned her attention back to her work.

He was getting under her skin and he liked that.

Lyra left Seamus's house with a pile of local history books tucked into Daisy's basket and started cycling up the hill. It was a lovely warm summer evening, with a gentle breeze in the air, wildflowers dancing on the edges of the road. Laughter tumbled out from the gardens as people hung out with their friends and families. She could smell the scent of a barbeque somewhere, making her stomach rumble. The mince for the lasagne she was going to make later was already cooking in the oven but it would be a while before they sat down and ate. She cycled away from the main part of the village and followed the road over the hill towards her cottage. It was quieter here, the only sound that of the birds in the trees. As she reached the top of the hill, she could see the turquoise blue sea stretch all the way down the coast until it disappeared in a pinky heat haze in the distance. She would never tire of this view.

Nix was waiting for her in her garden when she got back to the cottage and she couldn't help her heart leaping at the sight of him. She told herself that was just because she was excited about finding the tunnel or the treasure, nothing to do with the man himself. Dexter was lying on the doorstep.

'Hey,' Lyra said.

Nix waved and Dexter came running over to say hello. She squatted down and stroked his soft head, and his whole body wagged with excitement. Maybe he knew they were going to go on a treasure hunt too.

'I've had such an interesting chat with Seamus about this house, well about all of the island's history actually,'

Lyra said. 'He's given me a ton of books to read. Although I'm not sure any of it will help us find the tunnel. He said the entrance was down an old well. I certainly don't have...' she trailed off as she watched Nix's eyes light up.

'A well? I might be able to help you there.'

'What do you mean?'

'When I bought my land, the deeds made it obvious that the fields used to belong to your cottage but were sold off separately many years before. The old maps I saw when I was researching the land use showed the garden of the cottage was much bigger than it is now.'

'Are you saying we need to look on your land for this tunnel?'

The haystack had suddenly got a lot bigger.

'I'm saying I have an old well on my land. Just on the other side of this fence, as it happens.'

Lyra stared at him. Surely it couldn't be that easy.

'Can we put Dexter in your house and then take a look?' Nix asked.

'Sure.'

She stood up and unlocked the front door. Dexter went straight in and sniffed around. She quickly went into the kitchen and put down a bowl of water for him and then stepped back outside, closing the front door behind her.

'Come on,' Nix said, already climbing over the wooden fence that separated her garden and his land.

She hurried to join him and he helped her over the other side. He gestured to an area that had been boarded over, with large rocks on top of the wood. She couldn't help feeling a tiny bit disappointed that it wasn't the old-fashioned type of well with a little tiled apex roof and a pulley for the bucket that she'd been expecting.

'I covered this when I first bought the land. I didn't want George or his family to fall down it, although from what I remember there wasn't much of the well left.'

He started removing the boulders from the boards and she knelt down to help him. Soon they had shifted all the rocks and Nix carefully lifted the boards to one side.

Lyra could see a deep hole that had been lined with rocks all the way down. There were metal rungs in the side of the walls that fell away into the darkness. She couldn't see the bottom of the well, but she could see that much of the walls had collapsed and crumbled and that many of the rungs were missing. If it was that bad up here at the top, what would it be like at the bottom where it would be wetter?

'I don't think these ladder rungs would be up to holding much weight any more,' Nix said as he kicked out at one, and to prove his point the rung came clean away and fell down into the darkness. They listened as it bounced off the walls but it took a good five seconds or more before they heard it clatter into the bottom.

'That's very deep,' Lyra said.

'Yeah, I wouldn't be surprised if it went all the way down to the caves on Crystal Sands, or at least did at one point.'

'Yes, I think you're right. It makes sense location-wise. Isn't it fascinating to think they really used this for smuggling things onto the island all those years ago?'

'It's exciting but I don't think we're going to find any treasure in there, even if it was safe to climb down. Do the books mention the treasure at all?' Nix asked, as he bent down to re-cover the well.

'I've not had a proper look yet. Seamus says the treasure is more of a legend than historical fact, but he thinks it's where the name Jewel Island originally came from,' Lyra said, bending down to help him. 'There's not a lot to go on other than hearsay. No one knows the name of the ship or where it came from, or what the origins of the jewels were. I'm not sure where we can go from here?'

'I've asked around about the treasure too,' Nix said. 'Legend says the fisherman who stole it left a map of where it was hidden so he could come back for it one day. Only no one knows where the map is, and no one ever saw the fisherman on the island again, so they think he might have died before he had a chance to come back and reclaim it.'

'An actual treasure map,' Lyra laughed. 'Come on, this legend is looking more and more unlikely.'

'Well we have the tunnel,' Nix said, gesturing to the great hole in the ground. 'That part is obviously true.'

'It could just be a well.'

'Why would a well need a ladder going down to the bottom?'

'In case someone fell in.'

'It's very deep if it was just a well,' Nix said.

Lyra conceded that. 'OK, it's possible there really was smuggling on the island, and it's possible that they used this tunnel. Doesn't mean the legend of the treasure is true. That sounds like a nice story to tell people about the origins of the name of Jewel Island.'

Nix shrugged. 'Maybe. Wouldn't hurt to look, would it?'

'But where do we start?'

'We need to find that map. I've been talking to some people in the village and I think I've got just the place to start looking for it.'

❧

Nix led Lyra across the field towards the old stone house that was no more than a shack now. Most of the roof had collapsed years ago but the walls were still in good condition if you ignored the ivy that had almost reclaimed the whole building. It was hidden in the trees and, the first few times he'd explored his new land, he'd missed it entirely.

'What's this?' Lyra said as they moved closer, stepping over brambles and other bushes and plants. He smiled at the hint of excitement in her voice.

'I'm not sure. I doubt anyone lived here, it's way too small for that and only consists of one main room, but maybe it was used for storage.'

There were quite a few large rocks littered around the building and Nix offered out his hand to help Lyra across them. She took it easily and he couldn't deny how nice it felt.

The door had long since gone and they stepped inside cautiously. There was so much debris and leaves in here, broken parts of the roof hanging down from the remains of the ceiling. It was in a pretty bad state but Lyra looked really interested.

'God, I wonder what they used this for, it's so old,' she said. 'You're right, I don't think anyone lived here – there's no sign of a fireplace.'

'I was wondering if it had been used as some kind of ice

house at some point,' Nix said, moving carefully to the far side of the room.

'What makes you think that?'

'Because of this,' he said, brushing some leaves aside to reveal a hatch in the floor.

Lyra's eyes lit up as she crossed the room to stand next to him. He lifted the hatch and it creaked in protest over lack of use. Stone steps led away from them into the darkness. Nix fished his torch out of his pocket, switched it on and took Lyra's hand as he walked down into the gloom.

He shone his torch around to show her the stone shelves and some of the old pots, jars, and various tools. It wasn't exactly a treasure trove of historic significance but the look of wonder on Lyra's face was priceless.

'Here, hold this a second while I sort out some light,' Nix said, handing her the torch. He started lighting the candles he'd left there the last time he'd come here and then placed them around the small chamber. 'I came down here when I first bought the land, but I didn't know what to do with it, it seemed a shame to interfere. I came down here again a few weeks ago and cleaned it all up a bit, took a load of photos and sent them to a museum to see if they were interested in coming and having a look at it and if they wanted some of the artefacts, but they haven't come back to me yet. But other than cleaning it, and leaving candles down here, I've left it exactly as it was, just in case they ever were interested.'

The light from the candles flickered across the stone walls, creating a golden glow as Lyra walked around and picked up a few of the artefacts. 'I don't know enough about history to even begin to date this stuff but, from the glazing on the pot, I would guess it might be seventeenth or eighteenth century.'

'That's when all the best exploring was happening, when great clippers were sailing the world and bringing back treasures from foreign lands,' Nix said.

She placed the pot down on the shelf and looked at him, excitement dancing in her eyes. 'You think the treasure map is in here?'

'I think it's definitely worth a look. Based on what the villagers told me, the fisherman used to store the smuggled goods in his ice house. If this is that then there could be something here. Check for loose floorboards or loose stones in the wall. If it's here, it'll be hidden away.'

Lyra started stamping on the floorboards to see if any sounded hollow or moved, and for a moment he just watched her. He loved that she was getting into this. Nix began checking some of the stones, while Lyra turned her attention to the wall opposite where Nix was looking. He smiled to himself that she was taking this seriously despite her earlier protests.

'Oh my god, this one's loose,' Lyra said, after a while.

He turned to see her wiggling a stone out of its place in the corner of the room. It was big and quite visibly heavy so he rushed over to give her a hand. It came out easily and he grabbed a candle so they could see inside. There was space behind it and the light glinted off what looked like a dusty glass bottle.

'Look,' Lyra gasped, reaching into the hole and bringing out the bottle.

It was a dark browny-green colour, but it was quite obvious there was something inside. He reached inside the hole to check if there was anything else but it seemed the bottle was the only thing in there.

Lyra eased the cork out of the bottle neck with a satisfying pop and slid her finger inside to coax out whatever was in there. 'Got it.'

He watched as she twisted and pulled at what was evidently a piece of yellowy-brown paper and he found himself holding his breath as she finally released it from the bottle.

It had a shiny red seal on the outside, keeping the paper in a neat roll. He watched as she ran her fingers over the wax seal. 'I can't believe this.'

'Anything else in the bottle?' Nix asked.

She gave the bottle a shake and shook her head.

'Well, shall we go back to the cottage and have a proper look at it?' Nix said. 'Dexter will be wondering where we are.'

She nodded keenly.

He grabbed the torch and between them they blew out all the candles, then he took her hand and led her back upstairs and out of the house.

'I can't believe this place,' Lyra said, obviously in awe, as they walked back up the hill towards the fence. He liked that she was still holding his hand. She turned back to look at the little house. 'It's like a little moment in history, preserved forever.'

'That's why I haven't touched it. I want to keep it that way. I kind of hope the museum are as interested in it as you are.'

'I'm sure they will be.'

They climbed over the fence and hurried back inside

173

her cottage, Dexter greeting them like they'd been gone for hours.

Lyra went straight to the kitchen and placed the rolled-up paper very carefully on the table.

'You ready?'

He nodded.

She took a deep breath and then gently broke the seal, spreading the piece of paper out on the table in front of them.

She gasped and Nix grinned at her reaction.

The piece of paper was most definitely a hand-drawn map.

CHAPTER FOURTEEN

Lyra stared at the map, hardly daring to believe her eyes. 'This looks so new, as if it was only written yesterday.'

She ran her fingers over the torn yellowy page. The paper itself had clearly aged but the ink looked as fresh as a daisy.

'I guess that's because the bottle was airtight,' Nix said. 'It kept it in perfect condition.'

'Yeah, maybe,' Lyra said. It almost felt too easy that people had been looking for the missing treasure for years and now they had found the map after five minutes of looking. Still, she was too intrigued to question the whys. She supposed someone had to get lucky with the search eventually.

She studied the map and Nix leaned over next to her to look too, his delicious citrusy scent washing over her.

'This looks like a bridge,' Lyra said, trying to focus on the map and not his wonderful proximity. 'There aren't too many of those on the island.'

'There's one on my land, right at the far end before Crystal Stream enters the hotel land.'

'There's one near the village too, near where the stream meets the beach,' Lyra said. 'And a small brick one at the back of the school.'

'What about the causeway from the island to the mainland, would that count as a bridge?' Nix said.

Lyra thought about it. 'I don't think so. There are no railings on the causeway, and the bridge in the map looks quite small, whereas the causeway is fairly long. Also, we have what looks like a stream on the map, not the sea.'

'OK, let's leave the causeway for now. The brick one at the back of the school doesn't look like this drawing either, this looks like a wooden bridge with a railing.'

'So that narrows it down to two,' Lyra said. 'Look here, this looks like a waterfall.'

'Well that could be Ruby Falls, which is at the back of the hotel land. If it is then it could be pointing to the bridge that's on my land.'

'There's also a small falls near the one in the village.'

'Ah, OK, what other clues have we got?' Nix said.

'There's this little drawing over here but that doesn't seem to relate to anything.'

'Looks like a close-up of the bridge. There's a cross on this part of the railings, maybe that's where the treasure is hidden.'

'OK, well, I guess we can check both bridges out,' Lyra said. 'Wait, this is a compass sign over here.'

'That's pretty standard on maps, so people can orientate themselves accordingly.'

'But they've circled the E. So does that mean the bridge is in the east of the island?'

Nix fished his phone out of his pocket and brought up the satellite image showing the island. 'Well, my bridge is definitely in the eastern side of the island. And I guess it makes sense, that the fisherman would hide the treasure on land that he owned.'

'Come on then, let's go and look,' Lyra said.

'What, now?'

'Of course now,' she said, excitedly.

'That treasure has sat there for hundreds of years, I think one more night won't hurt.'

'Tell you what, I'll put the lasagne together now and then we can leave it to cook while we have a look at your bridge. It will only take ten minutes to walk down there and the lasagne should be nearly ready by the time we come back.'

'OK, can I help you with the lasagne?'

'You can chop some mushrooms.'

They worked alongside each other for a few minutes as she mixed the mince with the bolognese sauce and he chopped the mushrooms and grated the cheese. It was nice to have some company in her home again. It had been a while since she'd had that. Her brothers and sisters had left the family home as soon as they were able and it had just been her for many years, until the house had to be sold. Nix was easy company and she could talk to him comfortably. Then there was also the added bonus of being insanely attracted to him. He had beautiful eyes and a lovely smile and she had a hard time watching his hands and not remembering the way he'd touched her when they'd been in bed together.

She spent a few minutes layering the lasagne together and sprinkling on the grated cheese before putting it in the oven and setting it on a low heat, just in case the treasure hunt took a bit longer than she anticipated.

They walked back out of the house again and Dexter followed them this time. When they got to the fence, Nix lifted Dexter over to the other side and then helped Lyra climb it. He immediately took her hand as they started walking through the field. She looked up at him with one eyebrow raised.

'It's just a bit uneven underfoot, that's all,' Nix said, innocently.

'So you need me to lean on,' Lyra said.

He grinned. 'That's exactly right.'

Dexter ran on ahead, sniffing at everything, but he didn't stray too far. The sun was making its final descent across the plum sky, but it would still be a while before it was completely dark.

They walked on in silence for a time but it was companionable and easy between them.

'Why is Jewel Island so significant to you?' Lyra asked after a few minutes. 'Enough that you tattooed the co-ordinates on your arm?'

He was quiet for a while. 'I suppose it's lots of little things really. It's always been a special place. Holidays here when I was little were always fun. Good things happened here – I met my wife here and later we got engaged here. It feels like a lucky place. I had my very first kiss here too, when I was much younger.'

'With your wife?'

'No, long before that. I was twelve. We were just hanging around with a group of other kids and we started playing spin the bottle. I was dared to kiss this girl; I didn't even catch her name. She was nervous, shaking like a leaf. I probably wasn't much better. I took my hoodie off and wrapped it round her and then I kissed her and for a few seconds it was just the most perfect kiss.'

Lyra felt herself go cold with shock because she knew what was coming next. She remembered that kiss like it was yesterday because it had been her first kiss too, but also because of what happened next. Her cheeks burned with shame at the memory of it.

'And then she sneezed over you,' Lyra said, quietly.

Nix stopped dead, turning to look at her, his eyes wide in shock. 'Lyra,' his voice was a whisper. 'You were my first kiss?'

'I think you're missing the bigger picture here, I sneezed over you.' She remembered running away, crying with embarrassment and praying she would never meet the boy ever again. And now here they were, twenty-odd years later. God, she should never have mentioned it. She could have laughed along with him when he'd got to the punchline and he'd never have known it was her. 'Why are you not more grossed out about this? You should be running away from me, not staring at me with awe.'

'I'm not disgusted by something that happened nearly twenty years ago when you were a child. And last week's kiss was so wonderful, I think you've more than made up for it.' He touched his lips as if remembering what it was like to kiss her and she felt her cheeks flame red. 'That kiss was not like anything I've ever experienced before and the sex...' He cleared his throat as if realising this wasn't an appropriate conversation for two people who had agreed to be friends the night before. 'But don't you think it's significant?' Nix said.

'That my first-ever kiss ended with me sneezing over your face? I was so traumatised by it, I didn't kiss another boy for years after that.'

'It's a bit of a coincidence that we were each other's first kiss and then years later we meet again for the first time and we end up in bed together.'

'Strictly speaking, the first time we met after... *the big sneeze...* was at the job interview six weeks ago.'

'And that's a pretty big coincidence too. We met, we spent an incredible night together, and the following week we start a new job together. Don't you think it was fate, that we were supposed to meet?' Nix said.

'You honestly think fate or destiny or cupid looked down on us twenty years ago and said, I know, I'll make her sneeze on him, then they'll live happily ever after?'

He laughed. 'I'm sure they didn't plan for that.'

'God, no one could plan for that. What did you think of me?'

'Well, mostly I was worried about you, you ran off crying.'

She felt a pang in her heart. 'You were a gentleman even back then,' she said, softly.

'I'm no gentleman. If I was, I certainly wouldn't have pinned you to the bed and made love to you within hours of meeting you.'

'I wouldn't judge yourself so harshly, I was certainly

more than willing. Christ, if we ever get together and get married and people ask how we met, you'll be telling everyone how I sneezed on you.'

'I'll tell people that us meeting was written in the stars.'

Lyra let out a huff of frustration. 'You sound like my mum.'

She turned and walked down the hill towards the bridge.

Nix caught up with her. She couldn't deny that she was a little freaked out by this revelation.

'Us sharing our first kiss is nothing more than a very weird coincidence,' Lyra said.

She sighed. In her heart she wanted to believe that it was significant that they'd shared their first kiss all those years before, that, for a few precious seconds, it had been the perfect kiss before she'd ruined it all. But her mum was a big believer of fate and destiny and she didn't want to end up like her.

They walked on in silence for a while, Dexter blundering through the long grass.

'There is another reason Jewel Island is special to me,' Nix said after a while, apparently wanting to clear the air.

'Another moment of destiny?'

He was quiet for a moment. 'I suppose... As I told you over lunch, a few years ago I was very sick. I had a rare form of leukaemia.'

She stopped to look at him, the world suddenly fading away. Nothing else seemed to matter any more, not her mum's behaviour casting a shadow over everything in Lyra's life, not their fateful first kiss, not the lost treasure. This was important. When he'd mentioned that he'd been

181

sick, she'd suspected it might be something like this but hoped it wasn't. She had been touched by cancer in her life too; she knew what it was like to go through that.

'I needed a bone marrow transplant. I'd been waiting a while and was here for the weekend when I got the call to say there was a compatible donor.'

She felt relief rush through her, which was silly. Nix was standing there in front of her obviously very healthy. But she knew what it was like to get that call.

'I've never felt so much gratitude before. It's highly likely that transplant saved my life. I knew it was a long road ahead and it might not work but I had almost given up on ever finding a match. This complete stranger had gone on the bone marrow registry and was prepared to undergo surgery, which would have been painful, simply because we were a match. It was an incredible feeling.'

She swallowed. She just wanted to hug him. 'Did you ever meet the donor?'

He shook his head. 'I was allowed to write to them and my letter would have been passed on. It's up to the donor to get in touch if they want to. They never did. I have no idea what the donor's name is. I was so grateful for what they did, I couldn't even begin to describe what it meant to me.'

Lyra reached out, placing her hand on his cheek. 'I'm grateful for them too.'

He stared at her, his eyes dark with a sudden intensity. He moved closer and she wondered if he was going to kiss her. Suddenly she really wanted him to. But he seemed to stop himself.

'And you're OK now?' Lyra said, letting her hand drop.

He nodded. 'It took many months of treatment but, yes, fighting fit. And so the tattoo is part of that. When Emily left me and died and I ran away from the rat race, I was anchorless. The one constant in my life was this place. As I said, good things happened to me here and having the island's co-ordinates tattooed on my arm always gave me a place to come back to if I got lost.'

'I like that.'

He stared at her; his eyes locked on her face. 'And now it seems you're part of that history too.'

She swallowed. She needed to create some space between them, make light of this sudden intensity. 'So what you're saying is you got a tattoo to remind you of when I sneezed on you?'

He laughed. 'That's exactly right.'

She paused, wondering if she should share her own brush with cancer. It had been a complicated, messy, upsetting affair, and not just because of the hideous disease that had attacked her sister so horribly. It was difficult to talk about, but Nix had been honest with her about his experience and she wanted him to know she understood what he'd gone through. She didn't need to tell him the other details.

'My sister, Kitty, had lymphoma.'

'Oh god, I'm sorry,' Nix said.

'It's OK, she's OK now. It was a long time ago. She needed stem cell treatment but none of us was a match.'

His eyebrows rose. 'There's six of you and none of you were a match?'

'No. Well, it turned out Kitty was my half-sister. Something we didn't know when she got sick.' Lyra waved her hand to dismiss it. 'It's complicated but, anyway, we had to wait to find a match from the register too. Although not as long as you, it seems – we were matched very quickly, just a few weeks, but every day of waiting was torture. I know what that gratitude feels like when you get the call. We're all on the register now, to give back in the same way that Kitty's donor did. I was called last year because I was a stem cell match for someone else and of course I did it.'

'You donated your stem cells to a complete stranger?'

'Yes, of course. If I can help someone who's going through what we went through, of course I'm going to do it. It's not a big deal and it's not painful like removing the bone marrow can be, just a few days of feeling a bit rubbish.'

'It's a very big deal, Lyra. A really really bloody big deal.'

She shook her head. 'No, don't look at me like I'm some hero, I'm far from that.'

Nix stared at her. 'On behalf of the person you helped, on behalf of everyone who has received a bone marrow or stell cell transplant, thank you.'

'Oh no, it's not—'

She stopped as he stepped forward, cupped her face and placed the softest of kisses on the corner of her mouth. It wasn't a proper kiss and deliberately so, but the way his lips lingered on hers made her desperate for more.

He stepped back as if it hadn't even happened and turned in the direction of the bridge. 'Come on, we need to find this treasure before it gets dark.'

He carried on walking down the hill and she was left staring after him. Dexter, realising she wasn't following, bounded up to her and bounced around her, encouraging her to come. She quickly ran after Nix, catching up with him. He didn't say anything when she fell in at his side and she wondered if he felt he'd overstepped the line after they'd agreed to just be friends.

She slipped her hand into his and he looked down at her with a smile.

'I don't want you to fall over,' Lyra said.

He grinned. 'Thank you.'

She spotted the bridge up ahead, but the search for the jewels seemed a bit insignificant now after what she'd discovered. She and Nix were linked in so many ways. They were each other's first kiss. And then to meet again years later and end up working together did feel like a ridiculous coincidence. But the fact that they had both been touched by very similar cancers and probably at similar times did feel significant somehow. Their connection ran a lot deeper than she'd originally thought.

They approached the bridge, a small unassuming little wooden thing that crossed a narrow part of the stream. It was hard to believe the bridge had hidden the lost treasure all these years.

'OK, let's have a look at the map,' Nix said.

She pulled it out of her pocket and spread it out between them.

'Do you think it's buried under the bridge?' he said.

'No, I think what you said earlier was right. See how the railings each have two distinctive bigger posts on each side, with those acorns on the top? I think the treasure is hidden inside one of those four posts. Look on this close-up part of the map, the cross is on one of these posts.'

185

'OK, you take those two posts and I'll take these two,' Nix said. 'I guess we're looking for a hole of some kind.'

Lyra moved to the far end of the bridge and started examining the posts, but there were no holes, no secret flaps or compartments. There was nothing unusual about the posts at all.

'Any luck?' She turned to see how Nix was doing. He was examining every inch intently as if a chest of big precious jewels would be hidden among the tiniest cracks.

'Nothing.'

Lyra looked at the map again for any other clues. The cross was positioned directly over the bottom of one of the acorns. She ran her fingers over the nearest acorn and then tried to twist it. To her surprise the acorn turned like a doorknob and she realised it was screwed into the post.

'The acorns come off,' she shouted triumphantly, and she glanced over to see Nix frantically unscrewing his acorns from the posts too.

The acorn she was unscrewing came off in her hand and she could see it was hollow within. She peered inside but there was nothing in there. She quickly moved over to the other acorn and started unscrewing that one too. It moved a lot more easily than the first one and, as it came away from the post, she noticed another tiny glass bottle tucked inside. She grabbed it and pulled it out. Another rolled-up piece of yellowy-brown paper was hidden inside.

'I've found another scroll,' Lyra said excitedly, as she teased out the cork and then pulled out the scroll.

Nix quickly moved over to her side. Even Dexter came over to see what all the excitement was about. It was sealed with the same red wax seal as before.

'Shall we open it?' Lyra said.

Nix nodded and she cracked open the seal and then spread the paper out.

There was no map this time, just four lines of text in beautiful cursive writing, but as she looked closer she quickly realised that the words were in a foreign language, not one she'd seen before. She turned the paper over to see if there were any other clues but there was nothing, not even a little drawing.

Where did they go from here?

Nix watched Lyra across the table as she finished off the delicious lasagne. He wanted to know more about her, in fact he wanted to know everything. He wanted her to open up to him, to trust him, but he hadn't been entirely honest with her so he didn't really deserve that trust. He needed to confess everything before they got involved again. But telling her would probably stop any relationship before it got started. How was she going to react when she found out the truth?

She pulled out the next clue and then moved to sit next to him, spreading it out on the table between them. He couldn't help but smile at her evident enthusiasm.

'Well, this is obviously a year,' Nix said, pointing to 1697 at the end of the four lines.

'I agree. And this word here, *caelis*. I feel like I've seen it before,' Lyra said.

'Me too,' Nix agreed, watching her. He wanted Lyra to

work these clues out; she was clearly enjoying herself immensely.

'Our father, who art in heaven,' she muttered. '*Pater noster, qui es in caelis.* It's Latin, this word means heaven.'

He smiled. 'I love that you know that, did you study Latin at school?'

'No, not at all. But I remember studying the Lord's Prayer in Latin once in an English lesson, not sure why. It was something to do with language origins and the differences and similarities. *Caelis* is definitely heaven in Latin. But I have no idea what the rest of it means,' she said, thoughtfully.

'Well, if that word is Latin, that means the rest of it is, and fortunately, now we know what language we're dealing with, we have good old Google Translate for the rest,' Nix said.

'Brilliant idea,' Lyra said, pulling her phone out of her pocket. She spent a few minutes carefully copying the words over to Google Translate.

She slid the phone across to him once Google had done its job.

To find what you seek
  Look to our heaven
  Save our souls
  Beneath 1697

Lyra stared at it. 'Wow, should we be asking for divine inspiration to find the treasure?'

'It does seem like the fisherman was of religious persuasion.'

She frowned. 'Don't you think all this is a bit weird? Firstly, how many fishermen would have spoken fluent Latin, let alone be able to write it so beautifully?'

Nix shrugged. 'It's entirely possible that he was educated when he was younger but then decided to pursue a life on the sea instead of some academic career.'

'I suppose. But why leave clues for himself? This is a treasure hunt, not just a treasure map. Why would he go to this trouble to hide clues everywhere? He knows where he hid the treasure.'

'I don't know. Maybe he did all this so his family could find the treasure years later. If you were going to bury thousands of pounds' worth of jewels, would you risk doing one map, saying the treasure is here? What if the map falls into wrong hands?'

'I guess…'

'And don't you think following a treasure hunt is exciting?' Nix said, keen that she didn't give up on this just yet. The real Lyra was starting to emerge, the one who loved adventure. He longed to see more of this side of her and he wanted her to appreciate this part of her too.

The frown on her face slowly faded to be replaced with a huge smile. 'It is a bit.'

'Imagine being the ones to find it after all these years.'

'I know, it feels a little unfair for us to find it when we're the newcomers to the island. Do you think we should tell Seamus? I'm sure he would love to be involved with this.'

Nix considered how to answer this. He hadn't thought

that Lyra would want to involve other people in their little quest. He was enjoying it just being the two of them. Having spoken to Seamus about this, Nix was pretty sure the mayor wouldn't really want to be involved.

'I'll ask him,' Nix said.

She nodded, seemingly happy with this. 'OK, let's have a look at this clue.'

She read the lines again. '*Look to our heaven.* Does it mean the clue is in the stars? That's a bit obscure.'

'Is there some kind of observatory on the island?' Nix asked.

'Not that I know of.'

'*Save our souls.* SOS. That's the distress signal for when a boat is in trouble. Could the next clue be at the RNLI, the lifeboat station?'

'We don't have one of those on the island either. There's one on the mainland a bit further down the coast,' Lyra said.

'I suppose the clues will stay on the island,' Nix said.

She shrugged. 'Not necessarily. But I guess we should rule out different places on the island first before we go further afield.'

Nix nodded, studying the clue again. '*Beneath 1697* – could be some kind of plaque.'

'Or a gravestone.'

He pulled a face. 'I'm really hoping this treasure hunt is not going to lead us to start desecrating a grave.'

'No, good point, I'm not into grave robbery. If the treasure is buried with the dead, it can stay buried.' She thought for a moment. 'I suppose this clue could be more literal than we're considering. *Look to the heavens, save our souls*. It could mean the church, but I'm not sure it's as old as 1697.'

'I wouldn't let the date put you off, 1697 could refer to anything. Churches were heavily involved in smuggling back in the day. It's definitely worth a look.'

She nodded and he smiled when he saw her check her watch; she was obviously desperate to have a look now.

'Maybe tomorrow,' Nix suggested.

'Yeah, I guess the church will be closed now.'

'I'm sure it will be.'

Lyra played with the clue for a few moments, feeling the paper, running her fingers over the cracks. She was clearly enjoying this. He wondered how she would feel once it was all over. Would she be disappointed if there was no treasure? Would she go scuttling back inside her shell once the adventure was finished?

'Ooh, shall we have a look at those books Seamus gave me?' she said. 'There might be more information about the treasure in there.'

He smiled at her enthusiasm. Whatever concerns he had about what might happen when this was finished, he was going to do nothing to curb her passion and excitement for it now.

CHAPTER FIFTEEN

The next day, Lyra looked down her list of things to do for Heather and Jack's wedding. It was just over two weeks away and there was a ton of stuff left to organise. Clover had written an overview of everything that was left to finalise and Lyra had broken that down into a much more detailed plan of things to do. For example, where Clover had simply written flowers, Lyra had divided that into three more bullet points to tick off: collating different options, talking to Heather and Jack to discuss the different options, and contacting the florists to book the flowers. Lots of other points on Clover's list had been broken down like this. Lyra found it easier to work when there was a detailed plan. But her plan was now so big it was starting to look daunting.

She glanced over at Nix, who was working hard on something on the computer. He must have felt her watching him because he suddenly looked up and smiled. 'Hey, you OK?'

'Yes, well… are you busy?'

'I've always got time for you.'

She smiled. 'This wedding is coming up in two weeks and I think I need some help getting it all finalised.'

Nix wheeled his chair over without getting up, so he looked like he was waddling like a penguin as he made his way across the floor. It made Lyra giggle.

'What do you need?'

She passed him the list and he let out a whistle. 'This is quite an extensive list.'

'Oh, it probably looks worse than it is. I just like to plan things out to every tiny detail, that way I know I won't miss anything.'

'That's very organised,' Nix said, and Lyra wasn't sure if he was impressed or a little bit scared.

'I know,' she cringed. 'When Dad left and Mum fell apart, I sort of had to become very organised, very quickly, and I was always so worried about forgetting something and letting someone down that it helped to make lists and plans and schedules. It's a habit I've never grown out of.'

'So you're not a throw-caution-to-the-wind kind of girl.'

'Sometimes I wish I was but my mum is like that and she's not someone I'd like to emulate. In fact, the only time I've let my guard down was with you, you pulled down all my walls.'

He pulled a face. 'And then I made you quickly rebuild them when I left.'

'It wasn't your fault. What were you supposed to think when you woke up to find I'd gone?'

'It was never supposed to end that way. If I'd seen your note, I'd have been straight down to the lake to join you.

And then I'd probably have made love to you on the banks of the lake before we came back to Judy and I cooked you breakfast.'

She swallowed. That would have been a much better way to start the morning after the best sex she'd ever had. She hadn't been able to stop thinking about how she and Nix were linked in so many ways and whether by keeping Nix at arm's length she was turning her back on something incredible. She pushed that wonderful thought away because, regardless of how lovely that would have been, it never would have lasted, it never did.

'Then what?' she said. 'You'd have kissed me goodbye. Is that how it would have ended?'

He frowned and shook his head. 'I don't think it would have ended at all.'

'Oh come on, you said yourself you weren't ready for a relationship.'

'I said I wasn't ready for something big and life-changing. But love doesn't come along when it's convenient.'

She stared at him, her breath catching in her throat. 'Love?'

She watched him blush. 'I'm not saying I'm in love with you, I think real love takes time, as you said the other day. But I'm saying we would definitely have had something special. I don't think I would have walked away from that so easily, regardless of how inconvenient it was.'

Lyra thought about what Jack had said about meeting Heather the morning his divorce had been finalised, that another relationship hadn't even been on his radar and then there she was. Was that really how it would have gone for her and Nix? Was she missing out on something amazing because she was too scared to take that step? The morning after she'd met Nix, she'd woken up excited about what was going to happen next, but now she'd closed down any possibility of that ever happening because of a silly misunderstanding.

She shook her head. 'Being in a relationship was not part of my plan.' Protecting her heart from ever being hurt again was the main plan.

'Plans have their place, but there's also something wonderful about spontaneity. Sometimes the things that can happen by chance are far better than anything you could ever plan for.'

'What are you saying? That I should come round to yours tonight and recreate that wonderful evening?'

Nix's eyes darkened with need but he shook his head, clearing his throat. 'I'd like nothing more but I think, if we do give this a go, we need to go slowly. Go out on dates. Spend some time getting to know each other properly. Learn to trust each other. Making love can come later.'

She'd sworn that she wouldn't get involved with another man without getting to know him first, but how could she really get to know Nix unless she gave him that chance?

She shook her head. 'I'm not ready for another relationship. I don't want to get hurt again. You said if something were to happen between us it would be big and life-changing. That sounds like it would be even harder to get over when it ends.'

'*If* it ends. I can't make any promises about forever, but don't you think something as important as what we shared is worth taking that risk for? I have loved getting to know you better over the last few days; we have a connection that's a lot deeper than just great sex. Isn't that worth exploring?'

She wavered, because there was still a huge part of her that wanted that.

'Just think about it,' Nix said. 'Don't give up on us just yet.'

She nodded. 'I'll think about it.'

'Good.'

Her hand was on her knee and he reached out and ran one finger gently over the back of it. 'I'm really enjoying searching for the treasure with you,' he said, softly.

She turned her palm over, allowing her fingers to loosely entwine with his for a moment. She didn't know why she was letting this small act of intimacy happen but holding back from anything else. 'I am too.'

He held her hand for a few moments longer, his eyes locked with hers before letting her go.

He gestured to the list. 'What is it you want me to do?'

She turned her attention back to the list but now she could barely concentrate. It seemed she had a lot to think about.

There was a knock on the office door later that morning and Nix immediately knew who it would be. He glanced across at Lyra and, judging from the smirk on her face, she did too.

Nix got up to open the door and, sure enough, Sylvia

was standing on the other side, Snowflake next to her wagging his tail.

'Hello Sylvia.'

He had to smile as she swept dramatically into the office, her purple cloak flowing behind her.

'Beautiful morning, isn't it?' Sylvia said, admiring the spectacular view.

Nix came to join her at the window. The sea was a wonderful bottle green today and, beneath them on the beach, children were playing on the golden sands. It was funny to think that almost twenty years ago he had been on that exact beach kissing Lyra for the first time. He had felt a connection then, something he'd been too young to understand. And here they were now, and their connection was stronger than ever. But as much as he loved the idea of fate bringing them back together, Lyra wanted to run from that. Following her heart was something her mum had done, abandoning her children because of it. He wanted to show Lyra that letting go wasn't a bad thing, but he knew it would take time.

'It's lovely,' Nix said.

Sylvia turned back to face the office. 'And how are two of my favourite event planners getting on?'

He watched Lyra smile. 'Good, the job is fun, lots to do. We're actually organising a birthday party for the hotel, at the end of August – it's been one year since it's grand reopening. We're trying to find the right balance between something casual for the families and something a bit classier.'

'Oooh, I love a party, especially if I have a handsome

man to sweep me around the dance floor. Do you have a date for the party, Lyra?'

'Well, I presume I'll be going with Nix,' Lyra said, calmly, and his heart leapt. 'It makes sense that we go together, in a professional capacity, so we can sort out any problems that crop up.'

Sylvia let out a little grunt of disappointment and Nix felt the same way.

'But at the end of the night, when everything is done, you two could have a little dance together.'

'I think at the end of the night, when every box has been ticked, I'll be ready for bed, not a dance,' Lyra said.

'That's the spirit,' Sylvia said, mischievously.

Lyra laughed. 'To sleep.'

Nix sighed. He didn't mind the good-natured interfering, but it was probably more likely to drive Lyra further away than bring her closer.

'Was there something we can help you with?' he said. 'Were you here about the launch party?'

'Oh of course, I came to show you a cake I wanted you to organise for me. I saw it on the internet,' Sylvia said, taking a phone from her cloak pocket, swiping the screen a few times and showing him a picture of a fabulous open-book-style cake with stars spilling out from the pages. 'Only I'd want hearts, not stars,' she said. 'Or something to symbolise the magic of true love. Hearts are more in keeping for a romance author than stars.'

'Aren't your books more about sex than love?' Lyra teased.

Sylvia fixed her with a look. 'Don't you think the two

are linked? Incredible, once-in-a-lifetime sex can only really happen if two people love each other.'

Lyra cleared her throat. 'I'm not sure I believe that. I think you can have amazing sex with someone without love being involved. I think real love takes time, it's not something that happens overnight.'

'Have you ever been in love?' Sylvia said.

'Well, I guess so.'

'That's a no – you would know if you had. You might have liked someone, cared about them, had nice sex with them, but real love, that real heartrending, hit-by-a-bus, can't-breathe kind of love, you would know if you'd ever experienced that. Love at first sight is a rare and beautiful thing and it's so unexpected that sometimes we don't even see it when it happens. Or want to believe it.'

Lyra stared at her and Nix had no idea what to say to make this awkward situation better.

'And sometimes, you're right, real love does take time,' Sylvia went on. 'But it can only build from a deep connection and sometimes sex and friendship are a part of that.'

Lyra opened her mouth to say something but Sylvia ploughed on.

'If I was single and I was given a chance at real love, I'd snatch hold of it with both hands because it doesn't come along very often.'

Lyra nodded, too stunned to speak.

Nix cleared his throat. 'I can definitely sort out that cake for you; there's a bakery here on the island and she makes wonderful cakes. If you email me that picture I can show it to Kendra to see if it's something she could make and then I'll let you know the cost.'

'The cost is irrelevant,' Sylvia said.

'And may I recommend having stars *and* hearts coming out of the book,' Nix said. 'As that would be a more accurate way of symbolising true love.'

Sylvia nodded and smiled. 'Yes, I like that. Well, I'll leave you to it.'

And with that she and her dog swept out of the office.

~

Lyra hurried down to the church with Nix. They were on their lunch break so they didn't have long.

Her conversation with Sylvia earlier was still dancing around her head. She kept pushing it away but it kept forcing its way back in.

They were approaching the church so she put those thoughts aside again to focus on the treasure hunt. The church was an impressive old stone structure with a bell tower and the typical stained-glass windows, but the building itself looked like it had undergone a lot of modernisation and preservation over the years. It appeared in astonishingly good condition for something that was hundreds of years old.

They pushed the door open with a creak and stepped inside the cool church. It was almost completely empty apart from a vicar up the far end, dressed in jeans, black shirt and traditional white collar.

'Do you think he'll mind us being in here?' Lyra whispered, feeling the need to be quiet.

'I'm sure he won't,' Nix said. 'Come on, let's have a look around.'

They moved off through the wooden pews, which again looked fairly modern, Lyra checking the floor, the pews, the ceiling. But it wasn't long before the vicar came over to them.

'Ah Nix, lovely to see you again,' he said, holding out his hand for Nix to shake. 'And is this the lovely lady you were telling me about?'

Lyra frowned in confusion.

'Lyra, this is Father Lovegrove. Father, this is my friend Lyra. I bumped into Father Lovegrove yesterday and told him about the treasure hunt. He was the one who told me how heavily the church would be involved in the smuggling. Back in the day of course, nothing untoward happens here today.'

Father Lovegrove laughed. 'Of course not. Lyra, it's lovely to meet you.'

Lyra shook his hand. 'You too, Father. I'm not sure if you can help us. We believe the treasure maps and clues were left around the island hundreds of years ago. The latest clue seems to point us to the church, but this place isn't *that* old, is it?'

'It actually is around two hundred and seventy years old. Maybe a little older. But there was another church here before that and it was destroyed in a fire. Actually, most of the east side of the church was saved and they managed to use three of the original stained-glass windows in the new church. Those three over there were from the original church. You should go and have a look at them. They're very unique actually, for their era, in that they don't depict bible stories. As to whether your treasure is hidden here, I don't know. I've certainly never found anything.'

Lyra nodded. 'We'll take a look, thank you.'

They wandered over to the stained-glass windows.

'So these windows might have been here in 1697, even if the rest of the church wasn't,' Nix said.

'Let's hope the next clue wasn't buried in the old church and then lost in the fire, because that would bring our treasure hunt to a crashing end,' Lyra said. 'These windows are beautiful.'

One window simply showed a beach scene, with green cliffs, golden-yellow sand and bright blue sea and sky. The middle one was set at night, with white stars and the moon taking up the majority of the scene, presiding over a small stone building surrounded by grass. Her eyes moved over to the third one before snapping back to the middle one.

'Look to our heaven.'

Nix looked at her.

'What if you were right about the stars? What if it means the stars here in this stained-glass window?'

'Oh, it could be,' Nix said.

Lyra gasped as her eyes fell on something above the window. 'Look.'

There was a small stone plaque above the window that basically backed up everything that Father Lovegrove had said, that these were the original windows from the old church and dated from 1697.

'Oh wow, 1697,' Nix said.

'So, is the window our next clue?' She studied it for any indication of where they should go next. 'Wait, this is a picture of the school. I didn't recognise it at first because there are no other buildings in the picture and there are lots of houses and shops that surround the school now, but that is definitely the school.'

'OK, so we go there next?' Nix said, doubtfully.

'No, there has to be something else we're missing. Where do we look in the school? In the walls, in the grounds, inside somewhere? There has to be a clue here that tells us where specifically we should look.'

They stood in silence for a moment as they studied the window. It did seem likely that the school was the next place to search. But there was nothing here that stood out as to whereabouts in the school they should look. Lyra scanned the wall and floor underneath the window, to see if there could be anywhere that might hide another clue, but there was nothing and she didn't fancy pulling up floorboards or pulling out bricks in a church to find one. She didn't think Father Lovegrove would be too happy about that.

'Hang on, isn't this picture familiar to you?' Nix said.

Lyra looked back at it. 'Oh my god, this is the picture on the mosaic hanging outside the school, near the gate. Do you think that's where the next clue is?'

'It's worth a shot – we don't have anything else to go on right now. We can always come back here for another look if the mosaic at the school proves fruitless.'

She nodded. 'Come on, we haven't got a lot of time.'

They waved goodbye to Father Lovegrove and made their way up the road towards the school.

She was enjoying doing this with Nix, partly because she loved the thrill of finding the clues, but partly because she got to spend time with Nix and she loved that. She wanted to know everything there was to know about him.

'How is it you came to work in events management?' Lyra asked. 'From what I've seen you're really good at it, but with your love of nature and beavers I kind of thought you'd be working in a more... natural capacity.'

'I used to. I worked at a safari park. It was my first job at sixteen and I spent many years doing different jobs there, but my main job, when I was older, was arranging all the fundraising events for the park. It was something I just kind of fell into while I worked there but something I really enjoyed. We'd organise small theatre groups to entertain the children and camping nights, to sleep with the animals. It was my idea to start doing weddings and parties at the safari park, which helped to bring in a lot of money, and I was in charge of organising them too. But the park wasn't doing well in terms of profits and they started making job cuts. Sadly they made me redundant and then the park closed altogether the year after.'

'Oh, that's sad.'

'Yeah, I loved that job.'

'What did you do after that?'

'Oh, I got a job in charge of weddings at a specialised wedding venue for a short while, but then I got sick and, with all the hospital appointments, I couldn't give it the time it needed. They weren't particularly supportive either, as I'd only been working there a few months, so I quit. When I was better I took a number of virtual PA jobs – I was still organising things but for one person rather than a whole event – and I organised some fundraising events for the Countryside Trust too. It was unpaid of course, but I knew it was something I wanted to get back into.'

'You don't want to work with animals again one day?'

'I'll still do volunteer work for the trust and I have George and his family, so I have the best of both worlds right now.'

They had reached the school by now and they quickly made their way to the gate. Sure enough, the beautiful depiction of the school they'd seen in the church was replicated in a mosaic, embedded in the school walls. Carved in a thick wooden plaque underneath the mosaic was a name, perhaps belonging to one of the headteachers from the past, Mr Simon O'Smythe.

Lyra looked around for anything obvious to indicate where the next clue could be. She looked at the plaque and her heart leapt. 'Simon O'Smythe. SOS. It must be here.'

Nix nodded excitedly as he started running his hands over one side of the plaque and she did the same over the other. As she did, the frame of the plaque shifted in her hand. She looked around, hoping no one would see her vandalising a precious plaque. Promising herself she would repair it if she caused too much damage, she gave the side of the frame a gentle tug. It came away easily in her hand. The plaque was designed like a box and there was a space at the back where there was a flat bottle placed inside.

'Nix, look,' Lyra said, holding up the bottle triumphantly.

'Oh well done,' Nix said.

She tried to push the side of the frame back on and to her relief it clicked into place perfectly so no one would be any the wiser.

She passed the bottle to Nix so he could open it and watched eagerly as he carefully eased the cork free and tipped out the tiny scroll inside. She gestured for him to open it and she waited with anticipation as he cracked open the red wax seal. He moved to stand next to her and opened out the scroll.

There was a simple drawing of some ruins of the small fort that stood on top of one of the nearby hills. Underneath there was a clue.

Light and dark
   Ash and smoke
   Hot and cold
   Wood and coke

'Not in Latin this time,' Lyra said. 'Maybe the fisherman couldn't be bothered with a different language by the time he got to this clue.'

'Maybe he was running out of time and went for simplicity.'

'If he was going for simplicity, a treasure map with an X marking where the treasure was would have saved a lot of time.'

'Come on, admit you're having fun.'

She smiled. 'I'm having a lot of fun.'

His gaze locked with hers. 'I am too.'

She couldn't drag her eyes away.

He cleared his throat, focussing again on the paper in his hand. 'OK, what do we think of this latest clue?'

She read it again, looking at the drawing of the little fort too. 'Is it the fireplace? I've not been up there so I don't know whether it has one but this looks like it could be a chimney, doesn't it? If people lived there, I would think it would have some kind of kitchen. And the clues make sense if it is.'

'I think you're right.' Nix looked at his watch. 'But I don't think we'll have time to go up to the ruins now.'

She felt her stomach drop with disappointment. Each time they solved a clue took them one step closer to solving this quest and she couldn't wait to get to the end.

'Shall we go after work?' Nix suggested.

'Sure, I'm having dinner with my sister tonight but we can go before I go to hers.'

'Sounds good.'

She couldn't help smiling at the thought they were getting closer to the treasure. And at the thought of spending more time with him.

CHAPTER SIXTEEN

Lyra looked at her plans for the hotel's birthday party. She and Nix had spent some more time discussing their ideas but it still felt like there were quite a few loose ends. Jack and Heather's wedding had taken priority over everything else, which was how it should be, but that had been almost finalised now. The presentation for the birthday party was first thing on Monday morning, and though Lyra had an idea of what the party would look like, she wanted to nail down the actual presentation side of things too, especially as they had departed from the brief quite significantly. She felt there was a lot riding on this presentation, not least making Clover feel she had made the right choice in hiring them.

'Would you like to meet up this weekend?' Lyra said, staring at the ideas and feeling like they just weren't enough. She glanced up at Nix to see a big smile on his face.

'Like a date?'

She smiled. 'I meant to go through the party ideas and the presentation for Monday.'

'I was just thinking the same thing. It feels like we just have vague ideas right now, we need to drill it down and decide what we're going to present.'

'And come up with a budget too,' Lyra said.

He nodded. 'I don't have any plans for this weekend, I'd deliberately kept it free so we can meet up whenever.'

'Kept it free for what?'

He paused. 'For the presentation. I didn't think we'd get the plans finalised at work. Plus there's the treasure hunt, that's definitely worth keeping my options open for.'

'Yes, we could find ourselves multi-millionaires by the end of the weekend.'

A flash of worry crossed his face. 'If you're holding out for that, you're probably going to be disappointed.'

'What do you mean?'

'I think the chances of this treasure still being there are very small and, even if it is, it probably isn't going to be worth as much as we think.'

'Don't you think it's nice to dream though?' Lyra said. 'It's like playing the lottery – isn't it fun to imagine all the things you'd spend your money on? I mean, personally, if it was a massive win, I'd give most of it away to charity, no one needs that kind of money. But there'd definitely be a few places around the world I'd like to visit, I'd buy my own house so I wouldn't have to rent, and there's always room for more books.'

He smiled. 'I think having dreams is important, but it's probably better to enjoy the quest than pinning all your hopes on the treasure being something spectacular.'

'I'm enjoying the quest immensely but it doesn't hurt to imagine rubies as big as my head.'

He was silent for a moment and then nodded. 'And gold doubloons and emeralds and sapphires as big as your hand?'

'Now you're getting it.'

He smiled and turned his attention back to his work, but she couldn't help noticing that Nix was clearly worried.

Lyra walked into her cottage and quickly got changed. It was Friday night and she was meeting Nix soon to find the next clue. For some reason she felt like she was going on a date, which she had to keep reminding herself it most definitely wasn't.

Although it wouldn't hurt to put in a little effort.

She undid her hair from the bun and let it fall around her shoulders, fluffing out the poor suppressed waves. She put on a warm gold sparkly eyeshadow and a quick lick of her favourite lipstick. She'd thrown on one of her favourite green summer dresses and gold sandals. Hopefully this dress wouldn't get ruined like the last one had the week before. And she couldn't be too upset about it as it had led to her meeting Nix, and she could never regret that.

It was another warm sunny evening as she left the house. The sea was mirror calm, reflecting the cliffs and hills perfectly.

She hurried down the road and through the village, knowing that Nix and Dexter would be waiting for her at the other side, where a little footpath would take them up to the ruins.

She spotted Nix at the gate to the footpath, crouching down and stroking Dexter and seemingly having a proper conversation with him, or at least a monologue. The dog was wagging his tail as if listening intently.

Nix caught her eye as she approached and his face lit up in a big smile, making her feel warm inside.

He stood up and his eyes appraised her. 'You look lovely.'

'Thank you.'

He looked relaxed and happy, wearing shorts and a t-shirt. 'You look...' She searched for a word to describe him that wouldn't be too forward but only one came to mind. 'Huggable.' And he did; he looked so warm, friendly and comfortable in his own skin that she wanted to step up and hug him and let some of his laid-back, easy-going attitude seep into her.

'Oh well, I'll definitely take that,' Nix said, and, before she could stop him, he'd stepped up to her and wrapped his arms around her, enveloping her in the most wonderful bear hug. She slid her arms around him, leaning her head against his chest and closing her eyes for a second. It felt so good. There was something so solid, so reassuring about him. He felt safe. And coupled with his heavenly scent and the warmth of his body against hers, it was an intoxicating mix. It had been so long since she had been held like this. Even with the men she'd had semi-serious relationships with in the past, she'd never shared this kind of affection with any of them. She found herself snuggling closer against him, breathing him in, and he slid his hand up to the back of her neck, cupping her head. While he was holding her, every fear and doubt about getting involved with him fell away. This felt so right.

She suddenly realised how long they'd been standing like that and her cheeks flamed with embarrassment. He'd probably thought he was going in for a quick hello hug, he wouldn't have been expecting her to cling to him like a limpet.

She quickly stepped back. 'Sorry.'

'Don't apologise, I wasn't in any hurry for that to end. Hugs are medicinal and that certainly made me feel a lot better.'

She smiled. 'Come on, let's go and find the next clue.'

They walked through the gate onto the little footpath that would take them up to the ruins and immediately Nix took her hand again as if it was the most normal thing in the world. Maybe it was, as she couldn't even find it in her to object this time. Although her objections were never that serious before.

Dexter ran on ahead as if he knew the way and had been along this path before.

'I haven't been up this part of the island before, I generally stick to the roads when I take Daisy out exploring. Have you been up here?'

'Once or twice. The views at the top are quite incredible. You can see all the beaches on the island and the open sea stretching out for miles. It's a good place to come and think.'

'Well, that sounds like an excellent spot to solve a treasure hunt.'

They walked up the hill and soon the fort came into

view, quickly followed by the spectacular view Nix had spoken about.

The fort was a small place, no more than four walls now and large windows that held no glass. Most of the top had gone completely. There was, however, a chimney, which was a good sign when looking for a fireplace.

Outside there was a display board that had some information about the fort, with an artist's impression of what it would have looked like at its best. It had supposedly had three floors many years before and two chimneys, one each side, whereas it only had one now.

They walked through the large stone archway and it was clear that the inside had at one point been separated into several rooms, though the dividing walls had certainly seen better days, and some were missing completely. There was a stone staircase that led up to a second storey but there was hardly any floor at all now, and the bright blue sky could clearly be seen above them.

'So I guess we split up and try and find a fireplace in these downstairs rooms,' Nix said.

Lyra nodded. Nix moved off to the rooms on the left and she went off to the first room on the right. There was nothing in the first room so she progressed to the next room. Her heart leapt when she saw a fireplace but it quickly sank again when she saw it had been completely bricked up. She hurried over to it to see if any of the bricks were loose but they were all very secure. The mantel didn't move and there were no loose stones in the floor.

Nix joined her in the room. 'Ah, you found one.'

'Yeah, but it's all bricked up, and I can't see anywhere

else it might be hidden. What if it was bricked up after the fisherman hid the clue inside?'

Nix pulled a face. 'That's a possibility.'

Lyra ran her hand over the bricks again, disappointment flooding through her. This couldn't be the end.

'Was there anything in the rooms you looked at?'

He shook his head. 'Not even a chimney breast or a mantelpiece.'

She sighed and then frowned. 'Hang on, the picture outside showed the fort had two chimneys in its heyday.'

'That's right,' Nix said. 'Oh, that's weird.'

She pulled out the clue sheet they'd found at the school. The remaining chimney was on the left, but Nix had checked the rooms on the left and there was no fireplace. The drawing even had a tiny trail of smoke coming out the top of the left chimney, which she hadn't noticed before.

'Look at this – the smoke from the chimney. Is that a hint to say which fireplace the clue is in?'

'Oh it might be,' Nix said.

They looked at each other.

'It's upstairs!' they both said together.

They quickly ran up the stone staircase. There was only part of the floor left up here but they kept well away from the broken section. To Lyra's delight there was a large open fireplace to the left and thankfully this one wasn't bricked up. This part of the room seemed very solid. They moved over to it and began checking the stones at the back. There were signs of age but none of them was loose. The stones on the floor weren't moving either. Lyra moved back out of the fireplace and started examining the mantelpiece but there didn't seem to be anything there either.

She went back inside the fireplace to help Nix check at the back again. She looked up and the chimney stretched up above her, the blue sky peering through at the top.

'Maybe it's up there.'

Nix looked up. 'It could be, but I can't imagine it would be too high. Unless the fisherman walked in here with a really tall ladder.'

'Or he had a little chimney sweep with him,' Lyra said.

Nix laughed as he tried to climb up the chimney, not very successfully. 'We need a torch.'

Lyra rummaged in her bag to get her phone so she could shine the torch up into the darkness but the phone wasn't there. 'Ah crap, I've left my phone at home.'

'Here, I have mine,' Nix said as he came back down to the floor after climbing up two or three stones. He pulled his out of his pocket and passed it to Lyra.

She shone it up the chimney and, after a few moments of looking, the light glinted off something glassy about two or three metres up the shaft. Her heart leapt. She peered through the gloom, focussing on where she'd seen the glint, and to her surprise realised it was a glass bottle, perched on a stone ledge.

'Look, is that it?' she said, excitedly.

'It could be, but how the hell did he get it up there? It doesn't look easy to climb.'

'OK, we can do this,' Lyra said. 'I used to be top of my class in gymnastics.'

'What, twenty years ago?'

'Yeah probably, maybe more, but I did yoga until fairly recently, so I'm quite flexible. Give us a piggyback.'

Nix squatted down without question, and she jumped

on his back. He stood up and she reached over his head but she was still a good metre away from the bottle. She kicked off her sandals and, getting a good hand-hold on a large stone, and with a lot of wiggling around, she managed to climb onto his shoulders as he braced himself against the back wall of the fireplace.

'No peeking,' Lyra said, knowing that if he looked up, he would get a rather unflattering view right up her dress.

'I wouldn't dream of it,' Nix said.

She reached out for the bottle and could just about touch it with one finger but she couldn't pick it up. She leaned up further on tiptoes, feeling Nix do the same beneath her, and she finally managed to grab it.

'Got it,' Lyra said.

She tucked it inside her dress and walked her hands down the wall until she was in a position, with a lot of help from Nix, to climb down from him onto the floor. They came out of the fireplace into the daylight and she pulled the bottle from the top of her dress. Sure enough, she could see another scroll rolled up inside.

'I can't believe we've found another one.' She gave the bottle a little shake. 'This is so exciting.' She glanced at her watch and her heart dropped with disappointment. 'I hate to put a stop to this fun, but I promised I'd go round to my sister's for dinner and it's always an early thing for her. Can we pick this up later?'

'Sure. Come down to my boat after you've had dinner and we can have a look at the next clue then. Or, if you end up staying late, come round tomorrow morning.'

'I'll come tonight. It shouldn't be too late,' Lyra said. She was desperate to see the next clue and she knew she couldn't wait until the following day.

'I'll walk you to your sister's.'

'Probably not a great idea. She still hasn't forgiven you for how things ended between us last week.'

'Oh no, really?'

'I did explain, but she's very protective. I'll sort it out, don't worry, she won't hate you forever.'

'Well, I can at least walk you part of the way.'

She smiled. 'I'd like that.'

He offered out his hand and she took it.

'So things are better?' Lucas asked.

Nix put the phone on loudspeaker for a moment as he flipped a burger in the pan. 'Loads better. She's relaxed, happy. Most of the tension has gone.'

'Most of the tension?'

Nix glanced down at Dexter sitting hopefully next to the tiny oven. 'Well, now we have all this unresolved sexual chemistry bubbling between us. What we shared was not like anything I've ever experienced before. I'm pretty keen to revisit it again. But Lyra has been hurt in the past and she's scared of getting hurt again. She doesn't want to risk her heart by getting involved with me.'

'What are you going to do?'

'I have to respect what she wants. I've made it clear I'd be open to trying again but I'm not going to push her on it. She has to choose to have a relationship with me, not be badgered into it.'

'So just be your normal charming self,' Lucas said.

Nix laughed. 'I'm not sure how well that will work out for me, but I'm hoping that she just needs some time. She was prepared to throw caution to the wind before, hopefully she'll give me a second chance.'

And he knew, in his heart, it was only fair to tell Lyra the whole truth about his break-up with Emily, before it ever got that far. But he couldn't even ask his brother for advice on how to tackle that conversation as Lucas had no clue, nobody did.

'Is she really worth all this?' Lucas said. 'Or are you just seeing a connection because she's the first person you've slept with since Emily? There are plenty of other fish in the sea that probably wouldn't be this much hassle.'

'I think she is worth it. There's something really special about her. I mean, I guess we could get together again and find that our chemistry and connection was only worth one night, but I think she's definitely worth the wait to see.'

'Maybe I need to come down and meet her.'

'Maybe you need to mind your own business,' Nix said.

'OK, OK, I can take a hint.'

'No hint, just a great big flashing sign saying, "Butt out",' Nix laughed. 'I'm quite happy to chat to you over the phone about all this but that's as far as your involvement goes.'

'OK, but just… don't rush into anything. Most people in your situation would date several women before they settle down again. Don't go popping the question just yet.'

Nix laughed. 'No fear of that.'

'Hmm, I know my little brother. You're a bit of an all-or-nothing kind of guy.'

'I've told her that if we do start dating we're going to take things slow, we have to get to know each other first. Rushing into things is your style, not mine. How was your date with Helene?'

'Fine.'

'Are you seeing her again?'

'Absolutely not.'

Nix sighed. 'Why not?'

'She wanted to cuddle after sex.'

Nix remembered holding Lyra in bed after they'd made love; it had been wonderful. Was he weird for enjoying that? Or was Lucas right and he'd gone without intimacy and companionship for so long that he was seeing a connection there that really wasn't? He didn't know but he owed it to himself to find out.

'So come on, out with it,' Michelle said, as she ushered Lyra into the kitchen. It smelt of chocolate brownies and cookies again and Lyra's stomach rumbled appreciatively. 'All I know is that you took some of my brownies yesterday morning for a man who left you alone in a field after what you described as the best sex of your life.'

'Sex!' shouted Zach from his high chair as Ben tried to feed him and Lyra smiled. He couldn't say her name but he could say the word *Sex* perfectly.

Michelle didn't bat an eye; maybe Zach had said far worse before.

'And now you turn up here with a goofy smile on your

face as if all is right with the world,' she went on, hands on her hips.

It was a strange thing to be told off by her little sister. Growing up, it had always been the other way round. It was clear it was going to take a lot for Michelle to forgive Nix for what had happened.

'I told you, it was a misunderstanding. I went for a swim in the lake, he woke up and thought I'd gone and then left himself.'

'And you believe him?'

'I do. He was absolutely gutted when he realised what had happened and he felt awful when I told him how that had made me feel. He was so apologetic. Yesterday, he brought me some flowers and took me for lunch and he's been really lovely, which is kind of what I fell for when we first met.'

'I'd say he wants a round two,' Michelle muttered as she swept some multicoloured sprinkles off the counter top into her hand and then brushed them into the bin.

'That's what I thought,' Lyra said. 'But he said if we started dating, we'd take things slow, get to know each other, do things properly.'

'And you're tempted?' her sister said, in exasperation.

Lyra removed a toy car from the chair and sat down. 'I'd be lying if I said I wasn't. We have a connection, there's no doubt about that. There's something about him I've never felt before. He makes me laugh, he's kind, generous, funny. But I am scared. I've been down this road before and I always get hurt.'

'I think...' Ben said, carefully '... that if he's that special then he's definitely worth a second chance.'

'Ben!' Michelle said. 'This guy sounds like a complete ass. He charmed her into bed once and now thinks he can trick her into bed again.'

'I'm not naïve,' Lyra protested.

'You slept with a married man for months with no idea he had a wife.'

Lyra cringed. 'Thanks for that reminder of my complete stupidity.'

'I'm not saying you're stupid,' Michelle said.

'And to be fair, Michelle, we met Greg several times over that period and we had no idea either,' Ben pointed out. 'So does that make us naïve too?'

'I think this Nix is taking her for a ride,' Michelle said, completely ignoring the fact her husband was right. They'd both loved Greg when Lyra had introduced them. He'd played them all for a fool.

'I think we should trust Lyra's judgement and, if she thinks it was a genuine misunderstanding, then we should trust that too,' Ben said.

Zach was watching them with wide eyes, a fistful of cauliflower paused halfway to his mouth. If it hadn't been her own life they were discussing, Lyra might have felt like grabbing a box of popcorn and watching this unfold herself. Ben and Michelle never argued; Ben worshipped the ground Michelle walked on. But if Ben believed Michelle to be wrong, he was never afraid to say it.

'I just don't want her to get hurt,' Michelle said, as if Lyra wasn't even in the room any more.

'Lyra has definitely kissed her fair share of frogs, that's for sure, but doesn't mean the next man won't be a prince,' Ben said.

Lyra sighed and helped herself to one of the brownies sitting on a plate in the middle of the table.

'Love is a risk but she can't keep herself locked away for the rest of her life,' her brother-in-law went on. 'If it ends then of course it will hurt, but Lyra will get over it. She's strong and brilliant, just like her sister.'

Michelle immediately softened at the compliment. 'I want someone wonderful and amazing for her, just like you.'

'And it sounds like Lyra thinks this guy is all of those things,' Ben said. 'Isn't that worth the risk?'

Michelle stood for a moment, the wind visibly going out of her sails. Then she finally took a seat at the table next to Lyra. 'I want you to be happy and, if you think Nix will give you that, then go for it.'

Lyra smiled, still not sure if she was brave enough to take that step.

'And if he hurts you again, tell him Ben will break every bone in his body.'

Ben laughed. 'I'll definitely give him a stern talking-to.'

Lyra shook her head. 'I'll certainly pass that threat on, I'm sure he'll be quaking in his boots.'

'We want to meet him of course,' Michelle said.

'Do you think I really want to subject him to all this madness or your preconceived ideas of him? You can meet him on the wedding day, if it gets that far. After the ceremony. Then it's too late for him to run away once he's met my entire crazy family.'

'Probably wise,' Ben said.

'Hey!' Michelle said, indignantly.

'I love you,' he said.

'You don't get round me that easily,' Michelle said, her smile belying her words.

Lyra smiled at them. She wanted what they had.

'Anyway, let's change the subject away from my messed-up love life,' Lyra said. 'I have to tell you all about this treasure hunt me and Nix have been doing over the last few days.'

She started explaining about what Seamus had told her about the lost treasure and how they'd found the first clue in what might have been an old ice house, but she couldn't focus on it. Could she really start dating Nix, knowing that it would be something that was far from casual? She had never entered into a relationship before already knowing it would be something serious. The potential to get hurt was so much greater. And Nix reminded her of her mum in many ways, leading that carefree, exciting life she'd spent so many years trying to avoid. But Ben was right, she couldn't lock away her heart forever for fear of getting hurt. What she had with Nix was definitely worth exploring.

CHAPTER SEVENTEEN

She hurried down to the harbour as the sun made its descent across the sky. The windows of the cottages were sparkling with a rose-gold glow, reflecting the incredible sunset that trailed across the clouds.

There were lots of boats dotted around and Lyra had no idea what Nix's looked like. There were sailboats, dinghies, great luxury yachts, catamarans and everything in between. There were even more boats tied up to buoys further out in the sea but, as he was coming ashore every day, they were unlikely to belong to Nix. His would more likely be tied to one of the jetties or wooden walkways.

Suddenly she spotted Nix and Dexter sitting on the deck of one of the boats. She hurried along one of the walkways that would take her to his boat and as she approached his eyes found hers.

He quickly stood up, brushing down his t-shirt and running a hand through his hair. Dexter, realising there was company, put his paws on the side of the boat and started wagging his tail furiously.

She stopped by the boat, her mouth dry, suddenly unable to find the words she wanted to say.

'Lyra, I'm so glad you came,' Nix said. 'I've been looking forward to solving the next clue with you.'

She shook her head. 'We can get on with that in a minute, I have something I want to say. Can I come aboard?'

'Of course.'

He leaned over and offered out his hand. As soon as she took it she felt something spark between them. The flash in his eyes said he felt it too. And suddenly doubt and fear slithered away to the corners of her mind.

She climbed onto the boat and stood there in front of him.

'Is everything OK?' Nix asked.

'Yes, I think so... I thought about what you said today. About us.'

'Oh.'

She paused, wanting to get this right. She wanted to give them a chance but she felt like she needed to put some rules in place. Life always felt better when there were rules. But she hadn't put any thought into that.

He tentatively put his hands on her shoulders and goosebumps erupted across her skin, stalling all words in her mouth.

He smiled at her, his eyes gentle. For once, she was going to be brave.

'I'd like to give us a go – that is, if you want to.'

His smile spread right across his face and then he frowned slightly. 'Lyra, I need to say something.'

Her heart dropped. Had he changed his mind?

Then he shook his head. 'You know what, it can keep. I'd like that very much.'

He bent his head and kissed her.

God, the taste of him was utterly magnificent, the feel of his lips against hers was heaven. Lyra loved the way he cupped her face, holding her with such tenderness and adoration. She found herself pressed tight up against him, feeling the warmth of his body against hers. There was not a single part of her that thought this was wrong.

He pulled away slightly, kissed her on the nose and then left another lingering kiss on her forehead.

He moved his face so he could look her in the eyes, a large smile lighting up his face. 'This is the best news I've heard in a very long time.'

She smiled.

'Come and sit over here,' Nix said, pulling her down next to him.

Dexter sniffed around them, wagging his tail, and Lyra stroked his velvety head, glad of the distraction. Her heart was racing in her chest.

She glanced at Nix who was watching her with a smile. She reached out and stroked his face and he looped an arm round her shoulders and pulled her gently against his chest, running his fingers through her hair.

'I meant what I said today,' he said. 'We're going to take this really slow, get to know each other properly.'

She nodded. 'OK.'

Maybe that was all they needed, maybe they didn't need rules, just an understanding that they weren't going to rush into anything.

'And I can't promise this is forever—'

'You might get bored of me,' Lyra said.

'I think that's very unlikely, but in the event that I do want to end it, I will talk to you, I'll be honest. I can categorically promise that I will never ever cheat on you. This is an exclusive arrangement. There will never be anyone else while I'm with you.'

She smiled. She trusted him, at least with that. He still had the potential to break her heart, but at least not in the way that previous relationships had.

'And I will promise you the same thing.'

He stared at her, taking her in, as if he couldn't believe she was here. He placed another kiss on her forehead and kissed her again, gently, on the lips. She couldn't help smiling as the kiss continued.

He pulled back, stroking her face.

A thought occurred to her. 'I think we need to keep it quiet at work. At least for now. We've only just started there and I don't want them to think we're being unprofessional. Especially when they're considering us for a management position. Let's give it a few weeks so they can see that we're great at our jobs and then they won't care what we get up to in our private lives.'

'OK,' Nix said, slowly.

'It's not that I'm embarrassed about being with you or anything. I just don't think we should be blatant. We don't want Clover walking into our office to find—'

'Me making love to you on my desk,' Nix said, and she burst out laughing.

'I was going to say kissing but we should probably hold off on the sex at work too.'

He smiled. 'It's OK, I understand. Although I now have

227

a pretty wonderful image of making love to you on my desk in my head that I need to get rid of.'

She giggled. 'Well, we do have a lock on the inside of our door.'

He groaned. 'OK, let's change the subject, because I just promised you we would take things slow and now we're talking about sex.'

'On your desk,' Lyra teased.

He shook his head. 'Have you eaten?'

'Yes, my sister made sure I was well-fed.'

'That's good. Well, would you like the grand tour?'

'Sure.'

He stood up and took her hand. 'Well, it might take a while. It's quite big.'

She looked around and smiled. *Big* wasn't exactly the word she would choose to describe it. More like compact or cosy.

'This is the deck,' Nix gestured expansively, as if it were far larger than it appeared. She giggled. 'The benches all pull out to make a double bed or sunbed.'

'Oh that's cool.'

'It's handy for sunbathing or stargazing.'

'I'm definitely more of a stargazer than a sunbather,' Lyra said.

'Duly noted. There's storage space under here too, quite a large amount. And through here we have the galley, dining room and lounge.'

She smiled as she stepped inside to see a tiny stove on one side and a little dining table with two benches either side opposite the small kitchen area. It was neat and tidy but had a lovely cosy feel.

'And all the way up here,' Nix said, taking one step past the kitchen. 'Is the helm.' He gestured to the steering wheel and various other levers and buttons. It looked very high-tech for what appeared to be a very simple boat.

'This looks very complicated,' Lyra said.

'It's a lot easier than it looks. I'll let you have a go one day. Down here we have the bedrooms and bathroom.'

He took a step down next to the steering wheel and Lyra followed him to be faced with three very narrow doors. He pushed open the left door and Lyra could see a room with a smallish double bed. There was no space around the bed, just a tiny gap by the door. There were a few overhead cupboards though. The boat had quite a lot of storage for something which from the outside looked fairly small. But it was clear that living on board Serendipity would be a sparse existence. There was no room here for anything unnecessary. She thought about her beloved glitter-lamp sitting in the bedroom at her cottage, her small collection of snow globes from various places she'd visited around the world, the large coffee table decorated with bright colourful buttons in the middle of the lounge. There was no space for anything frivolous here.

'This is the guest bedroom.'

He pushed open the middle door and Lyra could see a large round bed in the middle of the room. This room was quite spacious and had lovely skylight windows above the bed.

'Master bedroom,' Nix said, then pushed open the third door. 'And this is the bathroom.'

This room was more like a cupboard but there was a

tiny shower cubicle and enough room for a toilet and a sink squashed in there too.

'Well, that's the extent of the tour,' Nix said.

'I love it, what a wonderful space to live.'

'It's a simple life, but I love that the open sea is out there ready for me to explore at a moment's notice. Life is short and I want to make the most of it. Eventually, I'd like to save up and get a house again, but I don't think I'd ever give up Serendipity or Judy. I love the freedom too much.'

'I love the idea of it,' Lyra said, although she didn't know if she would really want that life. Her mum would have loved it, which was a good reason to run in the exact opposite direction.

'Well, shall we have a look at the next clue?' Nix said.

She nodded and went back up to the dining area, excitedly pulling the glass bottle from her bag, popping the cork and easing out the small scroll. She took a seat and Nix sat down next to her. She broke open the seal and spread out the piece of paper.

There was another simple drawing of what appeared to be an island, although definitely not this one. Jewel Island had two distinct hills on either end and a valley in the middle where the village was, but the drawing had a jagged point right in the middle. There was what appeared to be a tiny figure of some kind at one end, with a cross underneath it.

There was another drawing of a mermaid underneath the picture of the island.

And that was it, there was no writing, no other symbols. It was pretty sparse.

'So I guess the next clue is not on Jewel Island,' Lyra said. 'Although I have no idea where this place is.'

'I do, I know it,' Nix said. 'This is Mermaid Island.'

'Mermaid Island, I've never heard of it.'

'I don't think it has an official name, but some call it Seal Island because of the sheer number of seals that live there. Some call it Shark Island because it looks like a shark's fin, but I've always known it as Mermaid Island on account of there being a statue of a mermaid there. No one knows where the statue came from, who put it there or how long it's been there, but it stands on the peninsula so you can see it from the sea. Many say she's cursed and sailors that used to traverse those waters would meet a very watery death.'

Lyra laughed. 'That sounds a bit far-fetched.'

'I agree, in fact that sounds like just the kind of rumour put about by a fisherman trying to hide his treasure. Imagine one fisherman tells another that he heard that Mermaid Island was cursed and he'd heard a few sailors had died there. They tell a few more. The rumour gets embellished and exaggerated over the years. Who's going to go anywhere near an island that's cursed?'

Lyra looked down at the piece of paper. 'Well, I guess we are.'

He grinned. 'I was hoping you'd say that. Only, it's about three hours down the coast from here.'

'Oh no.'

That was quite far.

He looked at his watch. 'What are your plans for the weekend?'

'No plans really. I thought I might explore some of the local area and obviously we need to discuss the birthday party at some point. What are you thinking?'

He grinned. 'That we could go on an adventure.'

CHAPTER EIGHTEEN

'To Mermaid Island?' Lyra almost squealed.

Nix grinned at her excitement. He had loved seeing her enjoying the treasure hunt over the last few days. 'Yes, if we leave now, we'd probably get there just before sunset. We could stay overnight and explore the island tomorrow.'

Her smile slipped from her face.

'Don't worry, I'll have you back at work first thing Monday morning,' he said.

'You want to go away for a weekend?'

'Yes, why not, be spontaneous.'

'I'm all for spontaneity but I don't even have any clothes,' Lyra protested.

'I have clothes I can lend you.'

'You can't lend me underwear.'

'Well I can, I have boxer shorts. They are clean, I promise.'

'I don't have a toothbrush,' Lyra said.

'I have a spare, it's brand new.'

'But…'

'I have enough food and fuel on board to accommodate us for our trip to Mermaid Island and back, or wherever else you want to go after we've retrieved the next clue.'

'We're supposed to be taking things slow.'

'I have two bedrooms; we don't have to sleep together.'

Lyra looked out over the horizon. The sky was a pale cloudless pink, the sun hovering just above the horizon. The sea was flat calm with barely a ripple breaking the surface. It was the perfect evening for a boat trip.

'Any more protests?' Nix said.

She was silent for a while and he got the distinct impression he was pushing her completely out of her comfort zone.

'I'll let you know when I think of them,' Lyra said.

'OK, although we might be a bit too far away from home to do anything about it by then.'

'I'm sure you can put my mind at ease,' she said.

He took her hand, stroking his fingers across her palm. 'I certainly can think of a few things to help you take your mind off it.'

'I bet you can.' She smiled as he kissed her but then she pulled away. 'Wait, I don't even have my phone with me.'

'What do you need your phone for? We can just switch off from the outside world. I have my phone and the boat's radio if we get into trouble. What else do we need?'

She clearly thought about it for a moment and then nodded. 'You're right, my phone doesn't stop beeping sometimes with Facebook updates from my family, silly videos of dogs from my youngest brother, Ethan, or photos of amazing cakes from my sister, Michelle. Sometimes I turn my phone on silent because it's non-stop and you just want some peace. They can do without me for one weekend.'

'Right, I think we better set sail, before you find any more objections,' Nix said.

He went about the preparations ready to leave, untying the knots that secured them to the jetty and pulling the fenders over inside the boat. Lyra was watching him keenly and he felt like he needed to do everything right.

He grabbed a life jacket and handed it to her. Her eyes widened as she took it. 'Are we going to need this?'

'I very much doubt it, this boat is as stable as a rock and the sea is flat calm out there. But I'd like to keep you safe.'

'Why aren't you wearing one?'

Nix didn't like to admit that he never wore one. He grabbed the second life jacket and pulled it on, zipping it up, and Lyra slipped hers over her shoulders. He spent a few moments adjusting the straps but if he was honest he was just using it as an excuse to be close to her, to touch her. Having her here felt so right.

He pushed away the doubts that said he still hadn't told her why Emily had really left him. It seemed such a ridiculous thing to talk about when they were supposed to be taking things slow. He knew he'd have to tell her at some point, but maybe they could enjoy the weekend together before he ruined everything with his secrets.

He started the engine and slowly manoeuvred out of the harbour. Lyra moved to the seat next to him, her eyes wide with excitement.

'Oh, look at the seals,' she said, pointing to a few fat ones lying sleepily on top of the floating pontoons.

'They're always there. They're so lazy, they spend all day there. We'll see loads more at Mermaid Island.'

Once they went past the buoys that marked the edge of the harbour, he put the boat into gear and accelerated out into the open sea.

Lyra gave a little shriek of delight next to him and Dexter came over to see if she was OK.

Nix glanced over at her as she took everything in and as she looked around she caught his eye.

'What are you smiling at?' Lyra said.

'I'm excited about this weekend.'

'About finding the treasure?'

'About spending it with you,' he said.

She smiled and he leaned over to kiss her but she squawked in protest. 'No, keep your eyes on the road.'

He laughed. 'The road out there is pretty bloody big; also, not a lot of traffic.'

She looked around. There was one sailboat out on the distant horizon, which they were heading away from, but other than that there were no other boats to be seen.

'A quick kiss then,' Lyra said.

Nix smiled and kissed her before she changed her mind again, and after a moment he felt her melt against him. God, this woman, there was something incredible about her. She made him feel warm inside.

'OK, that's enough,' Lyra said. 'I don't want you to crash.'

He smiled and turned his attention back to steering the boat.

'I can't believe we're doing this; I can't believe *I'm* doing this. It's you, you make me do things I wouldn't normally do.'

'Is that a bad thing?'

She didn't answer at first and then she smiled. 'It's definitely a good thing.'

∾

Lyra stared at the stars above them, millions of tiny crystals peppering the inky sky. It looked magical. They had followed the coast to the west, chasing the setting sun as it left a trail of cranberry and tangerine across the clouds. They had watched the sky turn from the deepest pink to purple to inky black as they continued to make their way west, the moon lighting up the water ahead of them, but not long after Nix had found Mermaid Island and anchored off for the night in a secluded cove. He had pulled out all the benches on the deck, which made a makeshift bed so they could lie down and watch the stars. Without streetlights here, the starry sky seemed to be endless and she felt like she could stare at it forever.

'Tell me more about your family,' Lyra said, watching a satellite move with purpose across the sky above them.

'I have one brother, Lucas. He's older than me and a complete tart when it comes to women. We're very different in many ways but I love him to bits. He was my rock when I was going through my toughest times. My parents are still together and as crazy in love with each other now as they were when they got married.'

'I'm glad you have great parental role models.'

'Oh they're amazing, I definitely want what they have,'

Nix said. 'Sadly I don't see them as much as I'd like because they live in Canada.'

'Yeah, it's hard, isn't it, when everyone is so spread apart. Most of my conversations with my siblings are over Zoom or WhatsApp. We try to get together at Christmas but even that's a bit sporadic, especially as Max is in Australia.'

'You said that Michelle has a little boy. What's his name?'

'Zach, he's this whirlwind of constant energy. I don't know how Michelle and Ben keep up with him.'

'Any other nieces and nephews?'

'No, not yet. I know Max is keen to start a family. Frankie and Ethan are still so young themselves so I don't think that's on their agenda. Ethan has just bought a house with his fiancée in north Devon so it's possible they might think about it in a year or so. I don't think Kitty will ever have any children.'

Nix was silent for a moment and she rolled over to look at him.

'Because of the lymphoma?' he said, finally.

'Because she doesn't like children,' Lyra laughed. 'She adores Zach but she says the best part about being an aunt is being able to give them back. I think the lymphoma made her really look at what she wanted from life and children wasn't on that list.'

'How old is she?'

'Twenty-six.'

'And how old was she when she was diagnosed?'

'Nineteen.'

'Oh god, so young.'

238

'I know. I was... twenty-three. Yeah, that was tough for all of us. Ethan was doing his GCSEs at the time so I was trying to help him with his exams and be there for Kitty throughout all her treatment.'

'And your parents never came back?'

Lyra shook her head and then gave a sad smile at the look of incredulity on Nix's face 'I know. Do I win the award for the worst parents in the world?'

'I think you'd come pretty damn close. How could they not care about their own child?'

'Oh well, that's when all the dirty laundry came out. It turned out my dad, the man who raised us, wasn't our dad at all. I'd had no idea. When I spoke to Mum about Kitty's treatment and how I couldn't understand how none of us were matches for her stem cell treatment, that's when the truth came out. Mum had already had me and was preg-nant with Michelle when she met my dad... the man I knew as Dad. Me and Michelle had two different dads who we've never met. Mum and Dad got married and Max, Kitty, Frankie and Ethan were the product of multiple different affairs over the next few years. Apparently Dad was crap in bed, or so Mum had great pleasure in telling me, so she had to go elsewhere to get her needs met. That's why he left when I was sixteen. He finally caught her out. I don't know to what extent he found out – whether he realised that none of us were his, or whether he caught her having another affair – but he'd finally had enough.'

'Oh your poor dad.'

'I know, I actually felt really sorry for him when Mum told me. And he still sent money over the next eight years after he'd left, which I suppose was pretty decent of him, considering he had no real connection to us other than he'd raised us.'

'That must have been so hard for you to find that out, especially at such a tough time,' Nix said.

'It was pretty heartbreaking,' Lyra said.

'And how did your brothers and sisters take it?'

'I... never told them.' She saw the look of surprise on Nix's face. 'I know, I'm a bad person. But it was such a shitty time and they were all finding it really hard that Mum and Dad didn't care enough to come back. I didn't want to add to that by telling them why. Michelle knows; I told her later. But with Max trying to kill himself, and Kitty's lymphoma, and Frankie and Ethan being so young when Dad left, I've always felt so protective over all of them. I just want them to know I'm always here for them and I don't want them to ever doubt that because I'm now technically only their half-sister. We all rallied round when Mum left, and later with Kitty's illness, I think we became a lot closer because of it. I didn't want anything to damage that.'

'Wow, that's a heavy burden to carry on your own.'

'It's always been that way, at least since my dad left. I've always carried the family and I probably always will.'

'Don't you think it's time to let go of this guilt?' Nix said. 'You have more than made up for any mistakes you made after your dad left, you spent eight or nine years of your life making up for it. And you're your own person now, there's no one relying on you, no one to let down. It's time to let go of the past.'

She thought about this for a moment. She wasn't sure if she could ever let go of that.

'Setting sail and going where the waves take us for the weekend doesn't hurt or impact on anyone,' Nix said.

'I know you're right,' Lyra said. 'I've actually really enjoyed tonight. I think you're good for me, in many ways.'

'I hope so.'

She rolled onto her back to stare at the skies again. Maybe he was right. She glanced over at him and he was still watching her. She snuggled up to him and he looped an arm around her, holding her close. Maybe he was the man to help her to move on, in more ways than one.

Nix woke in what must have been the very early hours of the morning. It was still pitch black, the stars sparkling above them. It was almost completely silent apart from the waves lapping gently against the side of the boat. Lyra was curled up lying facing away from him. Her shoulder was sticking out from under the blanket and, when he pulled the blanket up over her, he noticed how cold she was. The temperature had definitely dropped out here now that the sun had long since disappeared. Even Dexter had gone back inside.

Nix very carefully and gently curled himself around her, hoping to keep her warm without waking her, but she stirred in his arms and rolled over towards him, burying herself into his chest.

'It's cold,' she muttered.

He kissed her head, stroking her back to keep her warm. 'I think it's time we went to bed.'

'You said that last time and it didn't exactly end well,' Lyra said, sleepily.

'Oh, I have very different memories of that night – it ended very well.'

She grinned.

He climbed off the makeshift bed and offered out his hand. 'Come on.'

She sat up, stretched and stood, taking his hand. He led her inside and then closed the door to keep some of the warmth in. As he guided her down the steps, he could see her watching him carefully. He wondered if, like him, there was a huge part of her that wanted to rekindle that amazing night right now. But he would be good. He'd promised her he would take it slow. He opened his bedroom door and Dexter shot past them, launching himself at the bed and making himself comfortable right in the middle.

Nix turned his attention back to Lyra and cupped her face, kissing her softly. There was something so wonderful about kissing her, it felt like coming home, as if this was exactly where he was meant to be. It would be so easy to scoop her up and carry her into his room and make love to her for the rest of the night. He didn't think she would protest too much either. But he couldn't do that.

He gently pulled away, stepping back. 'Goodnight, Lyra.'

He took a step towards his bedroom and for a second she looked like she was going to object but she didn't.

'Goodnight, Nix.'

He smiled as she went inside her own bedroom and closed the door. He sighed, leaning his head against her door for a moment. Taking it slow was going to be a lot harder than he'd thought. He turned round to see Dexter giving him a look that suggested he was laughing at Nix's predicament. Nix shook his head and went into his own bedroom, closing the door. He'd loved spending time with Lyra tonight, but suddenly having her here for the weekend seemed like a bad idea.

CHAPTER NINETEEN

Lyra woke with the sun on her face, the sea sparkling through a little round porthole next to her head. She couldn't help but smile. Going away on a boat for the weekend on a complete whim, without any clothes or her phone, was something she'd never have done before she met Nix. Somehow he was pulling all her walls down.

She pulled on her dress and the boxer shorts Nix had given her the night before and grabbed the toothbrush he'd given her too.

She stepped outside the bedroom and could see Nix standing out on deck, glass of orange juice in his hand as he simply stared out over the waves. He was wearing shorts and a loose linen shirt that billowed in the wind. He looked happy. This was a man who was so relaxed, so laid-back he was practically horizontal. He was everything she'd run away from for the past ten or fifteen years, but for some reason she was inexplicably drawn to him.

She quickly washed her face and cleaned her teeth and then went out on deck to join him.

His whole face lit up when he saw her and he stepped forward and kissed her before he'd even uttered a word. This kiss was everything. She had never been kissed like this before, as if she was Nix's entire world. He stroked her face as the kiss continued and it was just so gentle.

He pulled back slightly to look at her. 'Hi.'

'Hello.'

He kissed her on the forehead, wrapping his arms around her, and she leaned her head against his chest as she looked out over the sea too.

'I could definitely get used to this,' Lyra said. 'Waking up to you and to this view every morning.'

'Well that could be arranged. Did you sleep OK?'

'Yes, like a baby. There's something very calming about the gentle lull of the boat on the water. Were you up early? I heard movement around six?'

He hesitated for just a second before he spoke. 'Yeah, sorry if I woke you. I couldn't sleep so I went for a swim.'

She looked up at him and for a fleeting second thought she saw worry in his eyes. 'Are you OK?'

'Yes, I just… I think we're coming to the end of this treasure hunt and… I worry you're going to be disappointed.'

She frowned. 'Why would I be disappointed?'

'I don't know. What if we don't find anything? The fisherman could have come back to get the treasure a few months after he'd hid it but never bothered to retrieve the clues. What if we do find something but… it's not what you were expecting?'

'But none of that matters. I was never expecting to get rich from this. I've loved going on this quest, the fun of solving the clues and finding the next one, but the best thing was that I got to go on this journey with you.'

Nix studied her face and smiled slightly. 'Come on, I'll cook you some breakfast. We need our strength if we are going to find this treasure today.'

He let her go, then walked back inside and started dragging out pots and pans ready to make breakfast.

She watched him for a moment. That was weird, why would he be worried about her finding the treasure? Unless he knew something that she didn't. She looked over her shoulder at the statue of the mermaid, standing on the edge of the island, supposedly presiding over the treasure, or at least the next clue. She guessed she would find out soon enough.

She turned and went back inside to help Nix with the breakfast.

Nix had managed to manoeuvre the boat very close to the beach so they could wade ashore without getting anything other than their legs wet. Nix had a couple of little trowels with him for when they needed to dig, which Lyra hoped would be enough. She wasn't sure how deep the treasure or the next clue would be buried. If she'd been the fisherman, she certainly wouldn't have buried a chest of priceless jewels just below the surface.

Nix was right: the seals loved this place and, as the island was completely uninhabited, she imagined they were relatively undisturbed most of the time, apart from the odd explorer who came here looking for adventure. Hundreds of seals littered the beach, most unmoving apart from the odd flick of a tail, or a roll as they tried to get more comfortable on the damp sand. As Lyra and Nix came ashore a couple shuffled a few metres away from them, but there was certainly no great alarm at their arrival.

'They're amazing, aren't they,' Lyra said. 'So beautiful.'

'Yes, I love watching them catch and eat fish. I snorkel off the boat sometimes and they're just so incredible to watch – so graceful in the water and very playful too.'

'I'd love to do that, that sounds incredible.'

'I have a few masks and snorkels on the boat, we can do it after we get back.'

'That would be great.'

Nix nodded. 'Do you want to explore the island a little while we're here or do you want to just get on with finding the next clue?'

'Let's get our treasure,' Lyra said, excitedly.

He smiled sadly, almost as if he didn't want to find this treasure after all.

She took his hand and they started walking towards the end of the island. They had to clamber over some rocks to get there but they were soon on a grassy patch of land and the mermaid was standing right at the end of it, towering over the rocks below.

'She's so big,' Lyra said as they approached. 'How the hell did she get here and why?'

'No idea. I tried to look into it once, thinking there must be some mention of her in the local history books. She crops up in several but there's no information on her. Other than the curse.' Nix's eyes widened as if he was scared and she laughed.

'I'll look after you.'

She pulled the latest clue out of her bag. 'If this drawing is accurate, this looks like the front of the statue and it looks like the cross is directly in front of it, so shall we start digging there?'

Nix nodded.

The area immediately surrounding the statue was more mud than grass, probably because the statue's presence had stopped anything growing in its immediate vicinity. Lyra knelt down and started digging with one of the trowels and Nix bent and started digging too. She was surprised by how loose the dirt was – she'd been expecting it to be fairly solid after years of not being touched, but it seemed to crumble very easily. They had only been digging a few minutes when her trowel hit something soft.

'There's something here,' Lyra said, excitedly, as she quickly scraped the dirt away from the thing she'd found.

It looked like some kind of cloth bag but it was buried pretty well. As she tried to pull the bag from the hole, she realised that whatever was in it was fairly large and heavy. It took quite a while to free it but eventually the bag came out. There was something square inside but it clanged against something else, like there was more than one thing in it.

The bag was tied at the top with some rope but, as Lyra tried to untangle it, it became very clear that the rope was heavily knotted.

She groaned in frustration, desperate to see what was inside.

'Why don't we take this back to the boat,' Nix said. 'I have a knife there we can use to cut the rope.'

She nodded and they started walking back. Lyra had to stop herself from running back in her enthusiasm to find out what was in the bag. 'Do you think this is it? Do you think this is the treasure?' she said, excitedly.

'It's fairly big if it's just the next clue,' Nix said. 'Considering all the other clues have just been inside bottles.'

They waded out to the boat, Lyra lifting up her dress as the water was up to her knees and Nix holding the bag. Nix climbed on board first, dropping the bag on the deck, then turned back to help her aboard. He went inside to retrieve his knife and let Dexter out onto the deck, leaving Lyra with the bag. She ran her hands over it impatiently and it was obvious her first thoughts were correct: there was a box inside, maybe made from wood, and a second object which felt like another glass bottle.

'Here we go, watch your hands,' Nix said, carrying a big knife. He cut the rope away and then passed the bag back to Lyra.

She eagerly opened it to find something that was undoubtedly a treasure chest inside.

'Oh my god,' she squealed. 'Look.' She pulled out the box, which felt quite heavy, and as she did she could hear things moving around inside. 'This is it, this is what we've been looking for.'

It was a smallish wooden chest, probably around a foot long, inlaid with gold.

'Go on, open it,' Nix said.

She ran her hands over the front but it was quite clear that the chest was locked and needed a key to open it.

She shook her head. 'We need a key.'

'Is there anything else in the bag?'

Lyra remembered that it had felt like there was a bottle inside. She opened the bag and, sure enough, there was a small glass bottle at the bottom of the bag. She grabbed it and pulled the cork out, releasing another yellowy piece of paper. She passed the scroll to Nix who broke it open and laid it out on the bench next to Lyra. It was another drawing, seemingly of a different island – it was definitely a different shape to Mermaid Island.

There was what appeared to be a pointy tower at the end of this island, with a cross underneath the tower. Next to the island there was a picture of a lion.

There were no more clues or writing.

She looked at Nix to see he was studying the drawing intently. 'I think I know this place too.'

'That's a relief, because the fisherman has definitely been a bit stingy with this clue.'

Nix smiled. 'This is a daymark to help mariners identify where they are. It's a really tall obelisk-type building and it has these great archways at the bottom, which you can kind of see here in the drawing. It's really distinctive. It's on another uninhabited island, more of a rock really. It's called Dagger's Point. It's not too far from Jewel Island actually, maybe an hour down the coast, but in the other direction from here, so we'd have to go past Jewel Island to get to it.'

'Do we have enough fuel to get there today?'

He nodded. 'I actually filled up the other day and I always get lots of spare. We'll have more than enough to get to Dagger's Point and back to Jewel Island again.'

'This is exciting. I bet this is where we'll find the key, now we've found the chest.'

'I'd imagine so and then the treasure hunt will be over.'

'I wonder what's inside,' Lyra said, trying to peer through the opening, but the crack was too small. She ran her hands over the chest, wondering if there was some secret button to open it.

A thought suddenly struck her and she frowned. 'Don't you think the chest is in relatively good condition for something that supposedly has been in the ground for hundreds of years?'

The wood was perfect, the gold not dulled or rusted at all.

Nix shrugged. 'I guess the bag protected it.'

'The bag is in good condition too and the rope looks brand new.'

'I don't know, maybe being buried underneath the mermaid, the mermaid might have protected it from the weather.'

She looked at the chest again. This just didn't add up and Nix didn't seem bothered by it at all. She glanced at him. He looked... uncomfortable, and that was confusing her more than the chest looking so new.

'Anyway, did you want to go snorkelling now? Or we could go further down the coast and snorkel on the way back?' Nix said.

Had he just changed the subject?

'We might see the seals if we go here,' he said.

Her heart skipped with that possibility. 'Let's go now.'

'Great, I'll get you some clothes you can swim in and I'll dig out the snorkels too.'

He disappeared back inside and she turned her attention back to the chest. There was something wrong about all of this, about the chest and bag being in pristine condition. And this whole quest, despite having been a lot of fun, had happened very easily: finding the first clue in Nix's abandoned ice house, solving and finding the other clues, after hundreds of years, seemed just a bit too... convenient. And now Lyra couldn't escape the feeling that Nix was hiding something from her.

She guessed all would become clear when they finally found the key.

∽

Snorkelling was one of the most amazing experiences of Lyra's life. She'd only been doing it a few minutes and already she knew she wanted to do this again. It had taken her a short while to get used to putting her face in the water and breathing through the snorkel, but Nix had been really patient.

Why hadn't she done this before?

The sea was so crystal clear it felt like she could see for miles, a world that she had never seen before except on nature programmes, although seeing it on the TV could never do this beauty justice. Below her on the sun-dappled seabed were hundreds of starfish of different colours and sizes, but some, as Nix told her, were actually sunstars, with twelve or thirteen arms spread out like the sun's rays. She'd never seen anything like it. There were lots of sea urchins perched on the rocks – lethal-looking black spiky ones and more friendly-looking pink ones with shorter spikes. There were a few crabs scuttling away from them, their claws held high as if ready to attack if the occasion called for it.

Dexter was swimming next to them, which was interesting to watch in itself, seeing his long, powerful, spotty legs propelling himself through the water, using his tail as some kind of rudder.

Nix suddenly tapped her arm, pointing frantically off to the left. She looked to where he was pointing and nearly squealed with delight. She could see two seals playing in the water, gambolling and swimming with such grace and elegance, the sun glinting off their silvery bodies. The creatures were very obviously aware of them, as they kept looking over in their direction, but they didn't come any closer, maybe because of Dexter who was happily swimming around with no idea what was happening under the waves. The seals were utterly enchanting to watch until they disappeared off into the depths of the sea.

Fish swam lazily past them, darting in and out of the rocks below, some coming very close but moving just out of reach when Lyra tried to touch them. Their scales were almost iridescent, shining in a beautiful rainbow of colours as the sun's rays hit them.

Nix suddenly nudged her again and pointed directly below, where there was a small mass of legs all curling around themselves like a nest of red snakes. Lyra quickly realised it was an octopus. It was incredible to watch as it moved itself across the seabed.

Lyra could have stayed there and watched the underwater vista all day, but soon the coldness of the water started to seep into her bones. She lifted her head, treading water, as she moved her face mask onto her forehead and Nix surfaced too.

'How was that?' he said, pulling his mask off.

She moved closer to him, wrapping her arms around his neck, and he slid his hands around her waist as she kissed him. He smiled against her lips as he kissed her back.

'That good, eh?'

'You are incredible. I feel like, since I've met you, everything has changed. This has been one of the best things I've ever done. Thank you for sharing this with me.'

He smiled. 'It's been my pleasure. And if you ever hate me in the future, you can remember this moment and perhaps think that I'm not that bad.'

'I don't think I could ever hate you,' Lyra said.

He looked sad for a fleeting moment. 'I think there could be a couple of things you could hate me for. But I guess we'll cross that bridge when we come to it. Come on, we better get a shift on if we're going to get to Dagger's Point before dark.'

He started swimming off towards the boat and she stared after him in confusion.

She couldn't think what could possibly cause her to hate him, because she was pretty sure she was slowly falling in love with Nix Sanchez.

Lying under a blanket of stars was something Lyra could get used to. There wasn't a single sound except the gentle lap of the water against the boat. Life on the open waves was something she could definitely enjoy. A life with no plan, no responsibility, was looking more and more tempting. Just complete and utter freedom.

They'd arrived at Dagger's Point just after sunset when the twilight of the evening was still allowing a fair amount of light, enough that she could see the impressive daymark standing in all its glory. Although sadly not enough to go exploring on the island. The next clue would have to wait.

She rolled into Nix's side, resting her head on his chest as she looked out on the mainland, twinkling with thousands of lights. Dagger's Point was quite far out to sea but they were close enough to land that she could still see home. Nix had pointed out Jewel Island, but, as the sun had been setting at the time, it had barely been a shadow on the horizon, though she'd been able to pick out the distinctive shape of it.

Right now, going back there on Monday, going back to reality, seemed very far away indeed.

Nix wrapped an arm around her shoulders and kissed her forehead.

She looked up at him. He seemed worried about something, distant somehow, even though he was as affectionate as ever. She wanted to talk to him about it but he had to trust her enough to open up and it was still early days for them.

She snuggled into his side and decided to ask him something else instead.

'Where do you see yourself in ten years' time?' Lyra asked, sleepily. It had been a long day and Nix had let her drive the boat, which had been exhilarating, scary and exhausting all at once.

'Are you interviewing me for a job?'

She laughed. 'No, I'm just interested in you. What's the grand plan?'

Nix was silent for a while. 'Ten years ago, I was twenty-one, I'd just got married. We had big plans, we were going to travel the world – which never happened because we didn't have enough money – we were going to buy a big house, overlooking the sea – that didn't happen either. And we were going to have a whole football team of children filling our home with laughter and happiness. Sadly that didn't happen. But the one thing I saw in my future, more than anything, was a happy ever after with my wife. If you'd asked me when I was twenty-one what life I saw for myself in ten years' time, it would not have been the one I have now.'

He was quiet again and she didn't know what to say. She hadn't intended to make him sad.

'Being diagnosed with leukaemia knocked me for six. I never saw that coming in a million years. All of those plans went out the window. But not to sound too philosophical, where there is darkness, there is also light. I survived where countless others didn't. And that kind of makes you reprioritise your life. What is it I really want? I didn't want another serious relationship. And then, last week, every-thing changed. I met you and that was one of the best things that ever happened to me.'

She swallowed down a huge lump in her throat.

'I don't think most of those original plans I had ten years ago will ever happen and part of me is scared to make plans for the future, in case they don't come true. Better to live for now than be disappointed by the future.

But I do know that I want that future, in whatever shape it comes, to include you, if you'll have me.'

She smiled. 'You are everything I wanted to avoid for so long, but you have shown me a world I want to be a part of. But as exciting as this life is, it wouldn't be the same without you by my side. I know it's still early days for us and we're taking it slow and, who knows, we might get bored of each other in a few weeks. But right now I want that future with you too.'

He smiled and kissed her.

It was exciting to think about a future with Nix but she couldn't escape the feeling that he was holding something back. How could they ever really move forward if there were secrets between them? But it was still very early for them. Lyra would give him time and she only hoped it would be enough.

As it was low tide, Nix was able to get the boat in close to the island again so they could get ashore quite easily and almost right next door to the daymark. It was an impressive octagonal stone building that towered into the sunlit sky. The eight arches took up half of the building and then it tapered off in a point some fifteen or twenty metres above them.

'It has a very wide bottom; how do we know where to start digging?' Lyra said.

'Let's have a look at the clue,' Nix said. She passed him the paper. 'There's this lion, that must mean something.'

'Let's go and take a closer look,' she said.

They walked all the way round the outside of the daymark but there were no lions or any markings of any kind. Lyra walked inside the daymark through one of the open archways. The roof of the daymark was way above her. On the floor there were lines of large paving slabs that led through the arches and out the other side, so it resembled a giant star, but none of them had any kinds of markings either. She looked up again and that's when she saw it. Above each arch were coat of arms carved into the top of the stone archway. Each one was different; some depicted various weapons, some showed plants, others different animals.

'Nix!' Lyra called and he came running in from outside. 'Look, coats of arms.'

'Oh wow, one of these must have a lion,' he said.

They started moving round, looking carefully at each coat of arms.

'It's this one,' Lyra said, triumphantly pointing to a small shield that had a lion and an eagle carved into the stone.

'It must be under here then.' Nix pointed to the paving stone that was directly under the archway.

She moved over to it. 'Do you think we can just lift the stone?'

'We can give it a go. Here, you take that side and I'll take the other,' Nix said.

Lyra was surprised that she could get her fingers under the stone quite easily and it wasn't embedded into the ground after years of being stuck in this position. They lifted it carefully out the way and, sure enough, directly under the slab was a small bottle buried in the soil. She levered it out with the trowel they'd brought with them and something rattled within.

'I think the key is inside,' she said.

'Let's go back to Serendipity and have a look,' Nix said.

They put the slab back into position and quickly hurried back to the boat. The chest was sitting on the dining table waiting for them and Lyra sat down, easing out the cork in the bottle and tipping out the contents onto the table. There was no paper scroll this time, just a small gold key.

'Oh my god, this is it,' Lyra said. She went to pick the key up but Nix stopped her, his hand over hers.

'What if we didn't open it?' he said.

'What? We've come all this way and you don't want to see what's inside?'

'I think the fun was in solving the clues and finding the treasure. I don't want whatever is inside to ruin what we've had.'

'Why would it ruin it?'

'Right now, that chest could be filled with diamonds, rubies and pearls. Emeralds as big as your hand. Isn't it nicer to imagine all that rather than open it and be bitterly disappointed to find that it isn't?'

'I want to see. It doesn't matter if the chest holds nothing more than a few old worthless coins, I want to see it. This is our reward for all our hard work – don't you at least want to see what we've won?'

He sighed. 'OK, but I just want to say, the last few days, going on this adventure with you has been incredible.'

She frowned in confusion. 'I've had a brilliant time too, it's been a long time since I've done anything like this.'

He took a deep breath and gestured for her to open it, taking a step back so he was leaning against the sink. He looked distraught.

She was beyond confused right now. She picked up the key and fitted it into the lock. It turned perfectly. She opened the lid and looked inside.

CHAPTER TWENTY

Lyra stared at the contents in confusion.

Suddenly everything made sense. Why they'd found all of the clues relatively easily, why these clues had been undisturbed for supposedly so many years, why Nix had always been keen for her to solve the clues or find the next one, rather than doing it himself, why the chest was perfectly preserved, the bag undamaged, why the rope looked brand new. And most of all she knew why Nix didn't want her to open it.

Inside were several gold chocolate coins, a cuddly toy dinosaur and the beautiful green leaf ring she'd pointed out to Nix in the jewellery shop a few days before.

'You did all this,' Lyra said, quietly. 'All the clues, the bottles, burying the chest, hiding the key, this was all you.'

'Lyra, I'm sorry, it was never meant to be anything malicious. I never meant to deceive you, I just... I saw the real you, the one who secretly wanted to be Indiana Jones and you kept her locked away. I wanted you to see that the real Lyra was someone to be proud of, that letting her out wasn't a bad thing. I wanted to give you an adventure, I wanted you to see that it's OK to let go and have some fun.'

She stared at the ring he'd bought for her because she'd said she'd loved it, she looked at the cute brontosaurus with its oversized eyes he'd chosen because he remembered that she loved dinosaurs. She couldn't believe all the work he'd put into this, preparing the clues and hiding them. For her.

'I know you're disappointed and I'm so sorry, I—'

'Stop talking,' Lyra said, her voice choked. 'Just stop.' She stood up and walked towards him. 'You did all this, for me?'

'Yes, I'm sorry—'

She reached up and put her fingers over his lips. 'This is… amazing. You have nothing to apologise for. Is this what you've been worried about telling me?'

He frowned in confusion for a moment and then his face cleared. 'No, that's, umm… something else. I was a little bit worried about this, I'm very worried about the other.'

'Whatever it is, after this, you have nothing to worry about.'

His frown turned to a scowl. 'The other thing is in a completely different league to this. It'll make or break us.'

How could anything be so bad that it could split them up?

'Whatever it is, we'll deal with it together,' Lyra said.

He shook his head. 'Can we have this weekend to just enjoy being with each other? I promise, I'll tell you before we go back.'

She nodded. She could give him that. 'OK. Thank you

for this. No one has ever done something like this for me before. No one has ever cared enough for me to go to all this effort. You're the first person to see what was underneath.'

'Lyra, you are definitely worth it. I... You mean the world to me.'

She swallowed down the huge lump of emotion in her throat as she stroked his face. She leaned up and kissed him.

He cupped her face as he kissed her and then his hands were in her hair as if he was desperate to touch her, to bring her closer. And she wanted that too. Their connection was not like anything she'd ever experienced before and suddenly it seemed silly to hold back. Right then, she knew everything she needed to know about Nix Sanchez. He was a kind, thoughtful, wonderful man.

She slid her hands down his arms and he wrapped his round her back, bringing her in closer against him. The kiss turned urgent and needful pretty quickly.

'Lyra,' he whispered. 'We need to stop, I promised you we'd take things slow.'

She kissed his throat and she felt the vibrations of his groan against her lips. She slid her mouth to his collarbone, relishing the taste of him.

Suddenly he lifted her and kissed her hard on the mouth. She wrapped her legs around him as the kiss continued and he walked straight into the bedroom. He laid her down on the bed, pinning her to the mattress, his body surrounding hers, his mouth not leaving hers for a second.

Clothes were dispensed with very quickly and he

started trailing his hot mouth over her body, worshipping her, adoring her, his every touch driving her to the point of insanity. She'd never had intimacy like this before. Sex had always been nice but over fairly quickly. But Nix was taking his time, seemingly enjoying kissing her all over as much as she was. He laid kisses across her stomach and a kick of shock and desire ripped through her as she realised where he was heading. The second his mouth touched her there, every nerve ending in her body exploded with pure need. She arched against him, crying out as that feeling tore through her so fiercely she could barely catch her breath.

Her breath was ragged as he leaned over to grab a condom and then he was over her, kissing her. She wrapped her arms and legs around him and he slid deep inside her, causing her to moan against his lips.

He pulled back slightly to look at her and smiled. 'Hey.'

'Hello,' Lyra said.

'I missed you.'

She smiled. 'You've been with me the whole week.'

'Not like this,' Nix said, kissing her briefly.

'I have to say, I wasn't expecting this to happen again, not so soon.'

'I knew it would happen again for us. The connection between us is too strong for us not to end up here eventually, and I was prepared to wait.'

She smiled. 'You're so sure of yourself.'

'I'm sure of us.'

She knew what he meant – this felt so right in every way.

He kissed her again and started moving against her,

every touch, every movement completely flawless as if they were made for each other. She moved with him, their bodies perfectly in sync with each other. She had never felt so completely alive before, every fibre of her body igniting, sensations rushing through her that she'd never felt before. She felt like she was soaring and when she fell over the other side she knew there'd never be any getting over this.

~

'I still can't believe you did all this,' Lyra said, gesturing to the chest that was spilling over with the gold chocolate coins on the bed. They were both hungry after making love but neither of them had wanted to leave the bed to make something to eat, so snacking on the chocolate coins had seemed like a good compromise. 'You went to so much trouble.'

She unwrapped another chocolate and broke it in two, giving one half to Nix before nibbling away at her own half.

'It was a lot of fun, but man, you were solving the clues far quicker than I expected. I had to stop you after the first night, because I'd not placed any of the other clues.'

'Did you use tea to stain the paper?'

'Yes, that was Seamus's suggestion actually. That's why I had that bag of teabags when I came into the office that day.'

'Seamus was in on this?'

'Yes, we'd planned to meet in Kendra's bakery that day so he could prime you with a slightly embellished version of the legend behind the treasure.'

'So the whole legend was a lie,' Lyra said.

'No, the part about the ship getting wrecked on the rocks and the fishermen going out there to steal the jewels is true – well, at least as far as the legend is concerned – but there's no mention of your house being involved. The stuff about smuggling through the tunnel is true, and your house was involved in that.'

Lyra thought about it for a moment. 'Hang on, you brought those teabags into the office when I was still barely speaking to you.'

'Yes well, I had no idea why you were upset on that first day, because in my mind you'd left me. You were so... free that night we met and so serious at work and I wondered if you'd woken up the morning after and regretted losing your inhibitions and done a runner. I know how much you like control and order after your mum did what she did and I wanted to do something for you that would... bring out that adventurous side again.'

She stared at him. 'You planned all this when I was being so horrible to you?'

'You weren't being horrible and I just wanted to make you happy again, even if nothing else could happen between us.'

She smiled with complete love for him.

'And how did you manage to have time to bury the clues on the islands?'

'I got up early in the morning and went ashore to bury the chest and the key before you woke up. When you said you'd heard me yesterday morning getting up around six, that's what I was doing. That's why I made sure we didn't get to Mermaid Island or Dagger's Point until after dark, so we couldn't go ashore to look for it before I'd buried it.'

Lyra laughed. 'That's why the soil around the mermaid was so loose – because you'd only dug it up a few hours before. I'm presuming the mermaid was nothing to do with you?'

'I'm not that good. That mermaid has been there as far back as I remember, there's no information on her. Although I might have embellished a little about the curse.'

She smiled. 'And what about the clue that was in the chimney, how did you get it so high up?'

'I climbed, with great difficulty, but actually there were bigger bricks sticking out the side of the fireplace that made it a bit easier.'

'You could have pointed them out to me so I didn't have to climb on your shoulders,' Lyra said.

'I considered it, but you were having so much fun and I was trying to appear a bit clueless about it all, so you could solve the puzzles, rather than me.'

She shook her head. 'It's been so much fun. And thank you for the dinosaur and the ring.'

She picked up the ring and slid it onto her wedding finger as a joke, but as she did she watched the smile fade from his face.

'It's OK. I was just joking,' Lyra said, quickly yanking it off.

He shook his head. 'Lyra, I need to tell you. Before we go any further into this relationship, I need to tell you the truth about why me and my wife broke up.'

She frowned. 'You didn't tell me the truth at the restaurant?'

He took her hand. 'I did, I just... left some details out.'

'Go on.'

He let out a heavy breath. 'As I said, when we planned our future, we wanted children – we wanted a whole house full of them. When Emily miscarried after we'd tried for so long to get pregnant, she was distraught. Well, we both were, but she was heartbroken. We never had time to grieve properly though, as I was diagnosed with leukaemia the next day. Then it was a non-stop ride of hospital appointments, meetings with doctors and specialists... and everything happened so quick, we had to start chemotherapy straightaway. But one of the things the doctors told me before we started was that... the intensive treatment I'd need, the chemotherapy, the bone marrow treatment, would make it highly likely that I'd never be able to have children.'

She stared at him in horror. It was safe to say she'd not seen that coming.

Nix hurried on. 'Emily was there for me throughout all my treatment but I could feel she was pulling away. I thought it was the stress of the situation – our nerves were fried, we were both exhausted. When I had the bone marrow treatment, things started getting better, healthwise at least – it was a very long road to recovery but there was a point where I could see the light again. But things didn't improve between me and Emily. She wanted children, she was desperate for them, and in the end that need to have a child far outweighed her desire to stay with me.'

'Nix—'

He shook his head, obviously needing to finish. 'I've had to live with that decision for the last three years. I've had to come to terms with whether I was completely worthless as a man if I couldn't father a child. And whether any woman would ever want me. And it's something I've never told anyone before, not my brother, my parents, no one, because I felt too embarrassed by it. I know I should have told you before, but it feels so strange to discuss having children with someone you've just met. And I was scared of losing you in the same way I lost Emily. But I had to be honest with you. If things go well for us, and you do see forever for us, then you have to know that our future won't involve children – or at least none that are mine.'

She stared at him in shock. The fact he'd been told he had leukaemia and that he could never have children in the same hit must have come as such a cruel blow. And even crueller was that after seven or eight years of marriage his wife didn't want to stand by him because of that.

'Say something,' Nix said.

'I understand why you didn't tell me. That's a hard topic to broach, especially when the last woman you told decided she didn't want to stick around.'

He was still looking at her with hope.

'Nix, I have no idea if I want children. Sometimes I look at my nephew and think, I want that, and sometimes I look at how exhausted Michelle and Ben are, and see how being a parent is non-stop, and there's a part of me that doesn't want it. I was mum to five children for eight or nine years. Ethan was only nine when Dad left, Frankie was ten, and I had no idea what I was doing. It was exhausting, physically, emotionally. And being their mum doesn't stop when they're eighteen, they still rely on me now. And I love them all to bits but I'm not sure if I'm ready to go through that again. But if I do, if we get two or three years down the line and we decide we want that, then we can adopt, we can use a sperm donor, or we fill our life with lots of little Dexter puppies or several colonies of beavers.'

He smiled cautiously.

'This is not a deal-breaker for me because I want to be with you more than anything else.'

He stared at her for a second and then leaned over and kissed her hard. He rolled her back onto the bed and, as the kiss turned to something more, she knew she had a secret of her own. She was pretty sure she was in love with Nix Sanchez and there was nothing that could change that.

'Right, let's go through this presentation,' Lyra said, firing up Nix's laptop after he'd given her the password to unlock it. 'I know I suggested a treasure hunt before, but all of this has given me an idea for how it could work. We could totally design a treasure hunt for the families to take part in. Write clues that will lead them all over the island to find more clues, just like this treasure hunt. I think perhaps we'll keep the clues in English only, instead of Latin, but it would be fun.'

'I love that idea,' Nix said. 'It'd also be a good way to promote our local businesses if we extend the invite to families who live nearby or are on holiday in the local area. We could direct the treasure hunters to different shops, have clues in the windows and spread out all over the island so people can appreciate the beauty of the whole island.'

'Yes and then we can have the barbeque on the beach once everyone has finished. We can get Angel to promote it as a family day out when he does all of his adverts.'

'Good idea. And then a casino and horse-racing night in the evening,' Nix said. 'We can make it classy so people have to dress up a bit, but still invite families along to join in.'

'And fireworks to close the night. Sounds perfect. I'll get all this typed up and then we can do costings so we can present what kind of budget we would need for the event. The main expense will be the fireworks so they might not agree to that. And then we need to hire a company to run the casino and horse-racing side of things. Everything else, like the barbeque and the evening dinner, can be handled by our own chefs.'

'We'd need a budget for small prizes for the treasure hunt too,' he said.

'Yes, good point,' Lyra said as she started writing all this down. She stopped for a second. 'God, I hope we're doing the right thing.'

'What are you worried about?' Nix said.

'It's just that the brief for the party was two days and we've done a plan for one. We were supposed to be working separately and we've worked together. The stipulations of the brief were simple enough but we've not even managed to meet them. I can't help feeling that they're going to be annoyed.'

'I think they will like our initiative and that the plan for the party will impress them,' he said.

'But they specifically wanted one events manager, someone who can take charge,' she said.

'And we're going to show them that we work better as a team. If they decide they don't want both of us on the managerial team, that's fine. We'll continue to report to them as we do now – nothing has to change.'

'OK,' Lyra said, although she wasn't convinced.

'They're not going to fire us because of this,' Nix said.

'I hope not, or I might be moving in with you on the boat.'

He smiled. 'And you'd be very welcome.'

'What if they insist on having an events manager, and they choose one of us? How would you feel if for example they promote me over you?'

'Lyra, you'd make a brilliant manager.' He kissed her cheek and then trailed his hot mouth down to her throat. 'And I have no problem whatsoever being *under* you.'

She laughed. 'And if you're promoted over me?'

'I have no problem being *over* you either. Look, it doesn't matter if one of us is the official events manager and we have to report to them in a weekly meeting, because we will carry on working as a team in the office, just as we are now. We've worked brilliantly together over the last few days and I have no doubt we'll continue to do that, regardless if one of us is officially more senior.'

'OK.'

'Stop worrying about the what ifs.'

She nodded. He was right. She had to stop worrying about the future and enjoy what she had now. What she had now was pretty bloody spectacular and she didn't want to do anything to ruin it.

CHAPTER TWENTY-ONE

Lyra had a serious case of post-holiday blues as she and Nix walked back up to her little cottage on Monday morning. The adventure was over and they had to go back to work because, sadly, bumming around on a boat for the rest of their lives wouldn't pay the bills. The reality outside of the perfect weekend was slowly seeping in, along with a whole ton of doubt.

She had fallen hard for Nix. What she felt for him was so much more than she'd ever felt before and that scared her.

She mentally shook her head. It was ridiculous to think that after one week and one incredible weekend she had fallen in love with Nix. There was still so much to know about him, to experience with him, before she could tick that box. She had been here before so many times, giving her heart away so easily and then having it broken. And yes, the feelings she had for Nix were so much deeper than anything she'd experienced before but that didn't mean it was love. They'd had a moment the day before when he'd told her that his leukaemia had ruined any chance of him having a child, and she'd told him that it didn't matter because she only wanted to be with him, and now her stupid hopeful heart was seeing marriage and a happy ever after. Nix had given her no sign that he wanted that from her – things were good between them but it didn't mean they'd have forever.

It was crazy to believe in some kind of fated, written-in-the-stars relationship too. They'd been each other's first kiss, nearly twenty years before, but that was just a weird coincidence. It would be silly to think that fate or destiny had brought them back together again, that a chance meeting that wonderful night the week before had started the ball rolling down a path that was unstoppable and predetermined. If they hadn't had that meeting, that one glorious night, would they be here now, holding hands, or would they just be work colleagues, friends, nothing more? That thought was unbearable but Lyra couldn't let herself believe in destiny either.

Her mum had decided she wanted to live in Thailand for the rest of her life based purely on a dream she'd had one night, that she was supposed to be there. She'd abandoned her six children on no more than a whim and Lyra never wanted to be that person.

'You OK, you're very quiet?' Nix said.

'Yes, fine. Just wish we could have stayed on that boat forever. I've had the most amazing weekend with you.'

'Well, we can do it again next weekend if you like, and every weekend.'

She smiled slightly at that thought.

She opened the door to the cottage. 'I won't be long; I just need to throw on some clothes.'

They'd already had a shower together on the boat that morning, which had turned out to be one of the funniest experiences ever, squeezing into that tiny cubicle. She just needed to change out of Nix's shorts and t-shirt he'd lent her and dress in something more professional ready for their presentation.

She ran upstairs and threw on some more appropriate office clothes and then tied her hair up, suppressing the waves that had been loose all weekend. She changed into some sensible footwear and ran back downstairs again.

Lyra spotted her phone lying on the side where she'd left it on charge Friday night before running out to meet Nix. That seemed a lifetime away now. She picked it up and her heart dropped to see she had seventy-six missed calls. Something must have happened. She scrolled through to see that most were from Michelle, but a fair few from Kitty, Frankie and Max too. Nothing from Ethan, but she suddenly felt sick to see that there were a couple from his fiancée, Naomi as well.

Shit, shit, shit.

With shaking fingers she phoned through to her answerphone to discover she had twenty-nine messages. She listened to the first one from Michelle, who sounded very teary. The call had come through early Sunday morning.

'Lyra, it's Ethan,' Michelle's wobbly voice came over the phone. 'He's been involved in a motorbike accident. He's been rushed to All Saints Hospital near his house but apparently the paramedics said he's in a bad way. Me and

Ben are heading over there now, give me a call as soon as you get this message.'

Lyra hung up. She didn't need to hear the next twenty-eight messages to know they would be from her siblings, in increasing levels of panic about the fact they couldn't get hold of her.

'My brother's been involved in a motorbike accident,' Lyra said, as she quickly dialled Michelle's number.

'Oh my god, is he OK?' Nix said.

'I don't know, they called me yesterday morning and my phone was here.'

She put the call on loudspeaker so Nix could hear. The phone rang a few times and then Michelle answered. 'Where the hell have you been?'

'I'm sorry, I went away for the weekend and I forgot my phone.'

'You went away and didn't tell anyone? We've been worried sick. Let me guess, you were with Nix.'

Nix rubbed his hand through his hair awkwardly.

'Michelle, I don't need a lecture. What happened? Is Ethan OK?'

'We don't know.' She sounded tired, emotional, tense. Lyra knew she should have been there to support them through all this. 'He was unconscious when they brought him in, he went into surgery pretty much straightaway. He has a collapsed lung and fluid on the brain and a ton of other injuries. They're prepping him now to go back into surgery again this morning.'

'Shit, I'll be there as soon as I can.'

She hung up before there were any other comments about her absence.

'I have to go,' she said, anger, guilt, worry and more guilt boiling up inside of her. She should have been there.

'I'll come with you,' Nix said.

'No,' she snapped, instinctively. 'I don't want you there. This is all your fault.'

'What?' He looked like she'd just slapped him round the face, and for good reason. But now she'd started, all her doubts and fears were rushing to the surface.

'If we hadn't been traipsing up and down the coast on your stupid treasure hunt, I would have been here. Instead, when my little brother was fighting for his life in hospital, I was lying in bed having sex with you. Do you know how that makes me feel?'

'Look, I know you're upset, I know you must be worried, but you don't need to shut me out. Let me help you.'

'I don't need your help. I've been fine all my life on my own, taking care of everything – you can't be let down when there's no one to rely on. I don't need you, Mr No Responsibility. You might not have anyone to look out for, no obligations in life, but I do and I can't just run away from them like you do. Christ, you are exactly what I've been running from all my life and this is why. I never wanted to be like my mum, but one week with you and all my rules, all my standards, went straight out the window.'

'Oh, I didn't realise you had to lower your standards to be with me,' Nix snapped.

'This is ridiculous. We were never meant to be together, we're too different. I like order and rules and a plan and you like chaos and spontaneity. That life isn't for me and I was an idiot for thinking it was. Soon enough you'd have got bored of me, you'd have wanted someone much more exciting. Like you said, you just needed someone to get back in the saddle with again and I ticked that box for you. Now you can move on, find someone much more thrilling.'

'So this isn't about Ethan at all, this is about you thinking you're not enough for me.'

'Just like you thought you weren't enough for me.'

'Oh, I'm sorry I didn't bring my crap sperm up in conversation the first time we met. "Here's your sausage sandwich Lyra, funny story about my sausage." I'm sure that would have gone down perfectly.'

She shook her head. 'I can't do this. I have to go. This was fun but let's just draw a line under this now before it goes any further.'

She grabbed her bag and stormed out the house, getting into the car, slamming the door and bursting into tears. Nix Sanchez was the best thing that ever happened to her so what the hell had she just done?

Nix arrived at work with his head in complete turmoil. He had no idea what had just happened. They'd spent the perfect weekend together and the thing he'd been so scared of sharing had turned out to not to be so scary after all. Lyra had said she was fine about him not being able to have children. But then Emily had said the same thing when they'd first found out and she clearly hadn't been fine about it at all. Lyra had been so quiet after they left the boat – had she rethought her decision?

He popped his head around Clover's office door and

she looked up from her desk. 'Hi, I just wanted to let you know that Lyra's brother has been involved in a motorbike accident, she won't be in today.'

She nodded. 'She's just called in.'

Of course she had, Nix thought wryly. She'd had horrible news, she'd just broken up with him, and she could still find time to make a call to work to say she would be unable to come in. He shouldn't have expected anything less.

He was about to turn away when Clover came round the desk to talk to him. 'Is she OK?'

He shook his head. 'No, not at all. Her brothers and sisters are her entire world, as I'm sure you can imagine.'

She nodded, studying him. 'If you need to go and be with her then go, we can cover for you both here.'

'No, it's fine. It's not like that between us.'

He sighed. Not any more it wasn't.

'Are you sure? Because I got the distinct impression that there was something between you and Sylvia said—'

He smiled sadly. 'I think Sylvia sees what she wants to see.'

'Sylvia sees things that sometimes we're not even aware of. She's very perceptive, even if that comes across as nosiness. Her heart is in the right place. But if you're hoping that one day there will be something between you and Lyra, then you need to show her now that you can be there for her.'

'I'm the last person she wants right now. She has her family so—'

'When our dad died and Aria was left trying to run this place, she felt completely alone, even though me and Skye were right here with her. What she needed was the man she loved to hold her hand, but he was staying away out of respect for her grief, because he thought she had too much on her plate to be able to deal with him turning up. But that's not how love works. You give them space while holding them tight, you listen while they cry and wail and moan, you show them love is unequivocal.'

Nix didn't know what to do with this unsolicited advice so he just nodded and gave her a polite smile. 'Thank you but I think she's fine without me.'

When his wife had left him because he couldn't have children, and then subsequently died, he thought he had hit rock bottom, but this felt worse. With Lyra, he'd had hope for the future for the first time in a very long while and now that hope had gone. His confidence had been shattered when Emily had left him and now Lyra ending it between them had sent him spiralling down that well of uncertainty and doubt. He certainly wasn't going to pitch up at the hospital and beg her to take him back; he had more pride than that.

'Well, as you're staying, we have your presentation in a few minutes. I know Lyra isn't here, but you can present your ideas and Lyra can present hers when she comes back,' Clover said.

This wasn't how their presentation was supposed to go. They had worked on it together and it wouldn't feel right presenting it without her.

But they had already changed the brief from two days to one and worked together instead of separately. Despite the confidence Nix had expressed to Lyra about the presentation the day before, he wasn't sure their bosses would take too kindly to these suggestions. He didn't want to refuse to do the presentation on top of those things. And maybe it was better that he took the flack for changing the brief now rather than Lyra having to cope with it when she came back after her family emergency. She wouldn't be in the right frame of mind to have to deal with any disappointment or anger from their bosses.

He cleared his throat. 'I just need a few minutes to print out the presentation.'

Clover nodded. 'Meet us in the boardroom whenever you're ready.'

She moved off in the direction of the boardroom and Nix quickly ran to his office and printed out a few copies of the presentation they'd worked so hard on over the weekend, then stapled it all together. He was nervous. The boardroom seemed so official; normally their meetings took place in the restaurant, but he knew that breakfast was still being served there right now for all the guests, so it perhaps wasn't the most ideal place for a meeting. But as he gathered his papers together, all he could think about was Lyra and what she must be going through right now, driving to the hospital not knowing if her brother was going to make it. He felt sick for her.

Should he go?

He grabbed his phone and looked up where All Saints Hospital was, finding it in north Devon, which was where Lyra had mentioned before that Ethan lived. He typed in a few more things on Google. He could get a fast train from the nearby station on the mainland that would take him to the nearest town to the hospital and then a taxi from there.

The train left in half an hour and there wouldn't be another one for an hour.

No. She had made it very clear that she didn't want or need him around.

He made his way to the boardroom, knocked and Clover opened the door to let him in. They were all gathered up one end and Clover encouraged him to sit next to them at the top of the table.

He sat down and looked at the smiling relaxed faces of the rest of the team. He hoped he wouldn't soon be wiping those grins off their faces.

'So, I should probably explain a few things before I go through the ideas for the party. Lyra and I have talked at length about the one-year anniversary celebrations. We wanted to liaise to make sure we weren't treading on each other's toes with our ideas and, the more we talked, the more we ended up helping one another, and I'm afraid to say what was Lyra's ideas and what was mine became very blurred. We now have a plan for the celebrations that we worked on together.'

Clover frowned a little and Noah and Aria exchanged glances, which didn't look positive.

Nix sat forward. 'I know you were keen to have an events manager but you hired us as the events team and we wanted to show you that we actually make a really great team, just as we are. There is no reason why both of us can't be a valuable member of the managerial team. Clover, you said you could see both of us shining in the events manager's position and we intend to do that, but together. We won't let you down.'

'Well, this is slightly unexpected,' Aria said.

This wasn't going well and Lyra had probably been right; their bosses might not take kindly to the two-night event being reduced down to one. He was going to have to temper this somehow.

'We also thought it might be better if it was a whole-day celebration, with events taking place throughout the day and the night, instead of two evenings – but of course we can change that if you're sold on two days,' Nix said. That didn't sound quite so set in stone as perhaps it might have done before.

'Well, let's hear what you've got,' Noah said.

'We wanted something that would involve the community, as so many of the successful events here have before. There are a lot of families on the island and locally on the mainland and we wanted them to be a part of the celebrations. We thought we would hold a treasure hunt, with various different clues taking the participants to different parts of the island. In this way we can encourage any holidaymakers in the area to come and the clues will involve many of the local shops to hopefully drive business their way. But it will also include some more of the touristy places on the island, like the beaches, the hotel gardens, the harbour, the fort ruins – everything that will show off the best parts of the island. Once the treasure hunt is over we can hold a barbeque on the beach or in the hotel gardens.'

Aria smiled. 'I like it. It's fun and I love the fact that we are involving and benefitting the local community too.'

'We did some research in the village about what kind of event people would like to see,' Nix said. 'And it was about fifty percent who wanted something fun, family-orientated, casual, while the other half wanted something classier, a more formal kind of party. So in the evening we thought about holding a casino and horse-racing-themed night. Guests can dress up, there'll be champagne and a three-course meal, but it would also be something children could attend too. To end the evening there would be fireworks.'

He opened up the folder with the details of the plan and handed out copies to each of them. 'We've drawn up a budget for each item of the event and how much it would cost. Of course it's up to you if you want to go ahead with some or all of these ideas and we can finalise the party accordingly.'

They all studied the plan for a few minutes and there were a few murmured comments.

He started drumming his fingers on the table. What was Lyra going through right now? How was she feeling? He hated that she was driving to north Devon in a terrible state. He should have insisted on taking her, regardless of what was going on between them. God, he was such an idiot. It didn't matter what he was feeling right now, and sitting here feeling sorry for himself wasn't going to solve anything. He had to be there for Lyra. Even if she didn't want any kind of relationship with him, he could still be there for her as a friend.

He looked at the rest of the team and the presentation in front of him. None of this mattered.

Clover placed her hand over his to stop the incessant drumming. 'You need to go, don't you?'

Nix nodded. 'I do, I'm sorry, but I have to go.'

'Go?' Aria said in confusion, but Clover shushed her with a wave of her hand.

'It's OK,' Clover said. 'Go, we'll sort everything out here.'

He stood up. 'I need to get to the train station.' He looked at his watch, would he have time to call a taxi?

'I can take you,' Jesse said. 'I have my motorbike parked round the back.'

'Yes, that would be great.'

Jesse looked at his watch. 'You're lucky that's it still low tide, or the causeway would be closed.'

Maybe fate was on his side after all.

Nix passed Clover a grateful smile as he followed Jesse out the boardroom. He only hoped he'd get there in time.

～

Lyra sat on a hard, plastic chair, staring at a stain on the floor. Ethan was undergoing surgery right now but the doctors had said it would be a few hours before there was any news. Naomi, Ethan's fiancée, had popped home to get changed and get some things for Ethan. They only lived five minutes away and there was unlikely to be any change in that time.

When Lyra had arrived, the greeting from some of her brothers and sisters had been distinctly frosty. Nothing had been said, but there was a definite undertone. Max hadn't arrived yet but he was on his way. She felt a small amount of relief that she had got there before him. She'd never hear the end of it if Max had flown all the way from Australia and beaten her to it.

Her siblings all had their other halves with them,

holding their hands, and that amplified what she'd stupidly done to Nix even more.

She'd felt angry, scared and guilty, but she'd had no right to take it out on him. This wasn't his fault; he hadn't done anything wrong. These were her issues, her fears of turning out just like her mum. And she could hardly blame him for pursuing a carefree life, running away from responsibility after his near-brush with death. She glanced over at Kitty; she'd been the same after she'd recovered from the lymphoma – she'd travelled the world, done all the things she'd put on her bucket list. Life was short and it was made for enjoying.

Kitty caught her eye and got up and sat next to her.

'You OK?' her sister asked.

Lyra nodded, even though it was a complete lie.

'Michelle said you were away for the weekend with your new boyfriend.'

'Yes, sorry. I—'

'You have nothing to be sorry about, you're allowed to have a life. Tell me about him.'

It felt disloyal somehow to be talking about Nix when Ethan was fighting for his life, but she needed the distraction.

'He's warm, funny, just really bloody lovely. He created this whole treasure hunt for me, hiding clues in glass bottles all over Jewel Island, and I had no idea it was all him. He set it all up because he wanted to give me an adventure.'

Kitty nodded. 'We all need that in our lives.'

'Yeah, we do. I've been on at Ethan for ages about giving up that blasted bike, but he loves it, and even after this I

286

wouldn't want him to lose that passion for something he loves.'

'I agree. So what was the treasure?'

'Some chocolate coins and a cuddly dinosaur and this ring.' Lyra showed the leaf ring she was still wearing. 'Because we'd walked past a jewellery shop a few days before and I told him I loved it, so he bought it for me.'

She swallowed the lump in her throat because what Nix had done was so lovely and kind and she'd thrown it all away because she'd got scared. She had to make it right with him somehow but would he even be interested any more? She had freaked out for no reason. Who would want to deal with that baggage?

'I'm liking this Nix more and more.'

'We have this connection that I've never had with anyone before. Nix thinks we might be soul mates or something silly like that. We were each other's first kiss, many many years ago.'

'Wait, your first kiss was with the kid you sneezed over?'

Lyra groaned with embarrassment. 'Yes, that was him.'

'Oh my god, that's a weird coincidence.'

'It is, isn't it?'

'And he wasn't put off by that when he found out?'

'Well, hopefully my technique has moved on a bit since then.'

'True.' Kitty was quiet for a moment. 'Finding your soul mate is a very rare thing.'

'Don't you start. What we have is special but it's not fate or destiny that brought us together. That's something that Mum would say and I don't want to end up like her.'

Kitty took a sharp breath. 'Look, Mum was an asshole, we know that. She wasn't cut out to be a parent at all, but you don't ever need to worry that you'll be like her. You are everything that she was not. You showered us with love when she withdrew from our family and then disappeared off round the world, never to return. You were there for us every single day. You were kind and generous, giving your whole life to look after us. You could never ever turn out to be a thoughtless asshole. It's not in your blood. So allow yourself to cut loose now and again, go away for the weekend more often, believe in soul mates and destiny. Because why the hell not, safe in the knowledge that you are Lyra Thomas, not Mum – and Lyra Thomas is one of the most brilliant, amazing and wonderful women I will ever know.'

Lyra stared at her in shock.

'Absolutely,' Frankie nodded.

'Hear, hear,' Michelle said, which surprised Lyra. Her sister had been so frosty with her when she'd arrived. Michelle got up and moved closer to her. 'I'm sorry I gave you a hard time about going away. You've given us so much and we've come to rely on you probably a lot more than we should. I guess I got scared because, without you here, I felt like I was in charge and I didn't like that. You've taken on so much responsibility for us and I hate that that has made you feel like you can't live your life.'

Frankie nodded. 'You made sure we were always happy; you took care of us. Now it's time to take care of yourself.'

Lyra looked down at the floor, embarrassed. When she was a child she'd always thought her mum was amazing because of her carefree attitude and love of adventure. Lyra had wanted to grow up and be just like her. Until she'd grown up and realised that her mum was actually a bit of a dick. Lyra had spent the rest of her life fearful she would one day turn out that the same. Had those worries really been completely unfounded? Her determination to ensure her siblings were loved would ensure she'd never let them down, regardless of her lifestyle choices. Maybe it was time to let go of the reins just a little bit.

Kitty gave her a friendly nudge. 'Anyway, I want to hear more about your soul mate. What does he look like?'

'He's tall, has dark messy hair. He has beautiful, amber-coloured eyes and that gorgeous Mediterranean skin tone.'

Kitty's eyes slid to the door behind Lyra. 'Wearing a pale blue shirt with a sea-green tie?'

Lyra whirled around and then stumbled to her feet because Nix was there and she had no idea how to react to that.

CHAPTER TWENTY-TWO

Lyra ushered Nix down the corridor and round the corner away from her family, who were all very interested in the new arrival. She had no idea what to say to him. *Sorry* might be a good place to start. *I love you* might be even better. She couldn't believe he was here – she had pushed him away and he was here. She wanted to wrap herself around him and hold him tight.

'Nix—'

'Lyra, listen, I'm not here for us. We can talk about that another time,' he said.

He wasn't here to get back together? Her heart crashed into her stomach. She'd pushed him too far. She looked down at the floor, afraid she might now finally succumb to the tears that had been threatening to spill over for the last few hours.

He cupped her face gently, tilting her head to look at him. 'I'm here for you. Regardless of whatever else is going on between us, I'm still your friend and I think you could really do with a friend right now.'

And that was it, that was all it took to push her over the edge. Tears filled her eyes and fell down her cheeks.

He gently wiped them away and kissed her on the forehead, before enveloping her in a big hug. She couldn't help but sob against his chest as he stroked the back of her head, crying for Ethan, the relationship with Nix that seemed to be damaged beyond repair, and the fact that, despite that, he was here. He really was the loveliest man in the world.

He held her there for the longest time, not saying anything, just holding her until she was all cried out.

Eventually she stepped back. 'I have things I have to say.'

He shook his head. 'I do too, but let's do all that later once we know that Ethan is going to be OK.'

She nodded. There was too much to think about right now. Her head was a complete mess.

'Let me introduce you to my family.'

He smiled slightly. 'I'm looking forward to meeting them.'

She took his hand and went back down to the waiting area. She knew that having Nix here was going to be a huge help in getting through the next few hours. She had no idea what would happen after that.

It was a few hours later when the doctor came to talk to them to say that Ethan had come out of a successful surgery, but that it would be a few more hours before they'd be happy that he was out of the woods. It was another few hours before the doctor said that Ethan was awake and responding well but that the next few days would reveal how much he would fully recover.

It was very late that night when they were finally allowed to see him for a few minutes, which was upsetting as much as it was a relief. He was attached to so many machines and tubes that it made Lyra want to cry, but he was alive and even managed a smile when he saw them, his fingers curling weakly around Naomi's as she sat next to him, almost afraid to touch him. Lyra told him he looked like shit and he smiled at that too before the nurse eventually ushered them all out.

The next few days passed in a blur of dozing in hospital chairs, eating crappy hospital food and alternating shifts, a few of them taking turns to go back to Ethan's house to catch a few hours' sleep on the sofa. Max had arrived, which was wonderful, despite the circumstances. There were meetings with the doctors and fleeting visits with Ethan, who was looking brighter and better each time they saw him.

The one constant in all of this was Nix, steadfastly by Lyra's side no matter what. There was no suggestion of him going back to work or going home. In fact, on the first day when she'd told him he should go because of Dexter, Nix told her his brother had collected him and was going to look after him until Nix got back. Lyra and Nix had phoned Clover a few times, but she'd made it categorically clear that they should take as long as they needed and there was no rush to come back. Nix made sure that Lyra had eaten, he asked questions of the doctors that Lyra simply hadn't thought of, and, when she did sleep, in the tiny single bed at Ethan's house, Nix curled himself around her, holding her while she slept.

There had been no talk about them, of getting back together, and she didn't have the headspace for it. If she let herself think about the possibility that she had permanently ruined things between them, and lost him for good, the last strands of hope she was desperately clinging to would be gone. It would break her.

It wasn't until Thursday, when Ethan was sitting up in bed laughing and chatting and asking if anyone could smuggle him in some beer, that it became apparent her little brother was going to be absolutely fine. He had surpassed even the highest hopes the doctors had had for him after he'd come out of surgery. Kitty and Frankie decided they were going to go home and, although Max said he would stay on for a few days as he'd only arrived from Australia on Tuesday, Lyra decided she would go home too.

Nix was in the car with her rather than catching the train home, but although they spoke on the journey back, it wasn't of anything significant. She got the sense he was giving her space until she was ready to talk but she was too scared to even broach the subject now. What if they got back to her house and he waved her goodbye and from then on they'd just be friends? She couldn't bear the thought of that. When she pulled up outside her house she wanted to prolong his departure even more.

'Do you want to come inside? I can cook us some dinner.'

He hesitated before he spoke and her stomach lurched.

'Actually, I thought I might check on George,' he paused. 'Do you want to come with me?'

Lyra nodded. She had to say something to him – she needed to apologise, she needed to tell him how she really felt for him, that she couldn't let him go.

Her heart was hammering against her chest as they climbed over the fence onto his land and then made their way down the hill towards where he'd parked Judy the first night they'd met. What if he didn't want to give her a second chance? What if this was it?

Nix stopped her under the tree where they'd sat that night, eating sausages and talking until the sun had set before he'd introduced her to George.

He placed his hands on her shoulders, looking her in the eyes. Her mouth was dry.

'Lyra. I love you. I think I fell in love with you right here, that first night, but I know, spending time with you last week, and last weekend, I fell in love with you even more.'

She stared at him, tears filling her eyes. She hadn't been expecting that.

'You are the most incredible, amazing woman I have ever met. Your love for your siblings, your kindness, your spirit of adventure, even if you like to keep it hidden – I fell in love with all of it. We share a connection that is rare and beautiful and I don't ever want to lose it. I get that you're scared, and that your parents let you down so spectacularly you're scared to put your trust in someone again for fear of getting hurt. But you can trust in me. And you can also trust in yourself. I know your worst fear is turning out to be like your mum so you shy away from spontaneity and adventure, but you don't ever need to worry about that. You are kind, thoughtful and completely selfless – there's no way you could ever be anything but. And I fell in love with you because of all of those things.'

Her breath left her mouth in a shudder. 'Nix, I love you too, but I have so much baggage.'

A smile lit up his whole face. 'Say that again.'

'I have baggage.'

He grinned. 'The other, slightly more important thing.'

'Oh.' She cursed herself. 'I love you. God I love you so much. You have changed my life so utterly and completely and I want to spend the rest of my life going on adventures with you.'

'We are going to have so many adventures, Lyra Thomas, and your baggage doesn't scare me one little bit, just like my baggage doesn't scare you.'

'It doesn't. I love you, unequivocally.'

'Then I assure you I can cope with you freaking out now and again when you get a little scared. And although I want to spend every weekend or every holiday exploring the world with you, for the first time in a long time, I want to put down roots, get a house here, make the most out of this job. I don't want to keep moving on any more.'

She smiled. 'I like the sound of that. Dexter needs a garden.'

His mouth twitched into a smirk. 'He does.'

'And a big comfy sofa to sleep on.'

'Yes.'

'And I have both of those.'

'Well, your garden is quite small, and Dexter is a big dog, but we could take the fence down between your garden and my land and then we'd have a much larger garden.'

'This sounds like a great idea.'

He smiled and kissed her on the forehead. 'Life is an adventure, Lyra, but it's far better to have someone by your side to navigate it with.'

She nodded. 'Through stormy seas and calm waters.'

He smiled and leaned forward to kiss her.

His lips felt so good against hers and she knew, right here in his arms, this was where she was supposed to be.

CHAPTER TWENTY-THREE
SIX WEEKS LATER

Nix looked around the gardens of the Sapphire Bay Hotel with a smile. The last few families were finishing off their treasure hunt which, if they solved all the clues correctly, would lead them to getting their free ice cream courtesy of Skye and Jesse. Many families and couples had already completed it and were sitting around the gardens on benches and blankets eating their ice creams and tucking into burgers from the barbeque. The treasure hunt had gone without a hitch – between him and Lyra they had struck the exact right balance between making it accessible for all ages, without it being too easy. They had trialled it a few days before with the three sisters, their husbands and Bea and Orla, and they all had enjoyed it thoroughly.

In fact, the whole of the hotel's birthday celebrations seemed to be going well. The casino and horse-racing night the evening before had been brilliant fun. Everyone had enjoyed getting glammed up for a special evening and placing bets. Although they were yet to have the fireworks later that night, everything for the party had been planned meticulously so Nix wasn't worried about anything going wrong.

He glanced across at Lyra, who was sitting down eating a pink ice cream as she chatted happily with Skye. To be fair to her, she had been running around all morning to make sure everything was running smoothly, they both had. This was the first time she'd taken a break all day. Her clipboard was close to hand but she looked happy and relaxed.

Lyra had blossomed in the last few weeks. She was now much more like the spirited, freewheeling woman he'd fallen in love with the first night they'd met. Most week-ends, at Lyra's suggestion, they would set sail in Serendipity and explore the coast and the little islands that surrounded it. She was no longer afraid of letting go and having fun. It wasn't that she had changed, because this spirit of adventure had always been there, though buried deep. But now she was letting it out. Nix didn't think he could take any credit for her letting her hair down, it was probably more to do with Ethan's accident making her realise that life was short, or perhaps it'd been what her sisters had said to her at the hospital, which she'd told him about. But, either way, it was nice to think he'd helped her out in some small way.

She kept the gold key to the treasure chest on a chain around her neck as a reminder of that wonderful weekend and the adventurous side of herself she had rediscovered. Doing that treasure hunt with him had given her the key to unlock that life, but she'd had to choose whether to open the lid or keep it slammed closed. Fortunately, she no longer saw spontaneity and a carefree life as something negative or to be scared of. She would always be there for her family and having a bit of fun wouldn't change that.

Lyra saw him watching her and, as Skye, heavily pregnant now, got back up to carry on serving ice creams, she came over to Nix, sliding an arm around his waist and giving him a quick kiss. He smiled against her lips. God, he loved her so much.

That was another thing that had changed. Lyra had been adamant that no one should know they had got together, that they would remain professional while at the hotel, but after he had left the presentation to be with her at the hospital, there was no point pretending that nothing was going on between them. To his surprise, Clover and Aria hadn't been bothered at all. As they said, neither of them could judge anyone for getting involved with someone at work when both of them had met their husbands through working at the hotel. And though Skye had met Jesse before he came to the hotel, they worked alongside each other every day now. As it had turned out so well for them, all three of the sisters were champions of mixing professional and private lives. Nix couldn't agree more; he and Lyra made a brilliant team in the hotel. And out of it.

'It's gone really well, hasn't it,' Lyra said. 'Thanks to you.'

He shook his head. 'You've planned this down to the tiniest detail.'

'This was all inspired by the brilliant treasure hunt you did for me. It was your idea.'

'This was a joint effort, we're a team,' Nix said.

'And a great team at that,' said a voice behind them.

Nix turned around to see Clover coming towards them. She looked tanned from having been in Dubai for the last week. She'd flown back for the party but he knew she and Angel were going off to New Zealand the following week to make the most of their time before their baby arrived.

'This party is brilliant, everyone says so,' Clover went on. 'We couldn't have asked for two better events managers.'

Nix smiled. When they'd returned to work after being at the hospital, Clover and Aria had made it clear that they were impressed with their unity and that they loved their ideas for the birthday party. Clover had still wanted it spread across two days rather than one, but that had been an easy fix.

'We knew when we interviewed you that you would both bring something special to the hotel, but together you have shone,' Clover said. 'Thank you for arranging such a wonderful party for us and for involving everyone on the island too.'

'We've enjoyed doing it,' Lyra said, giving Nix a warm smile.

Clover smiled and left them to it.

'I have loved working with you over the last few weeks,' Nix said. 'I have never had so much fun at work before, but you make getting up every day an absolute joy.'

Lyra grinned 'And the early-morning sex certainly helps with that.'

He laughed. He'd loved the freedom he'd given himself over the last few years so much that he had wondered if moving into Lyra's cottage and settling down would be a life he could truly embrace. He needn't have worried. They just fitted together perfectly. They shared the cooking, they walked Dexter together, they laughed and talked together, and he loved spending time with her. She had very quickly become one of his best friends. The sex was definitely a bonus, too – they were still in the honeymoon stage of not being able to keep their hands off each other. He didn't think that would ever end. With Lyra he had found a place to call home.

'I love you,' Nix said. 'You have changed my life so completely.'

She smiled. 'I love you too. You have given me my life back after I spent so long hiding away from it.'

Just then Sylvia came up to them. She hadn't been at the hotel for the last few weeks but she'd returned for the birthday party.

'I knew you two had a connection,' she said, without any preamble. 'Even when you hated each other, I could see the chemistry between you.'

'I never hated her,' Nix said. 'I was hurt when I thought she'd left but I could never hate her.'

He looked at Lyra to see if she would say the same thing.

'Oh, I was pissed,' Lyra laughed. 'And I wanted to hate you so much, but I couldn't, you were just too lovely.'

He grinned. 'Sorry about that.'

'You're forgiven.'

'I don't claim to be an expert on love – I've been married six times – but I can see that what you two have is forever,' Sylvia said.

Lyra looked up at him. 'He's my soul mate.'

Nix felt his heart fill with happiness. He had never

wanted to plan for a future in case those hopes were dashed like before, but now he could see it all so clearly. He and Dexter and the woman he loved with all his heart. Nothing else mattered. She was his future and he couldn't have been happier about that.

EPILOGUE

Lyra steered Serendipity around Jewel Island, Nix sitting next to her and Dexter lying between them. It was a glorious sunny autumn day, a lot warmer than was usual this time of year. A perfect day to celebrate her birthday. Nix had created a lovely treasure hunt for her which had taken her all over the island and then via Michelle's house for cake and a surprise lunch with all her siblings, where Max had joined them on a video call. All of her family adored Nix now, which was something of a relief, but it was very clear to see how completely and utterly happy he made her. She had never loved anyone as much as she loved him – he filled her heart to the very top.

She looked across at Nix to see he was watching her, his eyes filled with love, and she smiled.

'Right, where shall we anchor up?' Lyra said as they approached Crystal Sands, where the latest clue he'd given her had directed them to.

'This will do,' he said. 'Any closer and we run the risk of hitting the rocks.'

She cut the engine and Nix moved out onto the deck to throw the anchor over.

She moved out with him and looked at the little cove. 'We're still quite far out.'

'But here comes the best bit,' Nix said, stripping off his t-shirt and diving head first into the cool blue water. Dexter jumped overboard after him.

Lyra laughed as he surfaced. 'Isn't it cold?'

'It's bloody freezing, come on in.'

She rolled her eyes and stripped off her dress, so she was just in her bikini, diving into the water too. Christ it was cold, but it felt liberating as she swam under the waves. She surfaced next to Nix, looping her arms around his neck.

'I love you.'

He grinned. 'I thought the cold water might make you change your mind about that.'

'There's nothing that could ever change my mind about that.'

'Right, come on, let's go find your treasure.'

He turned for the shore and she swam alongside him, Dexter taking the lead as he powered through the water. There were a few rocks to avoid as they made their way to the beach but nothing too treacherous. They reached the shore and pulled themselves out onto the sand.

She looked around them at the towering cliffs. She could see their little cottage, Sunlight, sitting on the hills over Crystal Sands. It felt fitting somehow that the final clue would lead them here.

'Well, I believe the clue points to the cave,' Lyra said.

'Which hopefully should be the bottom of the smugglers' tunnel,' Nix said, as Dexter made it to the beach and shook himself, cold water spraying everywhere.

'Let's go and take a look.'

They clambered over the rocks and into the cave, which was quite big on the inside and would have been the perfect place to hide some treasure in years gone by. The roof opened out above them and Lyra could quite clearly see a great shaft going straight up into the cliff, lined with rocks and metal rungs for a ladder. This was obviously the bottom of the well.

'It's so exciting to think they really did smuggle stuff onto the island through this tunnel and that our house was some kind of smuggling headquarters.'

'It's like we have our own private entrance to the beach. One day, when we really do find that treasure, and we become millionaires, we can use the money to reinforce the well and the ladder again so we can come down here whenever we want,' Nix said.

'What do you mean, "when we find the treasure"? That's why we're here today, isn't it?' Lyra teased.

'You have to find it first.'

She smiled and looked around and her heart leapt. Up on a rocky ledge was a treasure chest, inlaid with gold.

'Could that be it?'

'It could be.'

She carefully climbed up the rocks and grabbed the chest, passing it down to Nix before climbing back down herself.

'Shall we go back to the boat, see if we can open it?' Lyra said.

'Yes, I'm hoping you'll like this treasure a bit more than the last lot.'

'Hey!' she said, indignantly. 'I loved the last lot of treasure and I'll love this treasure too, because it comes from you. Whatever it is, I'll love it.'

He smiled. 'Come on then.'

They swam back to the boat, which was a bit more difficult for Nix as he was now carrying the chest, but they were soon climbing aboard.

Lyra examined the box. 'Right, we need a key.'

Nix tapped his chin thoughtfully. 'Hmm, where would we find one of those?'

She laughed as she took the key from around her neck and unlocked the chest. She opened it up to see there was a blue silk cushion inside and, tucked into the top, was a diamond ring. She gasped with happiness. The diamond was perfectly round with small green leaves wrapped around it.

Her head snapped up to look at Nix and he was already getting down on one knee.

'Lyra Thomas, you have filled my life with utter joy. I never understood before what it meant to find my missing piece but I know now. You are quite literally the other half of my heart. I love you with everything I have. Will you marry me?'

She couldn't stop the smile from spreading across her face. 'Nix, you are my soul mate. And I thank my lucky stars every day that fate or destiny found a way for us to be together. I love you and I can't wait to be your wife. Yes, of course I'll marry you.'

He smiled and plucked the ring from the chest and slid it onto her finger, where it sparkled in the sunlight.

She bent down and kissed him and he gathered her against him, rolling her onto the deck beneath him. The kiss continued as clothes were quickly removed. He moved his mouth to her throat and she took a moment to admire the ring again.

'You're right, I do love this treasure more than the first lot. That was the start of the rest of my life with you, but this, right here, is our forever.'

He smiled as he kissed her again. This was her happy ever after: Nix, Dexter, and a little boat called Serendipity.

If you enjoyed *Sunlight over Crystal Sands*, you'll love my next gorgeously romantic story, *Mistletoe at Moonstone Lake*, out in October.

STAY IN TOUCH...

To keep up to date with the latest news on my releases, just go to the link below to sign up for a newsletter. You'll also get two FREE short stories, get sneak peeks, booky news and be able to take part in exclusive giveaways. Your email will never be shared with anyone else and you can unsubscribe at any time

https://www.subscribepage.com/hollymartinsignup

Website: https://hollymartin-author.com/
Email: holly@hollymartin-author.com
Twitter: @HollyMAuthor

Hope Island Series

Spring at Blueberry Bay

Summer at Buttercup Beach

Christmas at Mistletoe Cove

Juniper Island Series

Christmas Under a Cranberry Sky

A Town Called Christmas

White Cliff Bay Series

Christmas at Lilac Cottage

Snowflakes on Silver Cove

Summer at Rose Island

Standalone Stories

Fairytale Beginnings

Tied Up With Love

A Home on Bramble Hill

One Hundred Christmas Proposals

One Hundred Proposals

The Guestbook at Willow Cottage

For Young Adults

The Sentinel Series

The Sentinel (Book 1 of the Sentinel Series)

The Prophecies (Book 2 of the Sentinel Series)

The Revenge (Book 3 of the Sentinel Series)

The Reckoning (Book 4 of the Sentinel Series)

A LETTER FROM HOLLY

Thank you so much for reading *Sunlight over Crystal Sands*, I had so much fun creating this story and revisiting the beautiful Jewel Island. I hope you enjoyed reading it as much as I enjoyed writing it.

One of the best parts of writing comes from seeing the reaction from readers. Did it make you smile or laugh, did it make you cry, hopefully happy tears? Did you fall in love with Lyra, Nix, Dexter and George as much as I did? Did you like the gorgeous little Jewel Island? If you enjoyed the story, I would absolutely love it if you could leave a short review on Amazon. Getting feedback from readers is amazing and it also helps to persuade other readers to pick up one of my books for the first time.

Thank you for reading.

Love Holly x

ACKNOWLEDGEMENTS

To my family, my mom, my biggest fan, who reads every word I've written a hundred times over and loves it every single time, my dad, my brother Lee and my sister-in-law Julie, for your support, love, encouragement and endless excitement for my stories.

For my twinnie, the gorgeous Aven Ellis for just being my wonderful friend, for your endless support, for cheering me on, for reading my stories and telling me what works and what doesn't and for keeping me entertained with wonderful stories. I love you dearly.

To my lovely friends Julie, Natalie, Jac, Verity and Jodie, thanks for all the support.

To the Devon contingent, Paw and Order, Belinda, Lisa, Phil, Bodie, Kodi and Skipper. Thanks for keeping me entertained and always being there.

To everyone at Bookcamp, you gorgeous, fabulous bunch, thank you for your wonderful support on this venture.

Thanks to the brilliant Emma Rogers for the gorgeous cover design.

Thanks to my fabulous editors, Celine Kelly and Rhian McKay.

To all the wonderful bloggers for your tweets, retweets, facebook posts, tireless promotions, support, encouragement and endless enthusiasm. You guys are amazing and I couldn't do this journey without you.

To anyone who has read my book and taken the time to tell me you've enjoyed it or wrote a review, thank you so much.

Thank you, I love you all.

Published by Holly Martin in 2021
Copyright © Holly Martin, 2021

978-1-913616-23-6 Paperback
978-1-913616-24-3 Large Print paperback
978-1-913616-25-0 Hardback

Cover design by Emma Rogers

Made in United States
North Haven, CT
16 March 2024

50089547R00193